POSSESSIVE *heart*

BRIGHTON WALSH

COPYRIGHT

Copyright © 2024 by Brighton Walsh

All rights reserved. This book or any portion thereof may not be reproduced in any form or by any electronic or mechanical means, including information storage and retrieval systems, without written permission from the author, except for the use of brief quotations in a book review.

Edited by Lisa Hollett of Silently Correcting Your Grammar
Cover Design by Brighton Walsh
Cover Image: Cooper by Michelle Lancaster

This book is a work of fiction. Names, characters, places, and incidents are either products of the author's imagination or are used fictitiously, and any resemblance to actual persons, living or dead, business establishments, events, or locales is coincidental.

Digital ISBN: 978-1-68518-036-2
Paperback ISBN: 978-1-68518-037-9
Special Edition ISBN: 978-1-68518-038-6

CONTENT NOTES

Please be advised that this book contains content that may be upsetting for some readers. Should you prefer detailed information in order to have the best reading experience, please visit the author's website or scan the QR code below to view a full list of content notes.

For all the "unlikeable" heroines out there.

If you were a man, they'd call you assertive instead of bitchy. So hold your head high, adjust your crown, and keep it up, queen.

CHAPTER ONE

ADDISON

I SHOULD'VE KNOWN that waking up from a panty-ruining dream—memory, actually—featuring the one person in the world I wasn't supposed to be thinking about anymore was a bad omen for the day to come. And there was no denying today was shaping up to be a complete and utter clusterfuck.

I was juggling twelve thousand things, as per usual, but today, even more attention-demanding obligations were thrown into the mix. The wedding documentary that had been filming at the resort for the past couple months was finally wrapping up. Our beachside cottages were booked solid, even though we were fully entrenched in a Maine winter. And on top of all that, I was in charge of throwing my brother Aiden a party tonight to celebrate the release of book two in his blockbuster trilogy.

A party, by the way, that he knew nothing about. When it came to his pen name, he was touchy, to say the least. Had, in fact, kept it a secret from the rest of our brothers and me for *years*. But despite his fears of people finding out A.M. Kinsey, erotic fantasy author, and Aiden McKenzie, co-owner of the small-town, family-run Starlight Cove Resort, were one and the same, the reception had been better than even I'd imagined.

I was spread so thin, I was basically Swiss cheese at this point, so I'd stepped out of my comfort zone today and called in reinforcements. It was either ask for help or this party wasn't going to happen, and that wasn't an option. But I should've known better than to try to delegate anything to the men in my life. Especially when those men happened to be related to me.

Honestly, what good was having five older brothers if you couldn't boss them around? And what good was bossing them around if they didn't actually *listen* and do what you told them to? Some days, wrangling those five overprotective dumbasses was like attempting to corral wild monkeys. Except with monkeys, I had to be nice.

With my brothers? I did not.

Group text titled:
DO NOT INVITE AIDEN TO THIS OR I WILL KILL YOU
with Brady, Beck, Ford, Levi

3:24 p.m.

ADDISON:

BRADY

Where the hell are the supplies I asked you to get?

BRADY:

Asked is stretching it a bit, don't you think?

ADDISON:

That's not an answer

And I don't have time for your whining

So cough it up

BRADY:

I got called to a domestic dispute, so I passed it to Levi.

ADDISON:

LEVI

I need a status update

LEVI:

I didn't have time because I'm already doing all the other shit you told me to do today. I passed it to the twins.

BECK:

I'm a little busy over here, what with running the diner by myself and all. I told Ford to handle it.

ADDISON:

And where tf is Ford?

Because those supplies were supposed to be here an hour ago

BRADY:

Word around town is he's in the clinic's parking lot.

ADDISON:

Wtf is he doing there?

BRADY:

Making out with his wife in the back seat of his car, apparently.

"For fuck's sake." I tossed my phone onto my desk and closed my eyes on a groan, squeezing the hell out of my dick-shaped stress ball—a gift from Starlight Cove's pervy grandma, Mabel. Squeezed so hard, in fact, my nails dug crescent-shaped divots into the foam, creating craters in their wake. Or *more* craters, as it were. I went through these things like candy, and I had no doubt this one wouldn't see the end of the day.

"Fine," I said to the empty room, sitting up straight and rolling my shoulders back. "I'll do it myself. I'll run the inn, I'll handle the documentary wrap-up, I'll make sure this party goes off without a fucking hitch. And I'll do it all without breaking a sweat because I'm the one people go to to get shit done."

With every word, I gripped the foam peen a little harder, a little more aggressively, my nails digging farther into it, until finally it hit its limit and broke apart into pieces in my palm. Not the first dick I'd destroyed—and definitely wouldn't be the last.

"Well, that's just fucking great," I muttered as I tossed the remnants in the trash before pulling another foam penis from my top drawer.

"Are you already at the talking-to-yourself level of stress

today?" Avery—my best friend and Aiden's better half—popped her head into my office. "It's not even noon."

"I was this level of stressed before I even rolled out of bed this morning."

Her eyebrows hit her hairline, and she strode over to sit on the edge of my desk. "Why, what's up?"

I had been the only woman around here for so long that this—having actual conversations instead of being on the receiving end of little more than grunts—was entirely new... and actually pretty nice. My brothers' favorite method of dealing with my bad days was either to steer clear entirely, toss me candy from the doorway like I was a feral animal, or just take care of the problem themselves like the overprotective beasts they were.

God help me, but I loved those idiots.

"Just me handling shit on my own because everyone's bailing on me." With the hand currently squeezing the hell out of my new stress ball, I gestured wildly at the piles of work on my desk and the bags of incomplete party supplies stacked in the corner.

"That's nothing new. This—" she swirled her finger in a way so as to encompass my general being "—is something else. Spill."

Sometimes I hated how well my bestie knew me, but that was what ten years of friendship did for you. I sank back into my chair and blew a heavy sigh toward the ceiling. "I had a dream about *him* last night."

"Him who?"

I raised a brow at her. "*Him* him. *Him* who shall not be named. *Him* who's dead to me."

"Oh...*him*. Shit."

"Yeah, shit. Why the hell am I dreaming about him?" What I really wanted to know was why couldn't I *stop* dreaming about him?

She shrugged. "Probably because your vagina has cobwebs for all the use it's gotten in the past year, and it's feeling a little nostalgic for good dick."

I snorted. She wasn't wrong. "That's fair. But that can't be all it is. What do you think it *means*?"

"Nothing," she said without hesitation. "It means literally nothing. *He* means nothing. He's the worst mistake you've ever made, and we need to be done talking about the asshole or I won't be held liable for shipping him a glitter bomb. Again."

I bit my lip to stifle a smile, the urge to hug the hell out of her nearly overwhelming. Was there anything better than your best friend's sustained rage when someone did you wrong? Didn't matter if it was ten days or ten years ago, that shit was forever. And Avery could hold a grudge like a motherfucking champ...would no doubt take second place in the Grudge Holding Olympics.

Right behind me and my Dead to Me list where *he* was named Enemy #1.

EVEN WITH A CLUSTERFUCK of a day stacked against me, I'd still managed to tackle it all without breaking more than a stress ball. After my angel of a bestie told me she'd handle the stuff at the resort so I could grab the rest of the supplies and start setting up for Aiden's party, I was golden.

Everyone had shown up on time, and Aiden had been surprised, even though the only outward sign had been a twitch of his eyebrow. I knew his tells. Despite being a man of few words—which was ironic, since he wrote epic romantasy novels—he didn't have to say a thing for me to see how much this meant to him, especially considering how long he'd kept it a secret.

Besides that, this was turning out to be the best night I'd had in a while. Between throwing Aiden a party with those who loved and supported him and telling the prudish assholes who didn't to suck my dick and get lost, I was out here, living my best life, cobweb-covered vagina and all.

My brothers and I sat at a large table in One Night Stan's, Starlight Cove's local bar, along with their significant others. Levi and I were the only single ones left, the rest of our siblings already paired up and ridiculously, sickeningly in love. They all sat fused to each other as if they'd perish otherwise, while Levi and I exchanged eye rolls when no one else was looking. Which was often since they were so obsessed with each other.

Thank God I had a partner in him. We had a long-standing pact on these nights—never let the other's glass get too low and be the excuse to bail if we needed it. And after my day, I was thinking I'd definitely need it.

"So, Aiden..." Everly propped her elbow on the table and leaned toward Aiden from her perch on Beck's lap. "I know book three doesn't release until later this year, but..."

After several moments of silence, Aiden finally raised a brow in her direction. "But?"

"Well, I mean... Do you think—" Clearing her throat, she glanced away before returning her attention to him. "Would you maybe consider..."

"She wants the book, man," Beck said without hesitation. "And I want it, too, if you know what I mean."

"Hey, if they get it, so do we." Ford leaned forward, gesturing at himself and his wife.

"I would definitely take it," Quinn agreed with a nod.

Brady's girlfriend, Luna, brought her drink to her lips and shrugged. "I mean, if you're giving it out..."

"I'm not giving it out." Aiden rolled his eyes. "I can't just give you the book."

"But can't you?" Everly asked, hands clasped below her chin in a silent plea.

"If you did, I'd be willing to look the other way on your next speeding ticket," Brady said, shocking the hell out of me. Since when did the sheriff—aka my eldest, most rule-following, stick-up-his-ass brother—bend the rules just to get his hands on some smut?

Ford cut in, his tone hopeful. "I could build you something? Anything you want. I'll help with the lighthouse reno on my days off."

"And you can eat for free whenever," Beck offered.

"I already eat for free," Aiden said flatly.

Levi leaned close to me and muttered, "You believe these horny motherfuckers? Jesus." He shook his head before raising his voice to Aiden. "Shit, man. You've got all three of them begging for early smut? I'd maybe cash in on that."

The conversation continued around the table, with everyone pleading for Aiden's next book, but I blocked them out as best I could. I loved Aiden, and I was happy for his success. But I was zero percent interested in reading about sex that came directly from my brother's brain, no matter how hot it supposedly was. I was also zero percent interested in hearing about all the sex my other brothers were having thanks to Aiden's writing. It was a hard pass all around from me.

So instead of tuning in to them, I turned to Levi, ignoring everyone else as they carried on with their mini smut convention right here at our table. "Did you get Cottage Thirteen all taken care of?"

His shoulders stiffened the slightest bit, his mouth flattening into a thin line. Most people probably wouldn't have even noticed, but I wasn't most people. "Yeah."

I cringed. "Was it that bad inside?"

I wouldn't have been surprised if it was, considering our estranged father had been holed up in it for a decade without any outside contact until Aiden finally kicked him out last month.

I ignored the pit that opened up in my stomach, guilt niggling at the thought of renting out what had been his home for ten years, because that emotion didn't have any place here. He certainly didn't deserve my guilt. Logically, I knew he didn't deserve anything from me. From us. But my heart wasn't so easy to convince.

"It was fine." Levi took a pull from his beer. "It'll be ready for guests next weekend."

I shoved down the whisper in the back of my mind that wondered if that was a good idea and ignored it entirely. "Good, because we're going to need it. We're still booking out months in advance. I was worried about reservations waning during our slow months, but so far, that's not the case."

"Not when we have a famous smut author on the premises." Levi tipped his beer bottle toward Aiden, who was caught up in conversation with the rest of our siblings.

"That's definitely helped," I agreed. "But I still want to have something on the back burner for when—*if*—this interest and attention die down. I don't want us to be struggling for money again because we don't have any reservations coming in. I'm brainstorming some articles to pitch...see if we can get some more buzz about the resort. And I'm going to look into getting the ice rink back up and running. I'm not sure I can get it done this season, but—"

A roar of laughter went up around us, cutting me off, and Levi and I glanced at the rest of the table, dismissing them just as quickly before moving our attention back to each other.

"All we talk about anymore is work shit," he said. "We're pathetic."

He wasn't wrong.

Before I could respond, Mabel strolled up to our table, her smile bright, and rested her hands on the back of Aiden's chair. With her nose unapologetically in everyone's business, the older woman was Starlight Cove's surrogate grandmother...and sex toy dealer. It was quite the combo, but it worked for her. "So proud of you, Aiden," she said. "And I can't believe our little town produced two famous people! A *New York Times* best-selling author *and* a pro hockey player. Can you even believe it?"

I was so distracted by the *I like big balls and I cannot lie* sweatshirt she wore that it took a moment for her words to register. As soon as they did, I stiffened, all my muscles seizing at just the roundabout reference to *him*.

"Speaking of," Mabel said, pulling a copy of the *Starlight Cove Gazette* from her purse and dropping it on the table between Aiden and me. "Did everyone see the news?"

I glanced over at the newspaper, my entire body going cold as I scanned the headline.

HOCKEY PRO TO RETURN TO STARLIGHT COVE AFTER TEAM CONFIRMS HE'S OUT FOR SEASON

No.

No.

Abso-fucking-lutely not.

This could not be happening. Not now. Not *ever*.

Avery was shooting me worried glances, but I couldn't acknowledge her. Couldn't do anything but try to maintain my facade. The last thing I needed was my brothers—Levi, especially—sniffing out my reaction, because they'd lose their collective shit.

Without checking to see if Levi needed another drink, I pushed to stand and made my way toward the bar. I needed some help forgetting about this whole fucking day. Just as I stepped up to the bar, a loud cheer went up in the crowd. I glanced over my shoulder, figuring the commotion was coming from our table because once you got Mabel talking about spicy books, all bets were off. But everyone's attention —and I meant *everyone*—was on the door.

And the man who'd just walked through it.

He stood in the doorway, his ice-blue eyes already on me, as if he didn't have five dozen people surrounding him, all vying for his attention. I froze when our gazes collided, my stomach bottoming out at the same time my heart leaped into a pounding gallop, the thrum of it whoosh-whoosh-whooshing in my ears.

Standing a head above most of the patrons in the bar, he wore a navy hoodie and a pair of worn, buttery-soft jeans I knew from experience molded to his thick thighs and made his ass look fantastic. His light-brown hair was shorter than it'd been the last time I'd seen him more than a year ago, now cropped close and so different from the chaotic mess I was used to. Stubble dusted his sharp jaw, and lips I'd long since memorized the shape of kicked up on the side in that insufferable smirk I hated how much I loved.

Before I could tamp it down, a toe-curling flush swept over me from head to toe and all the neglected places in between as my nerve endings came alive with awareness. I knew exactly what those lips and that scruff would feel like across my collarbone, between my breasts, against my inner thighs...

And I fucking hated that I did.

Hated, too, that my body was already readying itself for him, despite my brain reminding it we were absolutely not doing that again.

But reminding myself did fuck all for the swarm of butterflies that had erupted in my stomach at the mere sight of him. Counteracting them was useless. I'd been having the same reaction to him for more than half my life, and I'd gotten damn good at hiding it in those early years.

Something I desperately needed to tap into now. Because what I *wasn't* going to do was show the man who didn't give a damn about me just how fucking much his absence hurt.

No matter how much I pretended otherwise.

CHAPTER TWO

CHASE

FOR THE PAST TEN YEARS, I'd lived by one mantra and one mantra only: *I have a wife. I'm just not married.*

If I had it my way, I'd already have *Addison McKenzie's Husband* plastered on the back of my jerseys, printed on goddamn business cards, and tattooed across my fucking chest, despite the fact that my best friend would rip off my balls if he knew the depraved shit I'd done to his baby sister.

Though my teammates were well aware of my obsession, they were the only ones. I was tired of not being able to call her mine, loudly and publicly, and I was really fucking tired of her ignoring me as she'd been doing for too damn long. But she was going to have a really difficult time ignoring me if I was standing right in front of her.

Unfortunately, from the murderous look the light of my life was shooting my way, it was clear she wasn't happy to see me. Fury burned in her green eyes, and I had zero doubts that if she had a shovel and some rope in the trunk of her car, she'd lure me behind the bar and murder me right here and now.

Best to give her a minute, though I didn't have much of a choice. I hadn't even taken two steps into One Night Stan's before I was swarmed by people and swallowed up in the crowd, the group of residents all too happy to welcome me home after my not having been back for more than a year.

Somewhere in the constant stream of *hello*s and *hey, how're you doing*s, Levi caught my gaze and lifted his chin in greeting, but that was all I was getting from my best friend. At least until I could extricate myself from the crowd.

A guy who graduated a couple years ahead of me clapped a hand on my shoulder. "Hey, man! Sorry to hear about the injury, but it's good to have you home. How're things going?"

It hadn't even been a month since I'd forgone coming home for Christmas and instead had lain on the floor of my condo, downing painkillers like candy and chasing them with a bottle of bourbon, just in the hope of being able to play through the pain to secure a contract, but I couldn't exactly tell him that.

"Getting better every day," I said instead.

"Good, good. We've been following the season, and you guys are doing amazing. You've got a good shot at the play-offs."

Another shot at the play-offs, because it wouldn't surprise me if they took it all the way for the second year in a row, even without me there.

"Yep. I'm proud of how the team's been hustling this year."

"We're hoping to get tickets if that happens. Any chance we'll see you on the ice by then?"

Media training wasn't my favorite, but I'd never been more grateful for it than I was in that moment. It allowed me to keep the smile on my face. To brush off the question with a vague, generic answer I'd practiced enough times that it was second nature to regurgitate it. "That's up to the medical team. I always want to be playing with my team."

That training helped me hide how my stomach churned at the unknown looming large and imposing in front of me. The truth was, I didn't fucking know when I'd be back on the ice. And that was scary as hell when hockey was all I'd known for so long. When it was all I was good at.

When it was who I was.

But if there was one good thing to come from all of this, it was that I now had four months back home to rehab the knee that was the bane of my existence. Four months in my hometown with my girl. And while the media-friendly answer for why I was here was that I was going to spend some much-needed time with my family while recovering from my second injury in a year, I was actually back in Starlight Cove to repair the most important relationship in my life.

Now, if only I could get her on board with that plan.

Despite the commotion around me and those attempting to engage me in conversation, I was acutely aware of Addison the entire time. Even though she'd downed a drink in the twenty minutes since I'd walked in, she remained rigid, her body tense, mouth pressed in a flat line as she tried her hardest to ignore me.

While I was listening to someone drone on about the Metropolitan Division play-off standings—it was January, for fuck's sake...anything could happen—Addison stood from the table and made her way down the hallway that led to the bathroom. And the back exit. I wouldn't put it past her to sneak out just to avoid me, so I excused myself and followed her. I belatedly remembered to double-check that no one was paying attention to the two of us—least of all the McKenzie boys. Thirteen months without her had made me sloppy. And greedy.

The raucous sounds of those gathered in the bar followed me down the dark, empty hallway to the single-stall bathroom at the end of the corridor. The door swung open just as I stepped up to it, and I barely had time to register the surprise on Addison's face before I curled my hand around her hip and guided her back into the room, closing and locking the door behind us.

She stared up at me, eyes wide, lips parted, and fuck me, but she was so goddamn gorgeous. A year was too fucking long to go without her.

She'd cut her hair since I'd last seen her, the dark waves falling loosely to her shoulders. I wanted nothing more than to bury my hands in it, tip her head back, and crash my lips against hers...capture her moans with my mouth.

It was only the rage burning in her gorgeous green eyes that stopped me.

After a brief, stunned silence, she snapped her mouth shut and glared up at me, all pursed lips, flushed cheeks, and eyes spitting fire. "*Move,* you overgrown jackass."

I nearly laughed—in relief and amusement. Addison's temper was nothing new to me. She'd always burned hotter than everyone else around her—passionate about everything she cared about—and it'd taken until right this second to admit I'd been uncertain about what kind of reception I'd receive from her. But I'd take her fury over indifference any day of the week.

Anger meant she still cared. Anger meant she had feelings for me, whether she wanted to admit to them or not.

Anger meant I still had a chance. *We* still had a chance.

"Happy to see you, too, firefly."

"Don't call me that," she snapped, her words like acid. "And get out of my way. I can have any one of my brothers in here in thirty seconds flat."

My lips twitched as I stared down at her, my fingers itching to reach out and touch her. Cradle her head in my hands, lower my face to hers until her glare melted into desire, and finally taste her again.

"You've never needed your brothers for protection."

She tipped her chin up defiantly, her mouth pressed in a flat line. "You're right. Does that mean you want me to test out my right hook on you? Because nothing would give me more pleasure."

"You and I both know that's not true," I said, voice low, recalling the last time I'd been in her bed. When I'd woken her up with my mouth before she'd dragged me up by my hair and begged me to fuck her. "But you're welcome to test out that right hook on me anytime. You know I love how fucking strong you are."

She narrowed her eyes even further, her lips pursing to the side as she crossed her arms over her chest. Her armor sliding into place piece by piece. "Sweet talk is going to get you fuck all with me, Lockhart."

"You sure? Because I—"

Before I could get out the rest of the sentence, she pressed her palms against my chest and shoved. Hard. "Yes, I'm fucking sure! It's been thirteen months, Chase. *Thirteen months*. You think you can stroll in after all that time and shit is just going to go back to normal? That I'm gonna fall at your feet and into your bed? Not happening, asshole."

The smile slid off my face as I finally saw beyond the anger simmering on the surface, that badass facade she loved showing the world. But deep down, she was hurt. And I had a desperate need to fix it. "Addie—"

She held up her hand to stop me and shook her head. "I don't want to hear it. And don't get any bright ideas while you're in town. Just because you're back home doesn't mean we have any reason at all to see each other—you already made it clear that's what you want anyway."

Without another word, she stepped around me, unlocked the door, and walked out of the bathroom, shoulders back, head held high. My fucking queen.

My queen who apparently had no plans to speak to me with anything other than insults, so that was just fucking great.

As soon as the door shut behind her, I scrubbed a hand down my face and groaned in frustration. I braced my hands on the sink and hung my head, curling my fingers around the porcelain basin. While I'd hoped our reunion would've gone better, I couldn't say I was surprised. This reaction was Addison, through and through.

She had this fierce outer shell, gave off major *go fuck yourself* vibes with a confidence that screamed *I will make your life a living hell if you cross me*. But she didn't fool me. I'd seen her face slack with sleep, all worries swept away. I'd seen her smiles when she thought no one was looking and her full lips parted in pleasure. I'd heard her soft pleas for more and her whispered fears in the dark.

Despite how much she no doubt hated it, she wasn't a mystery to me. She never had been.

I'd *always* seen her.

Even when I'd pretended not to.

CHAPTER THREE

CHASE

WAKING up on the family room couch in my childhood home was less than ideal. Especially as a 6'3", thirty-year-old professional athlete with a fucked-up knee. A knee that was screaming like a motherfucker this morning because of how I'd slept, cramped on a too-small sofa.

I groaned, stretching out and cringing at the sharp pain that shot down my leg. Fuck, I was going to pay for this today.

"Morning, sweetheart!" my mom called from the kitchen, poking her head into the pass-through window. "Did you sleep okay? How was the couch?"

"Great," I said, wincing as I stood.

Her brow creased, her lips pulling down in a frown as she looked me over from head to toe. "It doesn't sound great. I feel just awful about you staying out here, especially when you're paying for the renovations! You should take our room tonight, and your father and I can—"

"I'm not taking your room, Mom." I slowly made my way

into the kitchen, dropping a kiss on her cheek and accepting the glass of orange juice she handed me.

She wore an apron with *Queen of the Kitchen* printed across the front, her hair—more gray now than blond—pulled back in a ponytail, a scowl directed at me. "Well, that couch can't be good for you, especially your knee. You're a growing boy and—"

"I'm thirty," I said dryly. "I'm pretty sure I'm done growing."

Ignoring me completely, she continued, "Your body needs certain conditions to be in optimal working order. And you're supposed to be healing! If only we'd known you'd be coming home now. We could've—" She furrowed her brow, her train of thought shifting in an instant. She was definitely who I had to thank for my ability to do that on the ice. "*Carl*! Can we postpone the contractors? Maybe have them come back in a week or two?"

"What?" my dad yelled from his office—aka the twins' old bedroom before the two of them had headed to college this past August.

"*The contractors*!" Mom repeated at a decibel everyone in Starlight Cove could probably hear. Jesus Christ, I'd forgotten just how *loud* it was in my childhood home. "Can we postpone—"

"Mom," I said, raising my voice enough to be heard over hers. "You're not postponing the contractors. It's taken me seven years to get you to agree to this in the first place."

"Well, after all you've done for your sister—for this family..." She huffed and shook her head. "It's too much. I should've waited another seven."

That was a bone of contention between us. My parents never missed an opportunity to voice their gratitude for the monetary help I'd provided thanks to my first pro contract after my sister Morgan had gotten sick. And I never missed an opportunity to tell them that wasn't something they ever had to thank me for. It was just money, and I'd do everything all over again.

"And that's exactly why you're not calling off the contractors," I said. "You'll come up with all kinds of excuses to postpone again."

"Well, I don't like you cramped on that couch... It's not good for you or that injury you're supposed to be healing while you're home."

"I know. My furniture should be delivered by the end of the week, and then I can stay at my place. I'll figure out something until then."

"Like what?" she asked.

I shrugged. "I'll ask Levi if I can crash in his old room at the resort."

Mom's brows flew up. "*Levi*, huh? So your staying there wouldn't have anything to do with a certain spitfire who runs the whole ship?"

I took a sip from my orange juice, not going anywhere near that bait. "No idea what you're talking about."

"Mhmm." Her teasing tone was gone in a flash as she frowned at me. "Well, I don't know if I like you so far away.

You haven't been home in more than a year, and I've missed you."

I walked over and wrapped my arm around her shoulders, tucking her into my side and pressing a kiss to the top of her head. "I've missed you, too, but it's five minutes away. I can be over any time you want me to—especially if there's a roast involved. And I'm going to be in Starlight Cove for a hell of a lot longer than I usually get to spend at home."

She blew out a heavy sigh. "I guess that's true. I just wish we hadn't converted all the bedrooms into something else—Morgan's is full of exercise equipment, your dad's office is in the twins' old room, and yours—"

"Is a plant nursery. I know. It's not a big deal, Mom."

"What's not a big deal?" my dad asked, walking straight to the coffeemaker to get a refill. His dark hair streaked with gray was swept neatly to the side, his face freshly shaven, save for his signature mustache, and he wore a dress shirt paired with fish-patterned boxer shorts and black socks hiked up to his knees. The picture of professionalism. Since he'd begun working from home, he'd been in heaven. He gave me a once-over, his brow pinching when he saw how I was standing. "That couch wasn't good for you. You take the bed, and we'll—"

"He's already got it handled, Carl," my mom cut in as if she hadn't been trying to figure out the same exact thing. With a pat to my stomach, she slipped out from under my arm and walked to the pantry. "Let me get you some breakfast, and then I'll whip up some banana bread for you to bring to Levi. As a thank-you for letting you stay at the inn.

And for helping your dad move all the furniture around in here to get ready for the contractors."

"He told me you already filled his freezer with meals as a thank-you for that."

She waved her hand through the air. "That was nothing. I was making those dinners anyway. And what are your father and I going to do with all that food? Now that the twins are off to college and you and Morgan are out of the house, we've got more than enough. And anyway, where else is he going to get a nice home-cooked meal?"

"Oh, I don't know. How about at the diner they own? His brother is a literal chef, Mom."

"Beck's food is very good, I'll give him that. But it still doesn't have that mother's touch."

I knew there was no arguing with her, and from the way my dad subtly shook his head, he thought the same.

While my mom gathered the ingredients she needed, muttering to herself the whole time, Dad leaned back against the counter beside me. Keeping his voice low so my mom wouldn't hear, he murmured, "Your knee hurts like a bitch this morning, doesn't it?"

I breathed out a laugh and scrubbed a hand down my face. "More like a motherfucker, but yeah."

His brow furrowed as he regarded me seriously. "You sure it's good for you to be back here instead of with the team? They got you whipped back into shape in no time after your knee surgery in July. Seems to me you'd want that with this new injury, too. Especially when Starlight Cove can only dream about the kinds of resources they have."

Was it probably better for my recovery to be there? Maybe. But I didn't care. In one way or another, this injury had kept me away for far too long because I'd let it dictate my life for the past year—had to let the medical team dictate my recovery, too. This had been one thing I wasn't willing to bend on. If they wanted me to take four months to rehab my knee instead of allowing me to have the surgery I wanted, I was damn well going to do it on my terms, and that meant being near my girl.

"It's fine, Dad. Between the calls, video chats, and coordination with the medical team and the physical therapist here, I'll be good. Back in playing condition in no time."

I hoped. Because God knew I had no idea what I'd do otherwise.

"Yeah, well, you're my kid before you're a professional hockey player. It's my job to look out for you, no matter how old you get. Just make sure to take care of yourself first and foremost."

"I am, Dad." I held up my fingers in the sign for Scout's honor, even though we both knew damn well I'd never been a Scout. "Promise."

"Good, good." He clapped a hand on my shoulder and took a sip of his coffee. "So, when's your next check-in with the team?"

"I've got a video call with the rehab coordinator tomorrow."

He held up his coffee cup as if to cheers. "Love those video calls."

I raised a brow and pointedly glanced down at his ensemble. "I can see that."

"Oh shut up, you little shit." He pushed off the counter and headed toward his office. "If you didn't have to wear pants, you wouldn't, either."

With a laugh, I headed back into the family room, leaving my mom to her favorite thing—cooking. I grabbed my phone and sent a quick text to Levi to make sure I could stay there this week.

CHASE:

I know the resort's booked, but can I stay in your old room until my furniture gets delivered?

LEVI:

Marianne isn't treating you right? Told you she liked me better.

CHASE:

I'm on the couch, and it's a fucking nightmare.

LEVI:

That's what happens when you won't give her grandkids. She becomes a plant grandma and turns your old room into a literal nursery for them.

CHASE:

She told you about that, huh?

LEVI:

Gave me a tour and everything.

CHASE:

Of course she did. Can I stay there or not?

LEVI:

Yeah. When do you want to head over? I'll meet you there.

CHASE:

I've got appointments up the ass today. And I need to wait until your fresh baked banana bread is ready.

LEVI:

Marianne's fresh baked banana bread, all for myself? I rest my case.

CHASE:

Fuck off.

See you tonight.

CHAPTER FOUR

ADDISON

I'D BEEN off my game all day. Or, more accurately, since my encounter with Chase last night. I couldn't *think* with him around. It was as if he fried every brain cell I had, and I absolutely hated it.

In an effort to shove him out of my mind, I'd overworked myself. I'd managed to destroy only one stress peen as I'd reached out to several contractors in the area to get quotes for rehabilitating our decrepit ice-skating rink and surrounding buildings, recorded twenty new videos for our social media accounts, emailed back and forth with Levi's former bestie turned journalist, Harper, about possible articles on the resort, and started planning our spring marketing campaign. I wanted to do all I could to make sure the resort stayed at the top of people's minds. Just because things were going well right now didn't mean I'd forgotten exactly how tough times had been for us in the not-so-distant past.

It was nearly eight by the time I dragged myself upstairs

to my room, grateful I was on the other side of the house from Aiden after the looks I'd seen Avery shooting his way. I loved that they'd gotten together—hell, I was the whole reason they had!—but I absolutely did *not* need to know what my best friend sounded like during a night with my brother.

I shuddered at the thought and stepped through my bedroom door to find Levi lounging on my bed, ankles crossed, phone in hand. "Hey. Did we have plans tonight?"

"Nah. Just wanted to give you a heads-up."

I set my iPad on my dresser and kicked off my shoes, glancing at him with a raised brow. "About what?"

"Chase needed a place to stay, so I let him use my room."

I tripped over absolutely nothing on my way to the adjoining bathroom and turned around slowly to face my brother. "You what?"

He didn't lift his eyes from his phone, clearly not reading the sharpness in my tone. "Told him he could stay in my room this week."

"Why the fuck did you do that?"

He shot a look my way before shifting his attention back to his phone. "He's waiting for furniture to be delivered to his new place, and he can't stay at his parents'."

I didn't give a single shit about his furniture or the lack of accommodations at his parents' house. What I cared about was keeping my sanity intact. And that absolutely could not happen with him sleeping right next door to me. My entire avoidance plan would be out the fucking window.

"What about the cottages?" I asked, panic rising in my voice.

This time, Levi lowered his phone to his chest and met my eyes, his brows raised. He spoke slowly, as if he were explaining something to a child. "The cottages have been booked for months, as you continually remind me. What's the big deal?"

The big deal? *The big deal*? The big deal was I had absolutely no willpower when it came to Chase. I never had. And now he was going to be directly next door, separated from me by a measly bathroom shared between our rooms?

Absolutely not.

"Why can't he stay in Brady's old room? Or Beck and Ford's?"

"Because they're still filled with paper towel cartons—and Jesus Christ, how many did Aiden accidentally order anyway?"

"We can move them into your old room and send Chase across the house."

"Yeah...I'm not doing all that." He shook his head, dismissing it without thought. "What, are you worried about him bringing random women back here?"

Well, I hadn't been, but I sure as hell was now.

Levi shrugged. "I'll tell him to get his dick wet elsewhere. That work for you?"

Without my permission, images of Chase doing exactly that assaulted me. If the tabloids were anything to go by, it'd be someone leggy and blond with huge boobs stuffed into a child-sized jersey with his number on it.

"I don't care what he does with his dick." *Lie*. "When's he going to be here?"

In other words, how long did I have to prep for this absolute fucking catastrophe?

"Any minute. When you're done freaking out, how about you shut up so we can watch *Vampire Diaries*?"

"Not tonight." Any other time, I'd give my brother shit for being addicted to teen dramas, but I was preoccupied trying to determine a game plan. I needed to lock myself in my room and never come out. Figure out how to do all my work from right here in this 12' x 14' box.

Levi finally swept his gaze over me, his mouth pulled down in a frown. "What's wrong?"

"Nothing," I said too quickly. *Just trying to avoid your best friend because I'm done fucking him and fucking up my life in the process.* "I have my period, and I don't want you in my face."

He gave me a dubious look, and I threw my hands in the air. "Do I have to start throwing tampons at your head to get you to leave?"

"Fine. Jesus, you vicious little shit. You don't have to yell about it."

"I'm not yelling." I was *totally* yelling.

He stood from my bed and walked past me, ruffling my hair in the process. "I'll wait for him in my room and tell him to steer clear of the red beast. Text me if you need anything."

"Great. Thanks. Get out." I pressed my hands against his back and shoved him the rest of the way out of my room, slamming the door in his face and locking it for good measure. There wasn't anything I could do about the connecting bathroom door, though.

I just had to hope Chase wasn't stupid enough to come

through it. Because I might not actually have my period right now, but I could muster up some PMS rage if I needed to. And I had absolutely no problem directing it straight at him.

ADDISON:

I know you're busy getting freaky with my brother

shudder

But I have an SOS situation over here

ADDISON:

Seriously

You need to come to my room

Immediately

Probably daily for the rest of our lives

Since I'm never leaving here again

ADDISON:

I'm going to take your silence as a need for further explanation

Why am I trapped here forever?

Oh nothing major

JUST THAT HE WHO IS DEAD TO ME IS STAYING IN LEVI'S OLD ROOM

AKA the room directly next to mine

Connected by a bathroom

You remember how that worked out for you and Aiden???

ADDISON:

HELLO?

MY GOD

How long does it take my brother to get you off???

Does he need a manual?

I'm literally dying over here!

AVERY:

First, you're not LITERALLY dying, you drama queen. Second, he has no problem getting me off, believe me. He stopped at three this time thanks to your incessant text interruptions.

ADDISON:

oh my god

That's more than I ever wanted to know about my brother and his delivery of O's

AVERY:

You're the one who brought it up. But let's get to the issue here. What do you mean, He Who Shall Not Be Named is staying in Levi's old room???

ADDISON:

Exactly what I said

Tell my brother he can play porn star later

I need you now

AVERY:

Be there in 2

True to her word, Avery showed up at my door a couple minutes later, carrying the pan of brownies she'd baked earlier in the day. "I figured if you were going to stay in here for the rest of your life, you'd need sustenance."

"And all you brought were brownies?"

"What else matters, really?" She walked over and plopped down on my bed with the pan in her lap and immediately dug in. "I haven't seen you much since the bar, so you're gonna have to fill me in. How did we go from you glaring at him in One Night Stan's to him staying in the room next door?"

I joined her on the bed and grabbed a brownie for myself, stuffing nearly the whole thing into my mouth in an effort to make myself feel better. It didn't work. "I have no idea. Except for the fact that Levi is obviously out to get me."

"Sweetie, I'm pretty sure this lies squarely at He Who Shall Not Be Named's feet. Levi doesn't have a clue about you two and hasn't for years."

"Aiden doesn't either, right?"

She shook her head. "He asked about it after the bar, but I made up a story about Chase ruining your favorite dress freshman year, and then distracted him with a beej."

"Gross."

"It worked, didn't it?"

"Yeah, good thinking, I guess. Because I definitely don't want any of them to know." I pursed my lips to the side and glanced at her out of the corner of my eye. "Except I did think about telling Levi just to see if that would get the asshole to back off."

Avery scoffed. "I don't believe you for a second. Let's cut the shit, and how about you tell me what's really going on?"

What was going on was the only man I'd ever cared about had left me in the rearview without thought. What was going on was I'd allowed him to break my heart—not once, but twice—and I had no intention of allowing it a third time.

I threw my hands up in the air and lied through my teeth. "What's going on is the person I want to see least in the world is staying twenty feet away from me."

She lifted her brows, skepticism written on her face. "So this is the story you're going with, is that right?

"There's no *story*. It's the truth."

"Mhmm," she said flatly. "So, we're just going to ignore the fact that for the past however many years, you guys have hooked up every time he's been home?"

I cleared my throat and avoided her gaze. "Yes, I would like to ignore that, thank you very much."

"And how about the sobfest over margaritas last year after Christmas? Are we going to ignore that, too? Or the one in June after you found out he was injured and never texted you back? Or the one just a couple weeks ago when he didn't come home for Christmas without a word?"

When she laid it all out like that, it made me feel even more pathetic than I already did, and I fucking hated feeling like that.

I blew out a ragged breath, my entire body deflating as I shook my head, my gaze locked on a loose thread on my comforter. "I can't do it again with him. I need to move on with my life once and for all."

She studied me for long moments before nodding. "Okay. If that's how you really feel, then what you need to do is pretend he doesn't exist. He's dead to you, remember? If you hide away in your room, he'll know he's getting to you. Show him he's not." She grabbed another brownie and looked at me with raised brows. "And maybe if you do it long enough, you'll start to believe it, too."

CHAPTER FIVE

CHASE

IF THERE WAS one thing I knew with complete certainty, it was that when Addison set her mind to something, she didn't allow anything to stand in her way. It was one of the things I loved most about her.

Unfortunately, her mind was currently set on steering clear of me, which I didn't love quite so much.

She'd stayed in her room last night, her and Avery's muted conversation little more than muffled sounds through our shared wall. Levi had warned me Addison had her period and was on the war path. The war path part was confirmed by her listening to her *Fuck Off* playlist all night. But if I knew her—and I did—her anger had nothing to do with her cycle and everything to do with my staying in the room next door. That and the fact that she'd have to try a hell of a lot harder to ignore me now.

Especially when I had no intention of making it easy for her.

After having my ass handed to me at PT—I'd rather be slammed into the boards fifty times than spend another minute suffering my way through those exercises—and my weekly call with the rehab coordinator to update him on my progress, which wasn't much, I headed back to the main inn, sore and worn down.

I grabbed one of the half dozen ice-pack wraps I'd stored in the freezer and secured it on my knee. Then I popped some ibuprofen to mitigate the inevitable swelling I'd face tonight. My knee always ached more after PT, and it was just a reminder of how far I still had to go before I'd be ready to play again.

If I'd be ready to play again.

Not knowing the future never used to bother me. I could change plans at the drop of a hat, never needing to know what came next. But that had been what felt like a lifetime ago. Before my sister Morgan had been diagnosed with leukemia. Before our world had been thrown into chaos, none of us knowing what the next day—let alone year—would bring.

Considering all my hockey career had provided for me and my family, I didn't like not knowing what the future held when it came to my career. And that shit was especially scary when I was good at only one thing and had been doing it my whole life. What the hell would I do if playing hockey was no longer an option?

The inn was quiet except for the sound of furious typing —no doubt Addison's—coming from the parlor, so I headed that way. She liked her space—needed it, actually, and I was happy to give it to her. But I'd been doing that for a year, and I was tired of it, especially when I could read a thread of hurt beneath the anger she portrayed to the rest of the world.

I poked my head around the doorway to find her sitting on the couch, her legs folded, laptop perched on top, mile-high heels discarded on the floor in front of her. She didn't so much as twitch when I leaned against the doorframe, so she either didn't notice me or was incredibly good at ignoring me.

"Hey," I said. Long moments ticked by without a response. Ignoring me, it was. "What are you working on?" Ignored. "Social media?" Ignored. "I should have you take over mine because you're rocking the resort's."

"How about you have one of your puck bunnies do it instead?" she said without inflection, but I could hear the underlying tension threaded in her voice.

I pushed off from the doorframe and strode into the room, forcing myself not to favor my bad knee. "I don't have puck bunnies."

She snorted and rolled her eyes but otherwise didn't respond, which meant she didn't believe a word out of my mouth. That was fine. I had four months to prove otherwise.

I sat in the chair perpendicular to her—wanting nothing more than to sit next to her but loving my dick too much to chance it getting ripped off—and winced as my knee screamed in protest.

She shot me a sideways glance. "Your overexaggerated pain isn't going to make me feel sorry for you."

Leaning back in the chair, I stretched out my bad leg in

front of me and raised my brows at her. "I've known you your whole life, Addie. I already know you don't hand out pity."

"Then what's your angle here?" She circled a pen in my general direction, her eyes narrowed. "Because I'm working. And in case it's not clear, I have ten thousand things on my to-do list today, as usual, and entertaining a wounded man-child isn't one of them."

I knew it probably said something about me and our relationship, but her sharp, smart mouth got my dick hard. Every fucking time.

"That's why I'm here. My leg might be busted, but my fingers work just fine." I couldn't help but smirk when my comment made her fumble on the keyboard. "Word on the street is you need help, and I'm free labor. Put me to work."

"Word on the—*fucking Levi*," she spat, whipping out her phone to no doubt text my best friend to hand him his ass.

And fuck me, but even when her face was a mask of fury, she was so goddamn beautiful. If I looked at her every day for the rest of my life, I still wouldn't tire of the view. Especially after being denied it for over a year.

"I think I'll pass on fucking Levi," I said. "But you should know better than anyone he's not my type."

Without looking up, she said, "Actually, I don't pay attention to you or whoever it is you're fucking this month, so I have no idea what your current favorite flavor is."

Which meant she *had* paid attention and probably saw the completely fabricated pictures of my coach's daughter and me talking after a game—when she was informing me about the surprise party she was planning for her dad. Our five-minute interaction had been blown out of proportion and plastered everywhere. It hadn't helped that she'd been leaning close to keep her voice down or that someone had bumped into her from behind, sending her plowing straight into my chest.

My lips twitched as I stared at my feral little beast. "Careful, firefly, you're starting to sound jealous."

She scoffed. "Oh please. I care less about who you stick your dick in than I do about the migration pattern of birds. Which is to say, I do not have a single fuck to give."

"Never say that!" Mabel said, joining our conversation as if she'd always been part of it. She shuffled into the parlor wearing a purple velour tracksuit and a shirt beneath it that had silhouettes of various sex toys on it and read, *good vibes only*. Ford strode in behind her, giving me a two-finger salute. "Fucks are the very best thing to give, honey."

I didn't even try to hold in my laugh, and neither did Ford. Apparently, the older woman was still as feisty as ever and had, if possible, gotten even more blunt in the time I'd been gone.

Mabel turned toward me, her eyes sparkling with interest. "Chase! You're just the man I needed to see. I wanted to proposition you..."

Holding up my hands, I shook my head. "No can do, Mabel. George might be getting up there, but I think he can still take me. Especially when I have a busted knee."

She waved a hand through the air, dismissing my words. "I'm not propositioning you for sex. Honestly, honey, I don't think you could keep up with me. No, this is for charity. Since so many of our eligible bachelors in town have settled down this past year—" she shot a pointed look to Ford, who just grinned back at her "—I'm looking for some fresh sausage to auction off at our local meat market."

Ford snorted and shook his head. "What this trouble-maker means is she wants some men for the bachelor auction happening in the spring."

Mabel sniffed. "Well, if you want to be delicate about it, yes, that's what I mean. So, what do you say, honey?"

With my eyes still locked on Addison, who was trying valiantly not to pay any attention to us, I asked, "Who usually bids for the bachelors?"

I had no idea why I was asking. There was a less-than-zero percent chance the only woman I wanted to win a date with would bid on me. Especially if this event was public. And especially if she continued pretending to hate my guts.

"Well, I got a wife out of the last one." Ford waggled his eyebrows and held up his left hand, showcasing a black band on his ring finger.

"That he did," Mabel said. "It's one of our biggest success stories. Which is why I think this year's will be hoppin'. My friends are all saving up for it. Plus, lots of the eligible bachelorettes in the area will be there, so you just might find a love match! Wouldn't that be great? What do you say? Want to find yourself a girl?"

I already had a girl. One I'd been tied to for a decade, even without an actual commitment. But before I could tell Mabel I wasn't interested in a love match because my body, heart, and soul were already taken by the tiny tornado in the room, Addison slammed her laptop closed and gathered up her things with a little more force than necessary.

“Not sure why you're asking him, Mabel.” She walked toward the doorway, glancing back at me over her shoulder, her gaze as cold as ice. “I wouldn't count on him being here next month, much less in four. And Starlight Cove is a little light on the bunnies he usually goes for.”

CHAPTER SIX

ADDISON

A BACHELOR AUCTION? A fucking *bachelor auction*? He was a professional athlete and could go literally anywhere in the world, but he chose to come back to *my* town and ruin *my* life? And now I was supposed to watch him strutting onstage and stand by while some wannabe WAG bid on him?

I didn't fucking think so.

It made no sense why this bothered me so much. Chase wasn't mine, as he'd made perfectly clear. If this past year had shown me anything, it was that I wasn't important to him at all. Not enough to warrant a text to let me know he wasn't dying. Or that he'd come out of surgery okay. Or that he'd be back to his irritating, idiot self in no time.

Those hours following his brutal crash on the ice in game seven of the finals, where he went down like a box of rocks and had to be helped off the ice, had been some of the worst in my life. Only rivaled by the hours we'd spent searching the ocean in vain for my mom.

And then to have to find out from my *brother* that Chase was having surgery—then, later, was out of surgery and recovering at home...was at training camp and back on the ice...was set to play the first game of the season? It was salt in an open wound.

So, yeah. He could take his bachelor auction and shove it all the way up his ass for all I cared.

Mabel was probably down there right now giving him pointers on what to do and how to act at the auction, but that didn't mean I had to stick around for it. What I needed now was a distraction. If he wanted to put himself on the auction block, that was his choice. But no way was I going to let him know it bothered me. It was time to show him I hadn't been sitting around all this time, waiting for him to grace me with his presence. I needed to let him know his return to Starlight Cove had absolutely no bearing on my life, and I knew exactly how to make that happen.

I pulled out my phone, navigating to the dating app Avery had bullied me into downloading forever ago. Despite her telling me for the past nine months that I needed to start dating, I hadn't used it once since she'd set up my profile.

But there was no time like the present.

I clicked on the icon featuring a heart with a cupid's arrow through it, my eyebrows lifting when I saw what was waiting for me after logging in. "Damn. What the hell did she write about me?"

This app was unique in that it put everything in the woman's court—which was the only reason I'd agreed to sign up in the first place. Men showed their interest by sending a message, and the women could either ignore or accept. No unknowns. No unanswered swipes.

And what was currently in my court were seventy-eight unread messages awaiting my attention.

Most of the guys weren't in Starlight Cove but instead in the surrounding areas—some as far as a few hours from here —and since I wanted to do this *tonight*, I needed to find someone local. I scrolled through dozens before landing on a possibility.

Chad, age thirty-two, 6' according to his profile, which meant he was really 5'10". But that was fine, considering I topped out at 5'2" on a good day. He liked football—bonus points for not being a hockey fan—hiking, and hanging out with his friends. And the quote he chose to highlight was, "I'm not a professional photographer, but I can definitely picture us arguing about who should pay for dinner."

I wrinkled my nose. Who not only thought that, but then decided it was good enough to add to his profile in an attempt to snag some dates? This guy, apparently. There was no denying his profile wasn't great. And if I were in this for anything more than spite, I definitely wouldn't have picked Chad the cheapskate. But he was cute and local, and I'd bet money he didn't have the ladies banging down his door, so he was probably free tonight.

I opened the message thread, cringing at his intro message to me—*What's a guy like me doing without your number?*—not to mention his screen name.

God, this was going to be awful. Absolutely fucking terrible. But I was doing it. And I figured there was no sense beating around the bush since I was on a time crunch. So instead of pleasantries, I got straight to the point.

TinyTornado: *Are you free tonight at seven?*

It took less than thirty seconds before the dancing ellipses appeared, indicating he was typing a response.

69isMyFavoriteNumber: *Hell yeah I am. What are you thinking?*

Well, that was easier than I thought it would be. Though I shouldn't have been surprised. Single men—and even not-so-single men—were thirsty fuckers.

TinyTornado: *Dinner at Ambrosia. Pick me up at Starlight Cove Resort at 7.*

69isMyFavoriteNumber: *I'll be there*

The dancing ellipses told me he was typing another message, but I closed the app. It didn't matter what else he had to say. He confirmed our date for tonight, and I had shit to check off my to-do list before I could get ready for it, so I didn't have time to chitchat.

A couple hours later, after finishing what I could for the day, I texted Avery and begged for her help.

ADDISON:

I have a date tonight

AVERY:

You WHAT?

ADDISON:

I finally went on that app you set up for me

I picked one of the least cringey guys

Which isn't saying much

AVERY:

I see. And this wouldn't happen to have anything to do with a certain 6'3", incredibly built, extremely charming pro hockey player who's staying in the room next to yours, would it?

ADDISON:

I have no idea what you're talking about

AVERY:

Sure you don't

ADDISON:

Are you going to come over here and help me find something to wear or not?

I'd barely hit send before there was a knock on my door, and I opened it to Avery's bright smile. "How'd you get here so fast?"

"As soon as you said you had a date, I was already on my way." She hip checked me as she strode into my room, heading straight for my closet.

As she was sorting through my options, she called over her shoulder, "What kind of vibe are we going for? Do you want cute girl next door? Just one of the guys? Or are we going straight-up vixen tonight?"

I dropped onto my bed, leaning back and bracing myself on my hands. "I think you know the answer to that."

"Vixen it is," she said, shooting a mischievous grin my way.

After lots of mumbling on her end that I wasn't able to make out from where she'd burrowed her way into my closet, she pulled out a red dress I'd had for years. In fact, I was pretty sure she was the one who'd bought it for me in the first place. I'd worn it exactly once, to a New Year's Eve party after I moved back home following graduation. A party a certain hockey player had been attending and had gone absolutely feral when he'd seen me wearing it...

"You know Chase is going to lose his shit if he sees me in that dress, right?" I asked, raising my brows at her. I hadn't spared any details when I'd told her what had happened that night. How he hadn't been able to keep his hands off me and had fucked me in a darkened hall while half of Starlight Cove had been counting down to midnight.

She smirked, tossing the dress onto my bed. "Why do you think I chose it? Let's show him what he's been missing. And, more importantly, what he no longer has."

CHAPTER SEVEN

CHASE

IT WAS BECOMING BLATANTLY obvious that Addison and I were not on the same page. And I'd be lying if I said her display of jealousy—no doubt seen as irritation to anyone else—didn't please the fuck out of me. Because if she cared as little as she'd been pretending, she wouldn't have a reason to be jealous because she wouldn't care who or what I did, including participating in a bachelor auction. But she cared. A whole fucking lot.

Now I just had to get her to admit it.

My knee was throbbing like a mother, so thank God it was about time for my next dose of ibuprofen. I made my way to Levi's old room and the attached bathroom to grab the pills but stopped short as soon as I opened the door.

Addison startled at my intrusion, a squeak leaving her before her surprise turned to annoyance and she pinned me with a scowl. "Jesus, Chase!"

Her hair was wavy, the ends just brushing her bare shoulders, her eyes smoky and dark. She looked sexy as fuck, and I wanted to bend her over the counter and remind myself exactly how sweet she was. Exactly how well she took me.

I couldn't stop my gaze from sweeping over her, but with every inch it traveled down her body, my brow pinched more and more. She wore a skintight red strapless dress that left very little to the imagination. A dress I'd seen her in once before—the first New Year's Eve after she'd moved back home to Starlight Cove following college graduation. When we'd started hooking up on a consistent basis.

I hadn't been able to keep my hands off her that night. So much so that I hadn't even stripped her of the dress before fucking her in a darkened hallway not nearly far enough away from the rest of the partygoers. I'd shoved her panties to the side, tugged down the front of her dress to gain access to her perfect little tits, and taken her right then and there.

The memory alone had me hard as a fucking rock, and my gray sweatpants did very little to hide that fact.

"What the hell do you think you're doing?" she snapped. "You can't just walk in whenever you want."

"I needed some ibuprofen," I murmured, unable to tear my eyes off her. "Didn't know you were in here."

She blew out a frustrated breath and tossed a brush into her makeup bag. "This isn't going to work."

"You're right about that." That dress had to go. Preferably on my bedroom floor. Or hers. I wasn't picky.

She scowled harder. "If you're going to stay in the room next door to me, you need to knock before you come barging into the bathroom."

I ran a hand over my mouth, my gaze sliding over every inch of her, and shook my head, dazed and barely able to form words. "Figured you'd lock it."

She glared at me in the mirror, her eyes narrowed and her tone sharp. "I haven't had to lock this door in years. I forgot. And believe me, I'm cursing myself for that now."

I didn't bother to hide my slow perusal or appreciation of her. I *wanted* Addison to know exactly how much I wanted her. Exactly how much I craved her. Exactly how fucking gone I was for her.

Though her legs weren't very long, they were a feast for my eyes tonight. Especially with those black heels that had to add four inches to her minuscule stature. Her feet were going to be killing her by the end of the night, but I couldn't deny how fucking hot they looked. I wanted those heels propped on my shoulders while I fucked her, and I made sure my eyes conveyed exactly that when I met her gaze in the mirror. From the way her lips parted and her nipples tightened beneath that formfitting material, it was clear she wasn't immune to me, either. It was something, at least.

"What if I'd been in the shower?" she asked, her voice hoarse.

My cock was hard as a fucking rock, and it only got harder at the image her innocent question conjured. "Then I'd have been the luckiest motherfucker on the planet."

She huffed out an irritated sound. "That comment would be inappropriate on a normal day, but considering I'm getting ready for a date, it's exceptionally bad."

I snapped my head up to meet her eyes in the mirror. A

fucking *date*? I didn't even bother to hide my response to that bomb. Anger. Frustration. Jealousy. They all rushed through me, the thought of my girl going out with some other asshole unsettling me. I couldn't hope to hide my reaction, and she saw every single emotion as it flitted across my face, her responding expression a mixture of fury and satisfaction.

As soon as the latter registered, realization dawned. *That* dress? Those shoes? Her doing this after the little fiasco downstairs? No doubt about it—this date was designed solely to piss me off.

"With who." It was less a question and more a demand, but I couldn't help myself.

"That's definitely none of your business."

"How long has this been planned for?" I'd bet my good knee it was something she'd set up today—something that was a direct response to the bachelor auction discussion downstairs. The one I didn't give a single fuck about, the one I wouldn't be participating in, and the one that had no bearing whatsoever on the two of us.

I hadn't had eyes for anyone *but* Addison in more than a decade, and that wasn't ever going to change.

"Also none of your business."

I ground my molars together, biting back everything I wanted to say or do. Instead, I stood leaning against the door-frame, stewing and silent, and watched as she finished getting ready. Running her fingers through her hair and adjusting the loose waves. Applying another coat of mascara. Painting those lips I'd had wrapped around my cock more times than I could count a bright, vibrant red to match her dress.

Fuck me. No, seriously, fuck me in the ass with a cactus. It would be less painful than watching her go out with another man.

She was a fucking siren tonight. A drop-dead gorgeous hellcat, and some other bastard was going to be on the receiving end of it.

After giving herself a final once-over in the mirror, she turned and headed into her bedroom without a word. Since she didn't slam the door in my face, I took that as my invitation to follow.

Without glancing my way, she grabbed a small black purse and transferred items into it. Wallet. Keys. Lipstick.

A fucking *condom*.

She was doing this to mess with me, but it didn't stop me from clenching my hands into fists, my jaw tightening right along with them. Jesus Christ, if I had anything more than stumps for teeth by the end of the night, it'd be a goddamn miracle.

Without a word, she strode out of her bedroom, her ass and those legs a goddamn sight for sore eyes as she headed straight for the stairs.

"You're seriously doing this."

"Doing what?" she asked, feigning nonchalance, but it didn't work on me. Addison hadn't been nonchalant about a thing in her life. She was chalant as fuck, and I loved every ounce of it.

"Going out on a bullshit date just to fuck with me."

"Believe it or not, I'm capable of making decisions without considering you at all." She grabbed a black coat from the rack by the front door and shrugged into it.

I glanced out the window to the dark parking lot to find a car idling there, the douchebag sitting nice and warm inside. "He's not even coming to the door? *Seriously*?"

She rolled her eyes. "Relax, Grandpa. This isn't 1956."

"Give me a second to grab my shoes, and I'll walk you out."

"I don't need an escort."

"The fuck you don't. You're in four-inch heels, and the sidewalks are covered in ice. Give me a fucking second."

Instead, she waved to someone behind me and called out a quick, "Bye," before opening the door and slamming it in my face.

Fuck my shoes. Who needed them anyway?

I yanked open the door to follow after her, except a hand shot out and slammed it shut once again. I glanced over, coming face-to-face with Avery. A scowling, pissed-off Avery, who wore an expression that clearly said she wasn't impressed with me or any of my bullshit. Though that wasn't anything new—she'd looked at me the exact same way when I'd officially met her at One Night Stan's the other night.

"Addison's a big girl," she said. "She can handle walking to a car by herself."

I scoffed. "Did you see those shoes? She could break her neck."

"Better than her heart. Again." She shot me a pointed look and stepped in front of the door, arms crossed. "Addison's going on her date, and you're going to let her." Her voice was firm, hard, leaving absolutely no room for me to argue.

My mind was whirring with possibilities, but I saluted her and headed up the stairs two at a time, my knee screaming the entire way. Yeah, I'd let Addison go on the date, like Avery said.

But I never promised I wouldn't join her.

CHAPTER EIGHT

ADDISON

IT HAD ONLY BEEN twenty minutes, but I was already bored out of my mind on this spite date. I'd know from the guy's profile that he wasn't exactly a winner, but I'd hoped he'd be interesting enough to at least get my mind off a certain infuriating hockey player for five fucking minutes.

Sadly, this guy couldn't even manage to snag my attention for a *singular* minute. I was certain watching Levi hand-sand a boat for hours on end would be more interesting than sitting across from Chad.

What *was* interesting was Chase's reaction to me back at the inn. Having him walk in on me getting ready definitely hadn't been in the plans, but it should have been, considering his reaction. Witnessing the emotions flit across his face had made up for how uncomfortable this dress was and how precarious these shoes were and how absolutely little I wanted to be here.

Lust had blanketed Chase's features as he'd swept his

gaze over me from head to toe. Then had come the realization that he'd seen me in this dress before. And every one of those memories we'd made while I'd been wearing this the last time had played across his face, making me relive them, too.

When he'd shown up at that New Year's Eve party, his gaze had found mine the second he'd walked through the door. That always seemed to happen with us—we were like magnets, always being pulled together, no matter how hard either of us fought it.

His attention had never left me as he'd woven his way through the crowd, people attempting to catch his eye to no avail. He'd been popular, even back then, having just signed his second contract with Vancouver, which meant he couldn't stride up to me without being noticed. And if there was one thing neither of us wanted to be noticed, it was him stalking through the crowd toward his best friend's little sister, looking like he wanted to eat her for dinner.

As soon as we'd been tucked away in a secluded alcove, as hidden as we could be while being feet away from a raging party, he hadn't said a word before he'd cupped my face and kissed me. It'd started slow and sweet, just the brush of his lips against mine, before turning hungry in a blink.

The thing about kissing Chase was that it was *always* all-consuming. Every single time, without fail. He had a way of making me feel like I was the only person in the world...in the whole fucking universe. Made me feel like I was the only one he ever wanted.

But that was clearly me being disillusioned because he'd proven just how little he wanted me this past year.

"So, what do you think?" As if Chad knew I hadn't been paying attention, he rapped his knuckles twice on the table in front of me, pulling me out of my memories.

"What do I think about what?"

He lifted his brows and gestured toward the menu I was looking over. "You want to know what I like so you can order something from that list? That way, I can finish the meal for you. You're a tiny little thing. You probably don't eat much."

I flashed him my teeth in what he probably assumed was a smile but definitely was not. If he tried to eat my food, he'd be missing a finger by the end of the night. "No, I don't think I'll be doing that."

"Oh," he said, shock ringing in the single syllable. When I simply met his gaze with an unflinching stare of my own, he cleared his throat. "Okay. So, you got any plans for the Super Bowl next month? 'Cause I'm having a party if you wanted to come."

"I'm not really into sports." As long as you didn't count watching hundreds of hockey games featuring one very specific team over the past ten years. And I definitely did not.

He winked at me—actually winked, like a fucking creep. "Give me a couple dates, and I bet I could change that."

This guy certainly gave new meaning to the term cocky. Chase had exuded it for as long as I could remember, and while it had oftentimes irritated me, it had never made me cringe. The difference, though, was that Chase could back it up a hundred times over. And the guy across from me didn't have a leg to stand on.

I barely refrained from rolling my eyes. "How about we get through this first date before we start banking on any others."

Chad laughed as if I was joking, but I just raised a brow and lifted my drink to take a sip. God knew I was going to need every drop of alcohol I could get to make it through this date.

How long did I have to suffer through here? We hadn't ordered dinner yet, so maybe I could misconstrue what this really was and assume we'd just been going out for drinks and appetizers? Where was Avery when I needed her? I was so far out of the dating game, I couldn't begin to guess what was appropriate. Though, truthfully, did I really care what was "appropriate" with a guy who was going to fight me about paying and who told me to order his favorites so he could eat my meal?

Before I could send an SOS text to Avery to get me out of here, Chad said, "If you're not doing anything this weekend, maybe you want to come hang out. We can—*holy shit*!" His wide-eyed stare was fixed on something behind me. Without taking his gaze off whatever had caught his attention, he leaned toward me over the table and hissed, "You're never going to believe who's walking this way!"

My shoulders stiffened, my back going ramrod straight as goose bumps prickled my skin. With that reaction—one I was unfortunately intimately familiar with—I didn't have to guess.

I knew exactly who was headed in our direction.

Chase

ONE BENEFIT of being a professional hockey player was that I could get pretty much anything I wanted when I wanted it. Pair that with being back in my small hometown, and the fine people of Starlight Cove were willing to do just about anything to give me what I asked for.

I made it a point not to abuse that. Tried, in fact, to never use it at all. But when my girl was sitting in the middle of this restaurant across from some douchebag wearing a ratty graphic tee and a baseball hat when she looked like fucking fire, I intended to use everything I had at my disposal.

So, when I strolled into the restaurant I'd correctly guessed they'd be at—bonus points for small-town living—and requested the table that had just opened up one over from them, I got it, no questions asked.

The host was a kid, probably fifteen or sixteen, and he stared at me with wide, starstruck eyes and an open mouth. "Holy *shit*, you're—"

I dipped my chin in a nod and shot him a grin. "I am. And if you put me at that table right there—" I leaned on the stand and pointed at the table as close to my girl as I could get "—I'll sign whatever you want before I leave."

The kid was nodding vigorously before I'd even finished the sentence. He started walking that way before smacking a hand on his forehead and turning around to grab a menu while shooting me a sheepish smile.

I followed him, adjusting my cuffs as I kept my eyes trained on Addison. That meant I didn't miss her reaction when her date leaned toward her and said, "You're never going to believe who's walking this way!"

Her shoulders stiffened, and even though she hadn't turned around, hadn't even glanced behind her, I had no doubt she knew exactly who he was talking about.

With how short her hair was now, her shoulders and back were bare above the strapless dress, and it was fucking torture that I couldn't go up to her and brush my lips all over that smooth, soft skin. Couldn't suck that spot on her neck that always made her melt into me. Couldn't reach around, cup her tits, and run my thumbs over her nipples while kissing along every exposed inch I could reach...

"Let me guess," she responded flatly to the douchebag. "The NHL's biggest idiot."

"What?" he said, shaking his head. "No, it's—"

"Chase Lockhart," she interrupted. "Yeah, yeah, it's very exciting."

"How did you know it was him?" he asked.

"Lucky guess."

"Actually..." I stepped up to their table, bracing my hands on the back of her chair, my fingers lightly brushing against her skin. "Addison and I go way back. Isn't that right, Addie?"

"Unfortunately," she grumbled into her glass before downing the rest of her wine.

"Seriously?" Douchebag asked, his wide eyes flitting

between me and Addison. "That's fucking awesome! Do you want to... I mean, if you're eating alone anyway, do you want to join us?"

"*Excuse* me?" Addison hissed. Her tone was frosty enough to have a grown man's balls shriveling up, but Douchebag just looked at her as if he didn't have a clue.

I held up a hand. "I really don't want to impose."

Addison shot a glare at me over her shoulder. "Good, then you should—"

"Definitely sit with us!" Douchebag finished for her. Then he snapped his fingers at the host and pointed to the chair between him and Addison. "You can set that down right here, my man."

"I really don't want to interrupt your...date." I nearly choked on the word, and from the smug look Addison shot me, she could tell.

"Are you kidding?" Douchebag asked. "We want you to!"

"And does Addison agree with that?" I asked, since he didn't seem to care at all about her opinion.

"Of course she does!" he said. "Don't you?" Before she could answer, he snapped his fingers at the host again. "Right here, my man, like I said. And get this guy a drink." He hooked a thumb in my direction. "Whatever he wants! It's my treat."

My entire plan in coming here had been to sit close. Keep an eye on her. Make sure she was okay. And, yeah, hopefully ruin whatever vibe she had going with the asshole who was lucky enough to be on the receiving end of her presence tonight. But now? Fucking right I was going to join them.

This guy was an asshole *and* an idiot. I knew Addison could handle herself—especially with a guy like this. She'd chew him up and spit him out before he even knew she'd taken a bite.

But that didn't mean she should have to.

So, I unbuttoned my suit jacket and took the seat between them, my gaze locked on her the entire time. Though it was clear she was trying to ignore me, she shot several glances my way, her gaze flitting over every inch of me she could see. Her eyes were filled with unmasked irritation, but something else was hidden in their depths.

Hunger.

There was no denying how it heated her gaze, and my dick shot to attention immediately at her interest. That, combined with how snippy she was with Douchebag, and I knew there was no way she'd set this up as anything other than a revenge date, just as I'd thought.

And after hearing him cut her off, disregard her wants, and basically ignore her in favor of kissing my ass? Yeah, I was going to make sure this guy was put in his place before the night was through, and I was going to enjoy every fucking second of it.

CHAPTER NINE

ADDISON

GOING out on this date had been a horrible idea. Not only did I have to sit through multiple mind-numbingly boring conversations Chad dominated, but I had to suffer through it all with Chase sitting directly next to me while wearing a suit that looked like it was tailor-made for him. I was used to seeing him in jeans and a T-shirt or his uniform, but I couldn't deny what the sight of him dressed up did for me. Every time his knee bumped into mine, it shot a zing of awareness down my spine, my nipples responding in kind.

I'd been a fidgety, uncomfortable mess through dinner. And though I'd tried to minimize how often I glanced Chase's way, I could *feel* his stare on me, heavy and unwavering. And I hated how much I loved it.

Despite the fact that Chad had listed himself as heterosexual on his dating profile, I was beginning to wonder if he didn't have a little bit of a crush on Chase. Or, more accurately, a big-ass infatuation. He'd spent the entirety of dinner kissing Chase's ass. He'd talked Chase up about every great play he'd made this season, fawning over the injury that had taken him out in June during the play-offs and the reinjury a couple weeks ago that had sent him back home to Starlight Cove. Not to mention tripping over himself to get Chase whatever he wanted, as if the guy weren't a literal millionaire who could get it himself. And it turned out Chad and I hadn't had to argue about who was paying the bill because Chase had reached for it before Chad's finger could even twitch.

And me? Well, the only attention I got was from the one person I shouldn't want it from.

Shouldn't but couldn't help that I did.

All that combined meant this was going to go down as one of the worst dates I'd ever been on in my life. But that didn't mean I was going to give Chase the satisfaction of knowing that. And I sure as hell wasn't going to let him think he ruined this date, which had no doubt been his goal.

After Chase signed a couple autographs and the three of us strolled outside into the cold January air, I turned toward Chad and plastered on a smile. "What are you doing the rest of the night?"

"Yeah, you going to a sports bar later, or what?" Chase lifted his chin toward my date's ensemble, one that made him look like an overgrown little leaguer.

"No. Why, do you want to go to one with me?" Chad asked, as eager as a puppy with a new toy.

I definitely needed to steer this ship back on course if I had any hope of salvaging it.

"Actually..." I stepped closer to Chad and placed a hand

on his forearm. "I was thinking we could have a drink at my place."

Chase snapped his head in my direction, his mouth set in a firm line, his brows drawn down in a scowl. "I don't think that's a good idea."

"Good thing I didn't ask you, then."

"It's already late," Chase gritted out through clenched teeth.

I shrugged. "What I have in mind will be worth the lost sleep."

I was baiting him, every word I said designed to get under his skin. Make him feel an ounce of what I did whenever I saw the photos of him and the puck bunnies hanging off his arm.

And it was working.

"Fuck. No." Chase's words were little more than a growl as he stepped closer to me, eyeing my hand still resting on Chad's forearm. "You have work tomorrow."

I raised a brow at him. "I missed the memo where you became my boss. I'm an adult. He's an adult. We're going to do adult things. Now kindly fuck off."

Chad, for all his loudmouthed bluster in the restaurant, was doing little more than shuffling his feet and shooting worried glances at Chase. Though, there was a good reason for that, considering the anger rolling off him in waves. He was a big guy under normal circumstances, and I'd been right about Chad's misrepresentation of his six-foot stature, which meant he looked positively puny next to Chase's imposing frame.

Wearing ratty jeans, a well-worn—read: holey—graphic T-shirt that said something about his balls being bigger than mine—absolutely false—and a baseball hat, Chad looked like a kid playing dress-up compared to Chase. Especially considering Chase had shown up in an impeccably tailored black suit, the pale blue shirt beneath it making his even paler blue eyes pop. It was truly unfair how fucking good he looked tonight when all I wanted to do was claw those beautiful eyes out.

Chad cleared his throat. "I, uh, I don't mean to impose, man."

Without looking away from me, Chase said, "But you clearly are."

"Chase!" I snapped, hitting him with my purse for good measure.

"What?" He shrugged. "It's the truth. You and I have history. And I'm working really fucking hard to make it *not* history. I let you go on this date—"

"*Let* me?" I huffed out a harsh breath. "Excuse the fuck out of you."

Chase glanced to Chad for the barest moment, lifting his chin toward him. "And you spent the entire night with your nose shoved so far up my ass, you could smell what I had for breakfast instead of focusing on the most gorgeous woman you've ever had or will have the privilege of sitting across from."

Chad's gaze bounced between Chase and me, his eyes wide as he nodded vigorously. "You're right, man." He held up his hands in surrender. "She's all yours. I wasn't really interested anyway. But if you ever want to grab a beer or—"

"Are you a fucking idiot?" Chase asked, his words low and controlled, his eyes hard as he stared at the immature frat boy I'd asked out tonight. He took a step toward Chad, looming over him in a way that probably had him close to peeing himself. "You disrespect her like that, and you think we have a future other than me handing you your ass?" He jerked his chin toward the parking lot. "Get the fuck out of here."

Before I could even blink, Chad scurried off toward his car, glancing back every few seconds as if to make sure Chase wasn't following him.

Chad fleeing as fast as his legs could carry him meant I was left there, on the sidewalk, on a cold January night.

With Chase as my only way home.

THE RIDE back to the resort was silent, and I barely waited for Chase to stop the truck before I jumped out and hustled my way up the front walkway, uncaring of my four-inch heels.

"Jesus Christ, Addison," he called across the parking lot. "Would you wait a second?"

"Get fucked," I tossed over my shoulder without slowing down.

It was late, the inn closed down for the night except for the emergency after-hours number Aiden was monitoring. Thank God, because no one needed to see me yell at Starlight

Cove's golden boy before storming inside and slamming the door behind me.

Or attempting to anyway.

Chase caught it before it could provide that satisfactory thump in his face. He slipped inside the inn, his gaze finding me immediately, his brows drawn down in a scowl. "What the hell, Addie?"

I was already halfway up the stairs, and I whirled around to stare at him openmouthed. "*You're* asking *me* that?" With nowhere for the anger bubbling up inside me to go, I kicked off my ridiculously uncomfortable shoes in his direction, hoping like hell one of them landed against his stupid head. Unfortunately, my luck just wasn't that good tonight. "I can't believe you did that. You crashed my date, dominated all his attention, and then scared him off at the end of the night. You are *such* a jackass!"

Chase blinked up at me, mouth agape. "Are you kidding me? *He* was the jackass."

"I don't care if he came to the restaurant dressed in a fucking donkey costume. That wasn't your call to make!"

He ran a hand over the layer of scruff on his jaw, frustration written over every inch of him. "Don't even try to pretend you were into him. I'm intimately familiar with exactly how you behave when that's true, and tonight wasn't it."

"How about you become intimately familiar with my knee in your junk?" I snapped back. But instead of doing just that, I turned and stormed the rest of the way up the stairs. "I'm a big girl, and I can make my own decisions."

Chase was on my heels, even with his bad knee, and this

was one of the few times I hated our ridiculous height difference. "And the best decision you could come up with tonight was to revenge-fuck a dudebro?"

I headed straight for my room, not bothering to glance over my shoulder to find out how far he was behind me. That was how all the idiots in horror movies got murdered. And if Chase caught me? I feared my fate would be much, much worse than death. "I wasn't *actually* going to fuck him. I just said that to get a rise out of you."

As soon as I was over the threshold to my bedroom, I attempted to slam the door in his face. And, once again, he caught it before it could hit its mark.

He stalked toward me, a scowl firmly on his face. "Well, it fucking worked."

"Good." He deserved to feel even a sliver of what I'd felt every time I was faced with a picture of him and another woman. "It serves you right."

"It serves me right to see my girl out with another guy?"

"Your girl? *Your girl*?" I yelled, not bothering to keep my voice down. The only people who resided in the main inn were me, Aiden, and Avery, and they were all the way on the other side of the house. "Fuck all the way off with that bullshit, Chase. I'm not *your* anything, which you proved this past year. And now you want to sweep back into my life and pretend like you have some kind of hold over me? You *don't*."

I said the words even though every inch of me fought against the lie. Even though my heart was thrumming in my chest, the furious *thump-thump-thump* a reminder of just how big his hold over me was, despite how much I hated it.

"Well, you've got a fucking hold over me," he said, his voice low and rough, his gaze pinning me in place as he stood too close, too close, too close. "You always have, firefly, and you always will."

"Shut up," I snapped, not wanting to listen to his sweet words because they were a lie. "Take your horseshit and try to sell it to someone else. I'm not buying."

"It's not horseshit." He took a step toward me, and I stepped back, yanking my coat off and throwing it at him. Without breaking his stride, he caught it and tossed it on my bed. He kept coming, and I kept backing up until I was pressed up against my wall with nowhere to go. "I mean every word."

I held out my hand and pushed it against his chest, as much to stop him as it was to stop myself. With his scent surrounding me and the heat of his body seeping into my hand, I had to force myself not to curl my fingers into the material of his crisp shirt. Not to rip those buttons straight down the middle. Not to claw at his chest and make him feel even an ounce of the pain he'd put me through this past year. "If you step one foot closer to me, I'm either going to slap you or..."

"Or what? What are you gonna do, firefly?"

"Don't call me that," I said, without nearly as much force as I'd intended because the nickname swept over me, lighting up my insides and making my body hum for him. Just like always. And just like always, it reminded me of earlier times —better times—when we'd run around the resort as kids, catching fireflies at dusk.

"Tell me this date wasn't just to spite me."

"How big of an ego do you have? The date had *nothing* to do with you."

"And that's the story you're sticking with?" he asked, brows raised.

"There's no *story* because it's the truth. My going out tonight wasn't about you or your stupid face being in my town, in my inn, or sharing a fucking wall with me."

"If that's true, there's a very easy way to prove it," he said.

"Oh yeah? What's that?"

"Kiss me."

I huffed out an incredulous laugh and shook my head. "Excuse me?"

He shrugged like it was no big deal, although there was no denying the heat in his eyes as he stared down at me, or the rigid set of his shoulders. "If I don't affect you at all, kissing me should be no big deal. So, prove it."

"You're out of your mind if you think I'm kissing you just to prove something."

He stepped closer, despite my earlier threat. So close, his chest grazed my own, my nipples tightening at the heat pouring off him. Without breaking our gazes, he brought his hand up, moving slowly enough that I could've stopped him if I wanted to. But despite my bluster...despite the roadblocks I'd thrown up between us, I didn't.

I *couldn't*.

The second his fingertips made contact with the bare skin above the neckline of my dress, a shiver skated down my spine and goose bumps erupted everywhere. Every touch was weighted with his heavy stare, an air of reverence to it, as if he couldn't believe he had the privilege of touching me.

And that right there was why it had always been so easy to get lost in him. He made me feel like every whisper of his fingers against me meant something. Made it seem like he'd been starving for it, no matter how long it'd been since the last time we'd been together.

"Then don't kiss me to prove something," he whispered, tracing along my neckline, across my collarbone, over my bare shoulders until he cupped my neck, his thumb pressing softly but firmly under my chin. He tilted my head up as he lowered his face to mine. We were centimeters apart now, so close his breath ghosted over my lips. I could taste the mints he loved with every one of his exhales, and that, combined with the scent of him—all warm and clean and *mine*—and I was lost to him. "Kiss me because you want to."

I snapped, the frayed thread holding me back disintegrating with those handful of words. Without thinking about what this meant, how bad of a decision it was, or just how much I was going to regret it in the morning, I pushed up on my tiptoes, threw my arms around his neck, and crushed my lips to his.

To his credit, he didn't miss a beat. With a groan, he gripped my ass in both palms, lifting me up so he could pin me against the wall. He swept his tongue between my lips, sliding it against my own. His taste was so familiar it made my chest ache, and I couldn't hope to hold back my moan.

His hands were everywhere, sweeping over me. Gripping, clutching, caressing, like he couldn't get enough of the feel of me beneath his fingers. Like he was trying to prove to himself this was real.

Just like they always did, things between us escalated quickly, exploding into something neither of us could escape. With my legs wrapped around his hips, my dress hiked up indecently, and only a tiny scrap of lace separating us, I had no problem feeling exactly how affected he was by this. By *me.* His cock was thick and hard against my pussy, the head hitting my clit with every rock of his hips, and I wanted it. *Needed* it.

I moaned his name against his lips, and he groaned, digging his fingers into my ass as he held me tight to him.

"*Fuck.*" He kissed the corner of my mouth, then ran his lips along my jaw, his teeth scraping my earlobe, his panting breaths sending shivers down my spine. "You feel so fucking good, baby girl. Show me how much you want it. Grind that needy little cunt down on me. Just like that."

I whimpered, rolling my hips against the huge bulge in his pants, my body desperate and aching, my panties soaking wet. I wanted these clothes off. Wanted to feel him against me with nothing between us.

He adjusted his stance, pressing harder against me, and caught my moan with his mouth. He kissed me as if he'd never get enough, cupping my ass in his hands and guiding my movements, grinding me down harder against him. "That's it, baby. Take it. Take what you need and come. I want you to soak the front of my pants. Want to be able to smell your pussy on me all fucking night."

Locking my ankles tighter around him, I pressed down

harder against his cock. He grunted, gripping my ass, digging his fingers deeper into my flesh, like he was holding himself back. Like he was just as lost to this as I was. And knowing that was all it took.

I broke apart in his arms, my orgasm tearing through me as he whispered dirty words against my ear, but it wasn't enough. Heat still bloomed low in my belly, the answering ache in my clit reminding me just how much more he could give me. Just how much more I needed from him.

His breaths were harsh against my ear, his low groan reverberating through me. "I missed you so fucking much, baby girl."

His words—so innocuous in any other circumstance—were like a bucket of ice water dumped over my head. The reminder of just how long it'd been since we'd been together might as well have been a brick wall, and I crashed headfirst into it. Even despite the waves of bliss still rolling through me. Despite the ache in my pussy, still desperate for him.

I jerked away, shoving against his chest as hard as I could until he set me down on wobbly legs, resting his hands on my hips to steady me.

"What's wrong?" he asked, his voice raspy, his pupils blown wide, and his cock straining hard against the front of his pants. With a frown, he scanned me from head to toe as if he could find whatever the problem was and fix it.

But he couldn't see the ravaged pieces of my broken heart that he'd left behind, and I refused to show him an ounce of that weakness.

"Leave." I pressed both palms firmly against his chest and

gave him another shove toward the door. "I mean it, Chase. I want you out of my room. Now."

"Addie, what—"

"*Get out*," I snapped, shoving him one last time.

Whether from the surprise of it or because he finally relented, he stepped backward into our shared bathroom, concern blanketing his features as he stared at me with worried eyes.

And this time, when I slammed the door in his face, he let me.

CHAPTER TEN

CHASE

I'D WOKEN up with a lot of boners in my life, but this one topped them all. My dreams last night had been plagued by reenactments of the kiss—not to mention the orgasm—that shook the entire fucking world.

Kissing Addison was always intoxicating, but last night had felt different. Heavier. I didn't know if it was because it had been so long since I'd tasted her, since I'd felt her fall apart in my arms, or because I knew exactly what my intentions were while I was home. And those intentions meant if I had my way, I wouldn't ever again have to go that long without her lips under mine, without hearing her sweet moans.

But it had clearly gotten too real, too fast for Addison, and she'd retaliated by slamming that door in my face and then torturing me like the beautiful little terror she was.

Years ago, I'd stumbled across her listening history on Spotify, and ever since then, I'd made a habit before I crashed for the night to check out what playlist she'd been listening to that day. She had more than a dozen of them, everything ranging from *Missing Mom* to *Rage Machine* to *Horny AF*. It had always been a low-key, unobtrusive way to get an unfiltered peek at what she was feeling.

I always, *always* wanted the rawest version of Addison I could get. Whether that was anger or hurt or everything in between. If she was sad or missing her mom, I wanted to know. And I sure as hell wanted to send her something to cheer her up.

Years ago, I'd accidentally let one of her playlist names slip in conversation, and she'd pinned me to the bed, demanding to know how I knew it. I'd tried to deny it for all of three seconds before finally fessing up. Instead of getting pissed like I assumed she would, she just called me a creeper. And then things continued on as if nothing happened. She listened like I wasn't paying attention, I sent her little gifts without my name attached in response, and we never said another word about it.

Last night, though, she'd been making a point as she cued up her *Horny AF* playlist. She'd played it before, of course. Hundreds of times. And while every single instance had gotten me hard, I'd never been this close to her when it happened. It'd killed me, knowing she was on the other side of our shared wall, her little pussy wet and needy, aching after only a single orgasm when I never stopped at just one. But I couldn't—wouldn't—cross that threshold. At least not until she gave me the green light.

And last night it had sure as fuck been red.

So instead of giving her what I wanted to, I'd lain in my bed, fingers wrapped around my dick while pictures of every indecent thing I'd ever done to her had flashed through my mind. And I'd done a *lot* of indecent shit to my best friend's baby sister.

Since it was clear she had no intention of letting me help her with her soaked panties, I'd done the next best thing. Without a second thought, I'd placed an overnight order for a treat that would arrive for her this morning.

I grabbed my phone from the nightstand, a smile kicking up the corner of my mouth when I got an alert that her gift had already been delivered. I tossed the covers aside, cringing as I climbed out of bed—mornings were the worst for my knee after so many hours of inactivity. Once I'd stretched enough so I wouldn't grimace with every step, I pulled on a pair of sweatpants and an unzipped hoodie over my bare chest. I didn't care about walking around without a shirt on, but if any guests were in the inn, that might not be the best impression.

I made it down the steps and grabbed the package before slipping back upstairs undetected. Thankfully, the company I'd purchased from had a gift wrap option, so the black box came wrapped in a red satin bow. With a grin, I dropped it in the middle of Addison's bed and then strode back into my room through our shared bathroom.

Levi and I had plans to hang out today, and I was supposed to meet him at his workshop in thirty, which meant I needed to get my ass in gear if I was going to be anywhere near on time. And I needed to be because I somehow didn't think *I was waiting for the vibrator I bought your sister to be delivered* was a good excuse to give him.

After the quickest shower I could manage—one in which I didn't get the relief my dick was begging me for—I shut off the water, opened the shower curtain, and reached for a towel. Before I could grab it, the door leading to Addison's bedroom flew open, and there she stood, my tiny tornado, irritation written across her face.

"What the hell, Chase. You can't just—" She cut herself off as she finally registered that I was standing in front of her completely naked. And then I watched as her irritation slowly melted into desire.

There was no hiding just exactly how happy my dick was about that. I was surprised I wasn't light-headed from how quickly my cock swelled, growing thick against my thigh at her appraisal of it.

I didn't bother reaching again for the towel. Instead, I just stood there, dripping wet and hard as a fucking rock, as her gaze swept over me. Across my chest, down my abs, stuttering on the incessant beast standing thick and proud and jutting out straight for her. She shook her head slightly as if to clear herself from a fog and allowed her gaze even lower, her brow furrowing when she got to my knee and the not-yet-faded scars there.

When she lifted her eyes to mine once more, some of her bravado was gone, but I could still see the anger simmering behind those gorgeous eyes.

With her mouth pinched, she shoved the black box I'd

placed on her bed against my chest. "You seem to have misplaced something."

I shook my head. "'Fraid not, firefly. This is all yours."

"Definitely isn't. I hope you've suddenly grown a vagina because that'll be the only way it gets any use."

I raised a brow at her. "You just spent thirty seconds staring at my very-much-not-a-vagina, so I think you answered that question for yourself."

"It was *not* thirty seconds! It was—" She huffed and shoved the box harder against my chest until I reached up and took it from her. "Whatever, it doesn't matter. I've listened to that playlist a thousand times, and you've never felt the need to send me a vibrator in response."

"I was also never home to do anything about it. I am now, but since we're still in the freeze-out stage, I wanted to make sure you got what you needed."

"You don't know anything about what I need. Why don't you save us both the hassle and send it to one of your puck bunnies instead?" With that, she stormed off, flipping me off over her shoulder as she went.

The thing about Addison was she had a tendency to react before she really thought things through. And I knew that tonight, when her little clit throbbed because she was remembering what it had felt like to have me grinding against her pussy while I'd kissed the hell out of her, she'd wish she had this little toy to keep her company. To give her some relief.

So, with a towel wrapped around my waist, I strode into

her room, plucked the red ribbon off her floor, and retied it around the box.

And then I placed it on the center of her bed once again before ambling back to my room, grinning to myself the entire time.

CHAPTER ELEVEN

CHASE

STRIDING INTO LEVI'S WORKSHOP, the scent of wood and the sawdust swirling through the air, brought back memories from high school. When he and I would spend our weekends earning extra cash by rehabbing some of the locals' more worn-down boats.

Now, though, he did this for a living, while also leading any boat tours for guests at the resort. His family gave him a lot of shit for being a slacker, but Levi was one of the hardest working people I knew. Not only that, but he was selfless with his earnings.

When the resort had been down on its luck, the six of them struggling to make ends meet—especially while also trying to take care of their deadbeat dad, who contributed absolutely nothing—and I'd wanted to help dig them out of the hole, he hadn't let me. He'd said he had it handled and that I had other shit to worry about. Namely, my own family.

So, while I'd been sending money home, Levi had been

doing the same, funneling it back into the resort whenever he could and being sneaky as hell about it so his siblings were none the wiser. As long as it didn't go to his dad, he was happy to do it.

And I didn't blame him for that.

Sometimes my family drove me up a fucking wall. My mom overstepped, poking her nose where it didn't belong. My dad had placed the protection of all my sisters on my shoulders since I'd been old enough to understand the words. And my sisters? Well, let's just say I was no stranger to wearing lipstick or dressing up in a tutu to put on a show for our parents. Thank God that footage had never been leaked to the public, because fuck knew my teammates would never let me live it down. Levi was proof enough of that.

But even through the hassles and headaches, I'd never questioned their love or complete support of me. I'd never had to deal with the dysfunction the entire McKenzie family had faced every day for years.

The rhythmic sound of sandpaper against wood reached me as soon as I stepped through the door, and I headed toward it. This was the same workshop we'd used back in high school, an old warehouse Mabel's uncle had owned. Since it had been sitting empty for years, he'd let us use it, free of charge, in exchange for us slipping him burgers from the diner because he wasn't allowed them on his restrictive diet.

When he'd passed away several years ago, Levi had quietly taken ownership of the warehouse and had expanded his business, allowing him to take on more than sporadic projects.

A boat sat in the middle of the space, hanging by a solid system of pulleys and chains. The skeleton of it was complete but raw. And now the real work began.

I walked up behind Levi and clapped him on the shoulder. "I can't believe you still hand-sand this shit."

Without breaking the smooth, consistent strokes of the sandpaper against the wood, he said, "Believe it, because you're helping today. Your fucked-up knee won't save you from this."

I snorted and pulled over a chair, grateful I'd preemptively iced my knee and taken some painkillers before I headed over. "But seriously, why do you still do this? And on a boat this size? What is it, fifty feet?"

"Fifty-seven." He stopped sanding and looked at me with a raised brow. "And you know exactly why I do it this way. Because we fucked up Harvey's boat by screwing around with a power sander. The projects I work on now are a hell of a lot more expensive than his tiny fishing boat."

"Fair point." I leaned back in the chair, stretching out my legs and getting comfortable.

"What the hell are you doing?" he asked.

I glanced around, then pointedly looked from myself to him. "Bullshitting with my best friend."

He shook his head and grabbed a fresh sanding block before tossing it my way. "Not without putting some work in, you're not."

With a snort, I caught what he threw and then got busy.

The rhythm of this work, the repetitiveness paired with the soft scraping sound and the smell of sawdust, had always soothed me, and that hadn't changed in the twelve-plus years since we'd done this as a team.

Levi was always the calmest when he was working on this part of the job, so I figured if I was going to broach a touchy subject, now would be the time. Especially considering how he'd reacted when I'd last attempted this years ago. And since there was no delicate way to bring this up, I just went balls to the wall.

"So...how are things going between you and Harper now that she's been back in the Cove more often?"

His sandpaper stuttered against the wood before he refocused. "How do you know she's been back more often? Because I sure as hell haven't said anything."

I rolled my eyes. "You don't say shit about shit. Just because I don't tell you I've seen her doesn't mean I haven't. You made it perfectly fucking clear years ago that you didn't want to know."

His jaw ticked, a sure sign of his irritation. Whether over the fact that Harper and I had kept in touch or that I was bringing it up again, I wasn't sure. "I avoid her when she's around. Just like I always have."

"And why is that again?"

"You know damn well why. It's better for everyone if I stay out of her life."

"That's bullshit, and you—"

"Drop it, Chase." His voice was low and firm, and I knew that was all I was getting out of him. For now anyway.

"Fine. Then you fill in the silence, you broody asshole, because I didn't come over here to stare into your eyes."

"Whatever. You love my eyes."

I snorted and shook my head. "Mom told me you helped out over there, moving around their furniture before the reno started. Thanks for doing that."

He shrugged like it was no big deal. "She feeds me well. And I think finally being empty-nesters after thirty years is fucking with them a bit." He shot me a raised brow. "Hope you've stopped by to see your babies while you're home."

I laughed outright at that, recalling the sea of green my mom had filled my old room with—plants in all different shapes and sizes—because she was tired of waiting for me to give her actual grandbabies to fill it with. "Oh, believe me, I heard all about it."

"How're the twins doing at college? And how about Morgan? She still doing all right?"

"Yeah, Morgan's good. All clear." I sent up a silent thank-you to the universe for that. "And the twins are doing great. They never miss our weekly call—you believe that?"

"With those two? Definitely. They know what to do to keep you wrapped around their fingers."

"I'm not—"

He snorted before I could get another word out, and I blew out a sigh. My youngest sisters had me whipped, and they knew it.

"Fine, I totally am. But at least they make up for the shit Morgan gives me. You're lucky you only have *one* sister. Because dealing with three is a mindfuck."

"Speaking of my one sister...word around town is that you crashed Addison's date last night. That true?"

I forgot how quickly news spread in Starlight Cove. But thankfully, I hadn't done anything stupid in public...like dry hump her against the restaurant windows instead of her bedroom wall. "Yep."

"Well, thank fuck you're back, because my brothers have been so focused on their own shit, they've forgotten we have a baby sister to look out for."

"Happy to help," I said, the guilt gnawing at my stomach. If he knew the ways I'd *looked after* her over the years, he'd cut off my balls and shove them down my throat. "The guy she went out with last night was an absolute dick. He couldn't get his lips on my ass fast enough. I could've put up with that, but the way he disregarded and straight up talked over Addison anytime she said something wasn't going to fly."

"The good news is that even if you hadn't shown up, it never would have lasted because she wouldn't put up with that shit."

This time, it was my sandpaper that stuttered, and I could only hope he didn't notice. I cleared my throat. "She have any relationships that *have* lasted?"

"Nah. You know she'd never bring anyone around here. I think she was hiding something from us for a while, though—a secret relationship she didn't want us to know about, maybe. I'm pretty sure whatever it was is over now. She's been a fucking bear this past year. More so than usual, except for that one summer back in college."

Fuck me. Levi was looking directly at the other half of

her secret relationship, not to mention the cause of her mood the past year. And probably that one time in college, too.

"I wonder what that was all about," I said with as much conviction as I could muster.

"Don't know and don't care as long as it's done."

"What do you mean?"

"Come on. You, of all people, should know nobody's gonna be good enough for her."

I did know that. Intimately. I'd walked those halls with Levi in high school, scaring off any guy who'd dared to look in Addison's direction. Had done so thorough of a job, in fact, that no one would ask her out, even after Levi and I had graduated. Which was the entire reason this secret relationship had started in the first place.

If it hadn't been for Levi's and my scare tactics, Addison would have probably lost her virginity just like any other sixteen-year-old. Instead, she'd been eighteen, leaving for college the next day, and telling my sister Morgan in great detail her plans to, "just get it over with" that night at the send-off party.

And fuck no, I wasn't going to let her first time be with a fumbling idiot who didn't know his thumb from his dick and couldn't find a clit to save his life.

That night had sealed our fate. If I hadn't been with her... hadn't tasted her, hadn't been inside her, I might have been able to go my entire life without this ever-present hum under my skin that called out her name.

But that hadn't happened, I *had* taken her virginity, and

for the past ten years, she'd been my everything outside of hockey.

I cleared my throat, scattering the memories from my mind. "Not even someone like me?"

Levi barked out a laugh he didn't even attempt to temper. "Are you kidding? There's no way I'd ever let you date my sister, considering all the puck pussy you get."

I clenched my teeth, my jaw ticking in an effort to hold myself back from snapping at him. It didn't work. "Not everything they put in those shitty-ass tabloids is true. I wouldn't even fuck those women with *your* dick."

"Well, thanks for that," he said dryly. "But leave my dick out of it. And I don't care what you do with yours, as long as it stays away from my sister."

Too late for that. Way too fucking late for that.

CHAPTER TWELVE

CHASE

I'D ALWAYS KNOWN Levi wouldn't be excited about whoever Addison decided to bring home. And on some level, I knew I'd be included in that group because... Well, because I had a dick, for one thing. And because my best friend had been front and center when I'd been...undiscerning in high school and the two years I'd attended college before going pro, trying damn hard to forget about a certain someone who'd owned my heart for years. And because the media had a fucking field day with me, spreading all the bullshit they could about Vancouver's top forward, despite that none of it was true.

But thinking it in an abstract sense and hearing him confirm it were two very different things.

I loved my best friend like a brother and wanted to respect his wishes. But I loved Addison more. And I also trusted in her ability to make a decision about who she wanted to be with.

I could only hope, in the end, she chose me.

The inn was quiet and empty by the time I got back later that night. Aiden and Avery must have been holed up on their side of the house, and I hadn't been able to find Addison on my brief scan through the main floor.

I had no doubt she was still pissed off at me. It always took her a while to soften after someone got her good and angry. She'd get over it eventually—she just needed to be dramatic first.

I strode into Levi's old room, my gaze scanning the surroundings, checking for the black box with the red ribbon. It was nowhere to be found, which meant it was still tucked safely in Addison's room. I grinned at the thought of her finding it on her bed again, and I would've given just about anything to see her face when it happened. Unfortunately, that wasn't in the cards, so I'd just have to settle for her reaction whenever she—

A soft noise came from her room, and I froze, tilting my head in that direction to listen better. Now that I was paying attention, I could just make out a low, constant hum interspersed with other quiet sounds. My bathroom door was open—I never closed it because she was welcome in here anytime—but even so, I shouldn't have been able to hear anything coming from her room this well, considering she usually *did* shut her door.

I crept closer, pushing my bathroom door open fully and finding the door leading to her bedroom open as well. The sounds were more pronounced in here, and I quickly realized what I'd been hearing were Addison's whimpers and moans.

"Fuck," I whispered under my breath. Reaching down, I cupped my dick and gave it a firm squeeze as I slowly walked toward her room. With how mad she'd been earlier and how adamant she was that I knock, I knew there was no way she'd left this open by accident. Which meant one thing...

She wanted me to hear every bit of this. Wanted me to witness every one of her moans as she got herself off with the toy I'd bought her.

The real question was, did she want me to watch?

"Addie?" I asked, my voice scraped raw at the thought of what she might be doing just a few feet away.

"Chase..." she whispered.

I curled my fingers around the edge of the door, pulling it the rest of the way open, and then froze at the sight that greeted me.

She lay on her bed completely naked, her bedding pooled around her, all that beautiful skin on full display for me. I didn't know where to look first, my gaze hungrily taking in every bare inch of her gorgeous body. One of her hands was playing with her tits, her thumb and forefinger tweaking her rosy nipples just the way she liked, while her other rested between her spread legs, working the toy I'd gifted her this morning.

"Oh fuck," I barely managed through a tight throat. I ran a hand over my mouth, my gaze darting across every inch of her, trying desperately to take in what I hadn't seen in far too long. "Oh, *fuck me*, baby girl. What are you doing to me?"

"Getting my payback." Her voice was low, raspy, and the sound of it shot straight to my dick.

If this was her payback, I'd gladly suffer through it every day for the rest of my life if she'd let me.

"Addie." I took a step into her room, desperate to be closer to her. Desperate to feel her body under my fingertips. To taste her pussy on my tongue.

She shut off the toy and stopped all movement as she pinned me with a glare, her eyes heated and mouth set in a flat line. "Don't you dare. Consider that doorway a force field. You aren't allowed to take a step past it."

"Or what?"

"Or I quit."

Well, that would be a fucking travesty for everyone involved.

"And if I stay right here?" I asked, barely able to get the words out through my tight throat.

She lifted a bare shoulder in a shrug. "Then I'll let you watch me play."

My knee was screaming in protest after sitting in the same position so long at Levi's, and I was about five hours overdue for my next dose of ibuprofen. But the whole fucking world could've been on fire, and I wouldn't have moved from this spot.

I leaned against the doorframe, crossing my arms over my chest and ignoring the incessant throb of my dick inside my jeans.

"Go on, then." I lifted my chin toward the toy that was deep inside her, her pussy lips spread wide around it. "Take care of my perfect little cunt for me."

A shudder ran through her at my words, her nipples hardening even further. And then she turned on the toy again and sucked in a breath. Her lids grew heavy, her lips parted in pleasure as she thrust it in and out of her, her hips rocking as she increased the speed. "I didn't say you couldn't play, too. Take off your shirt and undo your jeans. Let me watch you while I get myself off."

Jesus Christ. *Jesus. Fucking. Christ.* At this point, I wasn't so sure I hadn't died and gone to heaven, because watching Addison play with her pussy, giving herself exactly what she needed while I witnessed it, was definitely one version of my nirvana.

Part of me wanted to just focus on her. Stand here and soak in every inch of what she was freely showing me. Study every crease of her brow, every arch of her back, every shift of her hips. I wanted to watch her come undone without the added distraction of my own pleasure.

But the look of pure hunger on her face as she stared at me, waiting for me to follow her directions, all while working herself up in a slow, steady build, made my decision for me.

Without taking my eyes away from her, I reached behind and gripped the neck of my shirt to pull it off. Then I undid the fly of my jeans, tugging down my boxer briefs until my dick sprang free, thick and hard and aching for her touch. It was going to have to settle for mine tonight.

"This what you wanted?" I wrapped my hand around the base of my shaft and gave a slow, firm stroke before swiping my thumb over the head. I was already leaking with how much I wanted her, and I gathered that wetness, using it to glide my downstroke.

"Yes," she breathed. Her gaze was glued to me, sweeping over me from head to toe before focusing on where I stroked my cock, her eyes going heavy, glazed, as she watched me watch her.

She was a fucking vision, lying there, her pussy on full display and spread wide around the toy I'd bought for her. All the while looking at me as if she wished I were the one filling her. As if she wanted to devour me whole.

"You still horny as fuck?" I asked, my voice strained.

After a moment, she nodded, her lips parting as she tugged harder on her nipple and moved the toy faster inside her.

"Tell me how it feels, baby girl. Tell me how well my perfect little pussy is taking that cock."

Instead of answering with words, she whimpered, her eyelids fluttering closed as she pressed something on the vibrator, the buzz growing more pronounced.

"Tell me, Addison," I said, firmer this time. "Does that feel as good as having my dick inside you? Does it fill you up as well? Does it reach that spot I hit every single time?"

"No..." she whispered, the word barely more than a breath as she stared at me with a need I hadn't seen from her in far too long.

"I didn't think so. Only I know how to get my baby girl off exactly how she needs, isn't that right? That piece of silicone might be nice to pass the time. Might give you a mediocre orgasm to take the edge off. But you and I both know if you want to scream, you come to *me*."

"Chase—" She broke off on a moan, her back arching, eyes still locked with mine, and I had to grip the base of my cock so I didn't erupt on the spot.

This was the closest thing I'd had to sex in more than a year. And while my dick was intimately acquainted with my right hand—considering it had been the only action it had gotten besides Addison for a decade—the scene in front of me took it to a whole new level.

"You're close, aren't you? My sweet cunt is fluttering around that toy, aching for something thicker. Something that could hit deeper. And you know just where to get it, don't you, firefly?"

Her eyes dropped to my cock, her lips parting as she watched me stroke it in the same rhythm she was fucking herself with.

"You see how much I want you?" I asked, my voice like gravel. "I'm hard as a fucking rock and dripping for you, baby girl. Want to be inside you so fucking bad. Want your throaty little moans in my ear while I sink deep and grind the base of my cock against that greedy clit, just like you love. I want the scratches you give me down my back and the bite marks you leave on my shoulders, and I want my ears ringing from how hard I made you scream."

"Oh fuck," she whispered, her eyes darting between my face and where I pumped my dick furiously, matching her pace. "Chase, I'm gonna—"

"Me, too, baby girl. Give it to me. Pretend I'm the one filling you up and let me feel you squeeze my cock."

She moaned low, her eyes fluttering closed as she covered her mouth with her forearm, her hips rolling through her release. I came at the same time, grabbing my discarded shirt and catching my release with it. My eyes never left her as I shot off into the cotton, wishing with everything I had it'd been inside her.

The buzzing stopped, and then just our panting breaths filled the space. Addison tossed her toy to the side before sagging against the bed, the bliss from her orgasm written over every inch of her sated body. She glanced at me then, wariness and trepidation in her gaze, that barrier she loved so fucking much slamming back into place.

I hated it, but I expected it. Addison was a hard one to win over, but I had months. And I wasn't scared of the difficult work.

She was worth it.

"This doesn't change anything," she said, her voice low and raspy.

Rather than argue with her about how wrong she was, about how this changed everything, I said, "You know you're the one in charge, firefly. Always have been, always will be. So, you make the call on what this is. If you want me to just tongue-fuck you every day, I will. You can sit on my face and let me drown in your sweet cunt for hours until you can't come anymore. You want me to suck on your perfect tits or finger you to sleep every night? Consider it done. Want me to watch every time you get yourself off with a less-impressive version of me? I'll do it every fucking time you ask, baby girl." I pushed off the doorway and pinned her with a heavy stare, my gaze never leaving hers. "But when you get tired of playing this game and decide you want the real thing, you know where to find me."

CHAPTER THIRTEEN

ADDISON

I PRIDED myself on being on time. After all, I couldn't exactly get on my brothers' cases for being late if I always was, too. Usually, it was fine. Usually, I was the first one up and the first one at our morning meetings.

But usually, it wasn't the morning following an evening wherein I made my—what? Ex-boyfriend? Ex-lover?—watch from the doorway while I got myself off with the toy he purchased for me. And usually, I wasn't doing everything in my power to avoid another run-in with said person, just to save a bit of my sanity.

Last night, after Chase had dropped the bomb that he'd be there and ready whenever I was, he'd left me. Naked and alone in my bed, where I'd proceeded to toss and turn all night, thoughts of just what that might look like if I took him up on his offer swarming me.

But we'd already been down that path. Had been for years. And where I'd once thought I could handle it again because *I* was the one in charge, this past year had proven otherwise. It had proven that Chase actually held all the cards. And I had no intention of blindly walking into that again.

So I'd done the mature thing this morning.

I'd hidden in my bedroom, waiting and listening, until Chase left for his PT appointment. Was it the coward's way out? Maybe. Probably. But so long as it meant I had some breathing room before I had to see him again, I didn't care.

Unfortunately, it also meant that I was late for the morning meeting, and I was going to get an earful about it from my brothers.

After waiting long enough that I was certain Chase had left the premises, I flew out of my room and through the inn. Beck had grumbled enough about where our meeting location was that we now switched off between the main inn and the diner. Fortunately, today's was here, which meant I didn't have as far to go.

I flew down the stairs, naturally avoiding the creaky steps—a holdover from my teenage years. But before I rounded the corner, hushed voices reached me, automatically perking my ears. Narrowing my eyes, I tilted my head as I tried to catch what was being said. My brothers weren't exactly known for their quiet, demure voices, so that meant one of two things—either they were talking about me, or they were talking about something they didn't want me to hear. Both of which I, obviously, wanted to know immediately.

I crept down the hall, careful to avoid any creaky planks

of wood and grateful Avery was doing her usual morning rounds so I didn't have to excuse my James Bond act to her.

When I was close enough to hear my brothers' conversation without straining, I plastered myself against the wall outside the dining room and held my breath.

"...said he checked himself in to rehab," Brady said in a hushed tone.

"Not the first time," Beck mumbled.

"For how long?" Ford asked.

"Not sure." Brady again. "Based on what I heard, my guess is he's already been there for a month."

"Not the first time for that, either," Aiden said, his voice hard.

There was no doubt in my mind who the *he* was they were talking about. Our father. I'd been young enough when it all started that I had no idea how many times he'd gone to rehab in my life. Four since I'd finally figured it out when I was in high school, but who knew how many of the "fishing trips" during my childhood had really been a stint in rehab.

I knew my brothers had had more time dealing with all the shit our dad had done, and it had eclipsed the good parts for them, but the good parts were what I remembered most.

His hearty laugh when my mom would tell a joke. His mustache tickling my cheek when he'd kiss me goodnight after reading me a bedtime story. Him scooping me into his arms and carrying me into my room after I'd fallen asleep on a long road trip.

I remembered the bad, too, in a vague kind of way. Which

was probably why the good overshadowed it for me, not allowing me to ignore it.

"No idea how long he's planning to be in there," Brady said.

"If history is anything to go by, he'll check himself out soon and be back at the liquor store a couple hours after that," Aiden grumbled.

Murmurs of agreement went up, and the pang in my stomach spread.

Brady blew out a heavy sigh. "Fortunately, either people around town don't know he's there, or they're keeping it quiet out of respect for us."

"At least until Mabel gets ahold of this, and it shows up on the front page of the newspaper," Aiden said.

"Don't see that happening, seeing as Mabel's the one who let me know in the first place." Brady cleared his throat. "As for Addison, I assume we're all on the same page..."

I furrowed my brow. On the same page about—

"She doesn't need to know," Aiden confirmed. "Levi, that means you need to keep your mouth shut."

"Fuck off," Levi said. "I know the drill."

And that was it. The conversation shifted to something else, and I stood frozen in place, shock and dismay and...hurt swarming inside me.

My brothers had always kept me sheltered since I was old enough to toddle behind them and poke my nose where it didn't belong. Sheltered me more than they should have, actually. More than I'd wanted them to. So much so that when I'd come back home after graduating college, my main goal had been to prove to them that I didn't need to be protected anymore. I was an adult. Strong as hell with a will of iron who could handle anything. *Anything*.

Apparently, they didn't think I could handle this.

After I shoved all my thoughts and emotions deep, shutting down any shadow of hurt so they couldn't see, I strode into the dining room and took a seat in the open chair they'd left for me.

"It's nice of you to join us," Levi drawled, an echo to what I said to him nearly every meeting he attended.

I flipped him off without glancing in his direction. "If you guys are finally ready, let's dive in."

Ford snorted and Aiden blew out a long-suffering sigh, but no one commented otherwise as Aiden dove into this week's budget numbers.

Usually, I was the one who ran these meetings. Kept everyone in line and on schedule, but I couldn't stay focused. My mind kept wandering, what-ifs and maybes bombarding me.

What if rehab stuck this time?

Maybe he would stay sober...

What if it could be different?

Maybe he'd want to come back here...move back in to his cottage, but this time, maybe he wouldn't shut us out...

"Addison," Aiden said, and it was clear from the irritation in his tone that it wasn't the first time he'd called my name.

"What?" I glanced around at the all-too-intuitive stares of my brothers.

"You okay, little D?" Ford asked. "You haven't yelled once, and that's not like you."

And I didn't even have it in me to snap back about his little dictator reference, either. "I'm fine. Where were we?"

Brady studied my face for far longer than I was comfortable with, considering he interrogated suspects for a living. Then he dropped his gaze to my closed iPad and the obvious lack of usual chaos spread in front of me, his brow twitching.

"I asked when we're going to start taking reservations for Cottage Thirteen," Aiden said.

I shifted in my seat, that pang of uneasiness inside me multiplying. "It's, um...it's not done yet."

Levi shot me a *what the fuck* look. "Since when? It's been done for days."

I kept my attention on anything but the five of them, finally opening the cover for my iPad and navigating to the reservations app just to give myself something to do. "I, uh...I wanted to do some stuff to it."

Silence hung in the air, and I didn't have to be looking at them to know they'd all exchanged *what the hell is going on* glances.

"What kind of stuff?" Aiden asked, suspicion heavy in his tone.

I shrugged. "Um...decorating stuff."

"Decorating stuff," Ford repeated.

"Yeah. Like...you know...throw pillows and cozy blankets and whatnot." I didn't dare lift my gaze—busy, busy, oh-so busy sorting through our excess of upcoming reservations—

because I had no doubt they'd be able to read everything in my expression.

I knew this was stupid. I knew there was absolutely no reason to keep this perfectly rentable cottage vacant on the off chance our father decided to get his shit together after decades of proving otherwise. But the pull that had been there—that tiny niggle of doubt whenever I'd discussed it—had grown into something I could no longer ignore.

"Cut the bullshit, Addison," Beck said, his arms crossed over his chest as he leaned back in his chair. "What's going on?"

"I just think maybe we jumped the gun with it. It might be a good idea to hold off on taking reservations for now."

Aiden narrowed his eyes on me. "Aren't you the one constantly telling us how booked we are and how we could be making a fortune if we had more cottages available?"

"If we had another dozen cottages to add, yes. But one more isn't going to make that much of a difference."

"What's this really about?" Brady asked, getting straight to the point.

I shrugged, still avoiding eye contact. "I just think it might be a good idea to have it open and available in case... someone needs it."

"And would that someone be the asshole who injured your best friend?" Aiden said.

"Don't be a dick," I snapped. "Avery already told you it was an accident."

"An accident that wouldn't have happened if he weren't a drunk." Aiden's voice rose with every word.

"Aiden," Brady said, his tone low and firm.

"Are you kidding me?" Aiden asked, incredulous. "Are you actually considering this?"

Brady shot me a look out of the corner of his eye, his mouth set in a firm line, and I knew his answer before he even uttered a word. He gave one definitive shake of his head. "No."

"No," I repeated flatly. "And that's it?"

"That's it," Aiden confirmed. "You're the only one here concerned about him. That should tell you something."

"What it tells me is that you're all uncaring, insensitive assholes."

"And you are allowing guilt to override your common sense," Aiden said. "Don't be a fucking idiot, Addison."

"Hey." The sharp voice startled everyone, and we glanced at the doorway. Chase stood there, looking as imposing as he did on the ice. His hands were fisted at his sides, his mouth set in a firm line as he glared at Aiden. Then, in a low tone that sent shivers skating down my spine, he said, "Call her a fucking idiot again, and we're gonna have a problem."

CHAPTER FOURTEEN

CHASE

WHERE MOST PEOPLE probably would've cowered in a room with five other grown men—all of whom were over 6'2" and more than two hundred pounds—glowering in their direction, I wasn't one of them. And Addison wasn't either, despite her pocket-sized stature. I had zero doubt that she could handle herself—hell, she'd been handling herself her entire life when it came to her brothers.

But that didn't mean she should have to.

I knew I was putting ten years of secrecy on the line by stepping in here, but I didn't care. My mind had blanked to anything but Addison as soon as I'd walked in the front door from my PT appointment and heard five grown-ass men yelling at my girl.

"What the fuck is wrong with you?" I spat, glaring at each of them.

"Excuse me?" Brady's voice was deceptively calm, but there was no mistaking the hard edge to it.

"Cut the sheriff voice, Brady. I'm not twelve anymore."

"Neither is she." Beck leaned back in his chair, arms crossed. "Addison can handle herself."

I dipped my chin in a nod because there was no denying that truth. "She can. But should she have to handle herself against her fucking brothers?"

That hit its mark, each of them shifting in their seats and exchanging wary glances as if just realizing how harsh they'd come off.

"Don't try to pretend you wouldn't hand someone their ass for speaking to her like that, so what in the actual fuck makes you think it's okay for you to do it just because she's your sister? Shit, if I talked to my sisters like that, they'd have teamed up to beat the snot out of me and done it all with a smile. But there's only one pint-sized version of her and five of you fuckers, so how about you lay off?"

There was a beat of stunned silence as they all stared at me. I met their gazes head on, arms crossed, mouth set in a firm line. They were in the wrong here, and they fucking knew it.

"Since when does Addison need someone to fight her battles for her?" Levi asked, his brows drawn down as he appraised me, and I really hoped I was imagining the suspicion in his eyes.

"He's got a point," Beck said.

Ford nodded. "Little D can handle shit on her own."

"If she has a problem, she can speak for herself," Aiden said.

Everyone's attention swiveled to Addison's chair. Addison's *empty* chair. Apparently, at some point during our argument, she'd packed up her shit and bailed without a word.

I turned back to them, brows raised. "What do you have to say now?"

"She's fine," Beck said.

"Best to leave her alone when she gets like this," Brady agreed. "She'll be back to biting our heads off by noon."

While the latter was certainly true, alone time was going to do fuck all for her right now. How did they not know that? Solitude would only serve to spiral her further into her feels, and that was a recipe for disaster where Addison was concerned. What my tiny tornado needed was a venting post, and I was all too willing to volunteer as tribute, just like old times.

Without another word to the assholes who'd run off my girl, I stalked out of the room, intent on finding where she'd snuck away to. After searching the inn and coming up empty, I stopped dead in my tracks as realization hit. If she wasn't here, there was only one other place she'd be. The same place I'd been taking her since we were both just kids.

Growing up, I'd spent nearly as much time at the resort as I did at my own home. My parents considered Levi another son, and Levi's mom had felt the same about me. That meant I was usually around when Addison's brothers pissed her off or when shit got too real with their dad. It was during those times when Levi would order me to get her out of the inn. Take her somewhere. Anywhere, so long as she didn't have to witness their dad's drunken fumblings.

Grabbing my coat, I headed out to my truck and drove the short trek to the other side of the property. Though someone still plowed this path, it looked as though it didn't get regular use. This part of the resort used to be the talk of the town in winter months, being the only outdoor and recreation-exclusive ice-skating rink in Starlight Cove and home to a camp for kids over winter break. But as I slowly drove down the overgrown path, it became all too clear it had been years—a decade, if I had to guess—since this place had been shown an ounce of love, and I hated that.

The Zamboni shack—aka Addison's and my hideaway—was just that. The building, if you could call it that, was in shambles, the wood splintered and faded, the roof sagging in the middle. The whole thing needed to be torn down and rebuilt from the ground up. Same with the bunkhouses that appeared to be in similar shape and the main building that used to house the rentals, warming center, snack bar, and changing rooms. And I didn't even want to think about the ice-skating rink.

Parking my truck, I glanced over at the open area, now covered with dead overgrowth and snow, and a pang hit me in the center of my chest. It was nothing but weeds and forgotten memories now, but that was the place where my dad had first taught me to skate. Where I'd then taught Addison. Where Levi and I had played hundreds of pickup games while she'd skated circles around us, begging to play, too.

I'd spent thousands of hours of my childhood right there on the ice or in the bunkhouses, and I hated that it had sunk to this. Hated that what was once a beloved part of Starlight Cove was now nothing more than a memory. A million options flitted through my head. Different things I could do or ways I could help get this back to its former glory... As good as some of those ideas were—I'd definitely be reaching out to my agent about an endorsement deal that would hopefully boost interest in the resort and thus its bottom line—they weren't my priority.

Addison was.

I followed her small footprints that led straight to the shack, scowling when I realized she'd walked all the way here rather than driving—no doubt in an effort to cool herself off. I'd bet money that hadn't done jack shit.

The loud creak of the battered door's old hinges announced my arrival, and I found her right where I thought she'd be. Facing away from me, she sat in the Zamboni, her back ramrod straight, her posture screaming *fuck off and never come back*. She didn't even shoot a glance over her shoulder at the interruption, as if she'd been expecting me.

At some point in the Zamboni's incredibly long life, the standard seat had been replaced with a wider bench that could accommodate two people, so I climbed up and sat next to her. Hundreds of times, she'd sat right where she was now, keeping me company as I cleaned off the ice. And hundreds more had been spent just like this...the two of us tucked away in this private, quiet place of our own, no one the wiser.

Not even Levi knew this was Addison's and my place.

I glanced over, studying her features. Her nose and cheeks were flushed a deep pink, probably because she'd walked her sweet little ass all the way over here in twenty-five-degree weather. Beneath a bright-red wool hat, her brow was creased, her mouth set in a firm line, and those eyes... Anger and indignation burned bright in her gaze. A lesser person would've run for the hills when she leveled that furious glower on them. But her scowls didn't scare me, so I just met her stare head on.

When it was clear I wasn't going anywhere, she blew out a long-suffering sigh and turned away, bringing her attention back to whatever was so fascinating on the wall. "What are you doing here?"

I could've lied to her. Made up some reason for why I just happened to be out here, at an abandoned ice-skating rink, but what was the point? Whether she meant here in this shack or here in Starlight Cove, it didn't matter. "I'm here for you."

If I hadn't been paying attention, I would've missed how her breath caught and the way she darted a quick glance at me before averting her gaze once again. And though it had been quick, I'd seen surprise and...hope? swimming in her eyes. I was all too ready to encourage that.

But instead of showing me an ounce of that hope, she leaned into her anger, her default coping mechanism. "I'm fine," she bit out. She was clearly anything but fine. Her hands were curled in her mittens, little balls of fury buried in fleece, and the pink of her cheeks darkened, having nothing to do with the chill in the air.

"Okay." I leaned back on the seat, propping my feet up and getting comfortable.

"I *am*," she said, more adamant this time. "It's my brothers who are the problem."

"Okay," I said again, ready to wait her out as long as necessary.

After several long moments of silence, she huffed out an irritated breath and turned to glare at me. "Why are you being so fucking quiet?"

I lifted a single shoulder in a shrug and tipped my head toward her. "This isn't my first rodeo."

"What's that supposed to mean?"

"It means I know you, Addie, and I know what you need. You don't need to be left alone like your brothers seem to think. You need someone to listen while you lose your shit." I shrugged, my shoulder brushing against hers. "Well, I'm here now. You can lose your shit on me."

She was quiet for a second...two, three...and then she threw her mitten-covered hands in the air and huffed out a frustrated breath. "They still treat me like I'm a child! Like they have to protect me from everything, and it's complete *bullshit*. I'm twenty-eight years old, not six, for fuck's sake."

If she were at a place where she was open to listening, I would've told her that while I didn't agree with her brothers' methods, they were probably doing it because they wanted to save her the heartbreak they'd gone through themselves. Their dad was a piece of work, and I was old enough to remember all his failed attempts at sobriety. Old enough to remember just how badly it tore her brothers up, too. But Addison didn't need me to try to fix this for her. She didn't need me to get involved or tell her what she should do instead or offer her any advice.

All she needed was for me to listen.

"They think I can't handle it." She barked out a humorless laugh. "I've handled *everything*. Everything they throw at me, I've taken care of. The resort...*them*. And then they try to keep this from me because they don't think I can deal? Well, fuck them and their dumb boy brains and their stupid, idiotic misconceptions. They're acting like jackasses, and they can all suck my dick."

My lips twitched, but I didn't dare smile. Instead, I sat silently, making sure she'd gotten it all out of her system. When her hands were no longer balled into fists and her shoulders weren't hiked clear up to her ears, I finally said, "Feel better?"

She pursed her lips and shot me a look out of the corner of her eye. Then she exhaled a weary sigh. "Yes."

"Why don't you sound happy about that?"

She fluttered her eyes closed and whispered, "I hate that you know what I need."

There was so much happening in my life right now that I had absolutely no control over and so much shit I couldn't do —like play the game I was getting paid millions to play— thanks to the injury that kept on giving.

But this? This, I could do. All day, every day. As long as she needed me to. For the rest of my life, if I was lucky.

I wanted desperately to pull her into my lap and kiss away that angry pout on her gorgeous mouth. Wanted to sweep her hair back, kiss along her jaw, and allow her to use me in a different way entirely in order to get out all that aggression.

Instead, I bumped her shoulder with mine and leaned into her, keeping our bodies pressed together. When she glanced over at me and our gazes locked, I murmured, "I don't."

CHAPTER FIFTEEN

ADDISON

IT HAD BEEN MORE than a week since that morning when my brothers made me lose my shit. I hadn't been able to take any more. So, without a word, I'd gathered up my things and hustled out of the room without anyone noticing—too wrapped up in their arguing to pay attention.

No one in their right mind would ever call me idealistic. I generally assumed the worst and had contingency plans for every possible negative outcome. But there was still a tiny part of me—a little girl buried deep inside who'd never had that special kind of father-daughter relationship portrayed in movies—that couldn't help but hold out hope that maybe this time would be different.

I knew it was stupid. And I knew they'd tell me as much if I voiced that to them. So, I'd bailed. Run off to the one place I knew no one would look for me.

Well, no one but Chase.

Having his reassuring presence next to me, his body heat

seeping into my bones as he sat and just...listened—didn't try to fix, didn't heap advice on me—had been exactly what I'd needed.

And he'd known that.

That scared the hell out of me. I could fend off cocky Chase. Could ignore jealous Chase. Had no problem taunting horny Chase. But thoughtful Chase? I was fucked.

Thankfully, his furniture had been delivered to his new home—a home I had no idea the location of, but that was fine by me. Less chance I'd accidentally-on-purpose find myself on his front step—which meant he was no longer staying at the inn. No longer sharing a wall with me. No longer witnessing me getting myself off to the visual of him.

I'd been so busy this week, I'd barely noticed his absence.

Yesterday, I'd received a call from an agent's office—why the agent couldn't call me himself, I wasn't sure. But the assistant I'd spoken to had let me know one of the agent's big clients was from Maine and was hoping to partner with some local businesses to endorse and give back to their home state. And, luckily, the resort had come up in conversation. This was exactly the kind of side project I needed in our back pocket for when—*if*—the resort started to backslide again.

When the assistant asked if that was something we might be interested in, I pretty much fell all over myself to say yes. Though the person I'd spoken to hadn't dropped any clues as to who this A-lister was, I couldn't help but wonder if it was the same top-secret person building a cabin on the bluff on the outskirts of Starlight Cove.

Ever since construction had started on it months ago, it

had been the talk of the town. The current rumor was that the owner was a certain superhero in a very popular film franchise. Thoughts of what that kind of partnership could possibly mean for the resort had been a constant whirlwind in my mind since I'd hung up after confirming our meeting for today.

Not wanting to get anyone's hopes up, I hadn't let any of my brothers know what this meeting was about. Part of me was still mad at them for their behavior and didn't want to talk to them, despite the olive branches they'd sent my way. Beck had sent over my favorite dinners, Brady had cleaned off my car every morning, Aiden had taken care of the shit jobs I hated doing, Ford had dropped off a care package full of my favorite snacks, and Levi had stocked the fridge with my favorite ice cream. Which told me they knew they'd fucked up.

The other part of me just wanted to make sure this opportunity was as good as the agent's office had made it out to be before I spilled the details to anyone.

The drive to the bluff was a little rough, snow coming down heavy and wet, but I'd lived in Maine my whole life, so this wasn't anything new. I could navigate wintery weather conditions like a motherfucking boss.

The road leading to this elusive cabin was secluded, a canopy of bare trees arching overhead and creating a makeshift tunnel that would've been kind of spooky if it weren't the middle of the afternoon. With how far on the outskirts of Starlight Cove this home was, I absolutely believed the rumors about who owned this place. Someone who wanted privacy and seclusion. Who didn't want to be harassed any time they stepped out their front door. And I was going to lose my mind if I was about to meet one of the Chrises today.

After a dicey uphill drive, I followed the long, winding driveway until I was in front of what could never be classified as a cabin by any stretch of the imagination. It was a lodge. Beautiful and impressive. Built of wood logs and stone with a steep, peaked roof, it stood proudly on the otherwise secluded property, with towering trees surrounding it. But what should have looked imposing somehow gave off a warm and inviting vibe.

I shut off my car and grabbed my bag before stepping out into the falling snow. My stomach was a mixture of nerves and determination, so I rolled my shoulders back, shook off any apprehension, and put on my game face. No matter what awaited me, I'd handle it because the resort deserved my best. My brothers, sporadic shitheads that they were, deserved my best. Especially after all they'd given me.

I rang the doorbell and barely had time to worry about what my first words were going to be to this Hollywood elite before the front door swung open...and the smile melted right off my face.

Chase stood in the doorway, blocking my view inside. He wore tattered jeans and a long-sleeved navy Henley, his feet bare as if he owned the fucking place.

I scowled at him, not prepared for this wrench thrown into my plan. Not prepared to face him so soon after I'd exposed my underbelly. "What the hell are you doing here?"

With that stupid, smug smirk on his stupidly handsome face, he reached out, hooked a finger in the pocket of my coat, and tugged me inside before shutting the door behind me. "What do you think I'm doing here?" he asked, grabbing my bag and hanging it on the rack next to the door.

I narrowed my eyes at him, crossing my arms over my chest. "Don't tell me you're here for a partnership, too. The agent's office never said the resort would be competing for attention."

"How about you come in, and you can crank up your anger to yell at Marty about that when he gets here."

My stomach dropped at the thought of being here with Chase...alone. It wasn't like I thought I'd jump his bones at the first opportunity. Probably. But it was best to err on the side of caution and stay as far away as possible. "He's not here yet?"

"Just me, firefly."

"Great," I said on a sigh.

"Take off those shoes you hate and stick around for a while."

As much as I didn't want to do what he said, I couldn't deny the truth of the statement. I *did* hate these torture devices. I also had no intention of stepping a foot into this immaculate home with my heels on. I kicked them off as I glanced around, taking it all in.

This place was...gorgeous. Basically everything I would put into a house if I'd had one custom-built. The main area, painted in soft grays with distressed wood floors, was one giant great room, with a white gourmet kitchen and a huge eat-in island, what looked like the fluffiest sectional I'd ever seen in my life, and a fireplace along one wall below a large TV. But the real showstopper was the wall of windows against the back of the house, running from floor to ceiling and wall to wall.

I stepped up to take it all in, my eyes widening at the view beyond. Driving up here, it had felt like this place was in the middle of the forest with all the trees surrounding me. But this proved otherwise. The house sat hundreds of feet above sea level, the ocean spread out below. My breath caught in my throat as I stared out the windows, watching as snow flurries swirled above a turbulent sea.

"You like it?" Chase asked, his shoulder brushing against mine.

"It doesn't matter if I like it."

He hummed but otherwise didn't comment on that. Instead, he said, "Why don't you give me your coat?"

I glanced over at him, narrowing my eyes. "Why are you acting like this is your house? Taking my coat and walking around barefoot—honestly, who does that?"

"And why are you—" Chase hooked a finger in my coat pocket and tugged me toward him once again, his hands landing on my hips to steady me "—being so difficult?"

I ignored how close he was, how fucking good he smelled, and how much I wanted to feel his lips on mine again as he slowly slid each button on my jacket through its hole, his eyes locked on mine the entire time. Without my heels on, I was more than a foot shorter than Chase, and where I'd once loved that height difference, I couldn't deny how vulnerable it made me feel. Something I couldn't afford to be around him.

I swallowed hard, trying to appear unaffected by him. "Because it's my favorite thing to be around you."

Chase laughed, free and unrestrained, and I hated how much I loved it. Hated, too, how much I'd missed it. He and Avery were the only two people in the world who could have me giggling at 3 a.m., punch-drunk on laughter, and it had been far too long since I'd done that with him.

"You know," he said, "I read somewhere that people always push boundaries the hardest with those they feel the most comfortable with. The safest with. Those they think will be there, no matter what. It's why teenagers are such assholes to their parents."

"I assume you have a point?"

He raised a brow, his lips kicked up at the corner. "My point is you push awfully fucking hard with me, Addie. And as much as I'm sure you hate it, that tells me just how comfortable you are with me."

"Have you ever thought that maybe I'm like this around you because I don't want to be around you?"

He shook his head, eyes boring into mine as he slid the last button on my coat through its hole. "Never once."

I pinched my lips together, shoving down the spark of heat his words had ignited, and glared up at him. But then he brushed his hands over my shoulders and down my arms, stripping the coat from my body, his touch featherlight and scattering goose bumps across my skin. Those were easier to hide with my long sleeves, but the shudder that ran down my spine wasn't. Apparently Chase valued his life too much to comment on it, though. Instead, he took my coat without a word and strode back to the entryway, hanging it on the rack next to my bag.

I watched him move around this home with ease, narrowing my eyes on him as various puzzle pieces slowly started shifting into place. "You're awfully comfortable in somebody else's house."

He shot an amused smirk my way, one brow raised. "Who said it was somebody else's house?"

CHAPTER SIXTEEN

ADDISON

I COULD ONLY BLINK at him as his words took longer than they should have to register, my mind rewriting everything I'd thought I had figured out and replacing it with this new information. There was no Chris. No A-list celebrity. Just a professional hockey player who called Maine home, who had been born and raised right here in Starlight Cove, and who had a soft spot for my family's resort.

"*What*?" I snapped, not bothering to hide the venom in my voice. "Are you being serious right now?"

"Sure am."

"So you're saying the rumors around town about one of the Chrises building this place are completely false? That you have, in fact, been the person behind this new construction the entire time? Is that what you're telling me?" My voice was too loud, my tone kicked up several octaves, but I didn't have any hope of tempering it.

This was not good. Not good at all.

"Yeah," he said with a nod. "I think that pretty much sums it up."

I curled my hands into fists at my sides and stomped my bare foot. "This isn't funny!"

He strode toward me, amusement lighting his eyes as he held up his hands in supplication. "I never said I thought it was, but this mini-tantrum you're throwing is pretty adorable. I love it when you're feisty."

I elbowed him in the stomach. "Don't try to be cute."

"I don't have to try, firefly."

"This doesn't make any sense. Why aren't you surprised to see me? And why am I the only one freaking out here?"

"Between the two of us, you're usually the only one freaking out."

I jabbed a finger in his direction, a scowl on my face. "You planned this. You tricked me into coming here! There's probably not even an agent. You made that call yourself, didn't you? What did you do, get a voice changer?"

Without answering my question, Chase turned around and strode into the kitchen, opened the commercial-sized stainless-steel refrigerator, and pulled out something from inside. Then he strolled my way, holding it outstretched to me.

I yanked the small, individually sized bottle of juice out of his hands, breaking my glare at him long enough to glance down at it. Orange pineapple. Fresh squeezed. My fucking favorite.

How dare he, honestly.

Under normal circumstances, I would've shoved this right

back against his chest and told him I didn't need it. But A) only idiots cut off their noses to spite their faces, and I was no idiot. And B) I was parched after all this yelling.

So, with a lot more attitude than necessary, I opened it and took a drink, my eyes narrowed on him the entire time.

Chase lifted his brows at me after I'd downed half the bottle. "Better? You always get a little cranky when your blood sugar is low."

"Or maybe I just get cranky when I'm around you. Have you ever thought of that?" Without waiting for his response, I continued, "And don't try to distract me. I want to know what the hell's going on."

He shrugged and slid his hands into his jean pockets. "My agent's been pushing me to up my endorsement game. The problem is, I'm not interested in most of the businesses he's suggested. I made a deal with him—one of mine for one of his."

"And one of yours is..."

"The resort," he confirmed with a nod. "So, he reached out to set up the appointment. How was I supposed to know you'd be the one coming?"

I shoved the now-empty bottle against his chest and scoffed. "Who the hell else did you think was going to show up? Levi? No, no...maybe Beck. Actually, I got it—you were expecting *Brady*. Of course!" I shook my head and scowled at him.

"What are you really mad about here, Addie? Because from where I'm sitting, this endorsement deal only benefits the resort."

When he put it that way, he had a point. But logic didn't take into account that he was my ex for all intents and purposes. And I was nowhere near the point of indifference I needed to be in order to work this closely with him.

Before I could come up with a lie about why I was upset, my phone rang, the sound piercing the otherwise quiet space. I pulled it from my pocket, glancing down to see Brady's name flashing across the screen.

I flipped it around so Chase could see who it was. "Look, here's the brother you were expecting!" I rolled my eyes and accepted the call. "Hello?"

"Why isn't your car at the resort?" Brady asked without preamble.

"Because I'm not at the resort. Why?"

"Where are you?" It was less a question and more a barked demand—the usual with Brady.

I shot a glare over my shoulder as I answered him. "Chase's new house, apparently."

"The one on the bluff? What the fuck are you doing up there?"

"Wait, you knew it was his?"

"You didn't?"

"No! I thought it was one of the Chrises like everyone else in Starlight Cove!"

"Who the hell are the Chrises?"

"Uh, Hemsworth, Pratt, and, the best Chris in the world, Evans? *Hello.*"

"I have no idea why you'd think a movie star would be at that house, and it still doesn't answer why you're there."

"I got a call from an agent's office—*Chase's* agent, apparently—with an endorsement opportunity for the resort, so we scheduled a meeting."

"Jesus Christ, Addison," Brady grumbled. "Did you look outside? Or even check a fucking weather app at any point this week?"

I glanced out the plethora of windows along the back wall of the house. The snow fell heavily, but it didn't look that bad to me. Of course, being this high made it difficult to gauge how much was sticking on the ground. From this vantage point, it all disappeared into the ocean below. "No, I wasn't checking the weather reports. You're supposed to keep track of that for me."

"Oh, I am, am I? Well, here's your forecast. You're fucked for forty-eight hours. Nobody's getting in. Nobody's getting out. Airports are closing, and planes have been grounded."

I gasped, my face draining of all color as I shot a panicked glance at Chase. That meant the agent I'd been sent here to meet was no longer on his way. And *that* meant I was stuck here with my ex. Alone. "*No...*"

"Yes," Brady snapped, aggravation punctuating the single syllable. "We're in the middle of the harshest nor'easter of the season. And you, apparently, didn't even know it was coming."

"I've been a little busy, all right?" Busy making it my job to avoid Chase, for all the good it did me.

"Yeah, and you're paying for it now. This could've been avoided if you'd adulted better and checked your fucking weather app. Jesus, Addison, it's February in New England."

"So?"

"*So*, we get snowstorms. A lot. And considering you've lived here your whole life, this shouldn't be news to you."

"Well, forgive the fuck out of me for missing *one* week of looking at a stupid app that's wrong most of the time anyway!"

"Don't get pissy with me because you fucked up."

I clenched my teeth together, closed my eyes, and exhaled sharply toward the ceiling. "I'm sorry. I'm upset and anxious, and I just want to know when you'll be here to get me."

Because there was no fucking way I could stay here, trapped in this gorgeous house with a man who still set my body on fire.

Worse...one who calmed my soul.

Brady barked out what could barely pass as a laugh. "I won't be."

"Like, for a while?"

"No. Like, ever. I can't get to you, so you're gonna have to deal with it."

"What do you mean, you can't get to me?" I asked, panic seeping in. "You're the fucking sheriff, and I'm the most important person in your life!"

Luna laughed in the background, her voice muffled as she said, "Um, excuse me," sounding more amused than affronted.

"Fine, whatever! *Second* most important person in your life. You're my big brother. You're supposed to be the rescuer!"

"Addison," he said, exasperation lacing his tone. "You really want me to pull resources away from the hundreds of people down here who need my help so I can rescue your singular ass?"

"Yes, exactly. That is what I'm telling you."

He blew out a heavy sigh, the *I can't believe I have to put up with this shit* silent. "You're in a literal mansion with, I'm sure, a fully stocked kitchen. You're not alone. You haven't lost power. You're going to be fine."

"I am definitely *not* going to be fine." Ignoring Chase's questioning gaze, I strode to the entryway, intent on proving Brady wrong. "I can get back down myself. I drive in this stuff all the time. My car will be—" I yanked open the front door and gasped at the sight that greeted me.

In the time I'd been inside arguing with Chase, four inches must've fallen. My car was buried, there was no sign of the road anywhere, and everything was a blanket of white as far as I could see. Which, actually, wasn't far, considering how hard the snow was coming down.

"Just looked outside?" Brady asked.

"Yep."

"That's what I thought. Stay inside. Stay safe. I'll see you in a couple days."

"If I survive."

"Don't be so fucking dramatic," he grumbled. "Call me if you need anything—and I mean *really, actually* need it. And don't die."

"Love you, too." The words were barely out of my mouth before the line went dead, and I was officially stuck here with the one man I was trying my hardest to avoid.

"*You*." I spun around to face Chase, stalking toward him

with as much menace as someone more than a foot shorter than him could exude. "You *planned* this."

Chase pointedly looked outside and then back to me, one brow raised. "Damn, the secret's out. I can control the weather. Just don't tell anybody else, okay? I don't want to become a lab rat."

"This isn't funny! I have stuff I need to do and a resort to run." Not to mention an unrelenting pull to ignore and horny memories I needed to forget immediately.

"That may be true, but it's not happening," he said. "So you might as well settle in, firefly. From the sounds of it, we're going to be snowed in and stuck together for a while."

CHAPTER SEVENTEEN

ADDISON

THIS WAS MY WORST NIGHTMARE. I had been able to handle Chase staying at the resort in the room directly next to mine because I'd had my own space. I'd been able to escape him anytime I needed to. But here? I was trapped. In his home. With nowhere to go.

The truth was, I didn't trust myself around him.

He had a way of breaking down my defenses. Of making me feel like I was the only woman in the world, as if he didn't have hundreds of puck bunnies throwing themselves at him every chance they got. He was playful and charming, the perfect counterpart to my fiery passion, and I'd fallen into that—into *him*—even though I'd known better.

After he'd taken my virginity and broken my heart when he'd dropped me off at college the following day and told me to have fun without him—that he had to give all his focus to his hockey career and he wanted me to live the college life without obligations—I swore I wouldn't allow myself to be vulnerable with him again.

But when we'd run into each other after I'd graduated college, there was no denying the sparks that still crackled between us. The difference was, I'd no longer been that stupid, naive girl who'd thought the guy she'd spent her teenage years crushing on actually wanted to call her his. I'd come into our new arrangement knowing exactly what it was and what it wasn't, and that had been because *I'd* been the one setting the terms this time.

But then one hookup had turned into two which turned into dozens. And before I knew it, years had gone by, and suddenly he was telling me we wouldn't have to get by on twice-a-year flings if I'd just marry him.

Marry him.

It was all too clear now, after being on the receiving end of nothing but silence from him for more than a year, that he hadn't been serious. He'd only been joking.

The worst part about that realization was I'd been contemplating saying yes.

God, what if I'd actually said yes? To a *joke*.

The knot in my stomach tightened, and I swallowed down the wave of uneasiness that washed over me. I sat on the closed toilet seat in one of Chase's many bathrooms, having escaped in here for a few moments of peace and quiet without the sexy bastard breathing down my neck.

A knock sounded at the bathroom door, and I yelped, nearly jumping out of my skin at the sudden intrusion. "What?"

"You doing all right in there?" Chase asked.

"Fine," I snapped. "Why?"

"Because you've been hiding in there for forty-five minutes."

"I have not been *hiding*. And it's only been—" I pulled out my phone and glanced at the time. Forty-seven minutes. Great.

"Are you intending to stay in there the entirety of the two days Brady thinks you'll be stuck here?" he asked, amusement clear in his tone. "You want me to figure out a food delivery system to you?"

He was just taunting me now. And if there was one thing I needed to do to make sure our time didn't go off the rails, it was prove to him that he didn't affect me at all. I was cool, calm, and collected and not at all knotted up inside at the thought of what we used to be...of what we could've been.

I whipped open the door to find Chase standing there, his hands braced above him on the doorframe. His biceps bulged beneath his shirt, the material clinging to every hard, heavily muscled inch of him, and I nearly swallowed my tongue at the sight.

His stance, combined with that flirty little smile he shot down at me, reminded me so much of him when we were younger. Back when I'd had illusions that something could come of us. When I'd thought that maybe, just maybe, he'd pick me.

"I don't know why you're smiling," I said. "We're trapped. I cannot be stuck here with you for days without anywhere to go."

"Why? Are you scared?"

"Yeah. Scared for your life because there's no way we can be in the same space for that long without me strangling you."

He laughed. *Laughed*! "Well, things are certainly not going to be boring, that's for sure."

"Is it even safe for us to stay here? You just moved in! What about food? What if we lose power? We need heat to survive in a nor'easter. And don't you dare say anything about sharing body heat, or I will murder you with my bare hands."

His lips twitched, and I didn't know whether to love or hate that he tried to suppress his laughter at my rant. He grabbed my hand and tugged me behind him into the kitchen. And I absolutely should not have been melting at the simple touch of his much larger hand engulfing mine or how his thumb swept over my skin, so soft and gentle despite his calluses. But as history had proven, all my best intentions flew out the window where Chase was concerned.

"We've got plenty of food." He opened the massive refrigerator, gesturing to the neatly stacked containers of what appeared to be fully prepared meals along one side. The other half of the fridge was stocked with fresh fruits and vegetables, a dozen bottles identical to the one he'd already given me, fresh rolled sushi, a charcuterie tray, and chocolate-covered strawberries—all my favorites. "I have a personal chef who drops off meals twice a week, and she just topped me off yesterday."

"Since when do you eat sushi?" I asked, shooting a questioning glance his way.

"Since never. That's for you. Same with the juice and the charcuterie and the strawberries."

"What? Why the hell would you stock any of that stuff for me?"

"Been doing it for years." He shrugged like it was no big deal. "Just in case."

"Just in case," I repeated, tone flat.

"Yeah, just in case you happened to show up starving. We both know how vicious you get when you're hangry."

I had to force myself not to openly gape at him, but there was no stopping the swarm of butterflies that took flight in my stomach at his admission. He could coat it in barbs all he wanted, but it wasn't going to overshadow the crux of it. He'd been doing this for *years*. Had been filling half of his fridge with my favorites on the minuscule chance I would *stop by*. To Vancouver. When I lived in Maine.

I pushed down the warmth that blossomed in my chest and cleared my throat. "I hope you realize how ridiculous that is. Just because you're rich and can waste all that food doesn't mean you should."

He huffed out a laugh and reached out, brushing a flyaway piece of hair from my eye, his thumb grazing the side of my face. "Have I told you lately how much I love it when you call me on my shit? It's pretty much impossible to find in my line of work."

I ignored the shiver his small touch caused and crossed my arms over my chest to hide my reaction to it. To *him*. "Well, I'm always happy to knock you down a peg or twenty."

"I know you are." And he didn't even try to hide the affection in his voice. "As for the uneaten food, my chef picks it up before anything can go bad, then takes it and a check from me to a local homeless shelter. I keep my girl's favorites stocked, just in case, and everyone gets a meal. Win all around."

My stomach flipped at his casual claiming of me...*his* girl. How was I supposed to stand a chance against him when we were trapped here for days?

"As for heat," he said, once again tugging me along behind him, "we can kill two birds with one stone."

"How so?"

"I want to make sure we have enough wood, just in case the power does go out, and I'm sure you'd like some material for the resort. You can film me."

"Doing what?"

"Chopping wood."

While I couldn't deny that content would have people frothing at the mouth like the thirsty fuckers they were—just look at any hot lumberjack's social media account, and the proof was in every innuendo-laced comment—we were currently in a snowstorm.

"Outside?" I asked, gesturing to the wall of windows and the sea of white beyond. "In *this*?"

His only response was a grin that shot straight to the center of my chest.

And that was how I found myself forty-five minutes later. Watching an incredibly capable Chase slowly shed layers of clothing as he chopped us a pile of wood that would probably last weeks.

There was a small, covered structure behind the garage with a rack for the wood, as well as a chopping block, so everything stayed dry as he worked.

Everything except my panties.

Watching his muscles bunch and flex with every swing of the axe, the way his face was creased in concentration... And kill me now, but the *noises.* Sweet Lord in heaven, the grunts and groans and everything that reminded me of what he sounded like when he was inside me...

Shaking my head, I cleared my throat and refocused on the videos I was filming for future promo—the whole reason I was out here with him in the first place. Once I was satisfied with what I'd captured, I opened my voice memo app, thankful I didn't have to actually take notes since my hands were currently bundled in mittens.

"I could use some sound bites and quotes, so can we go over some questions?"

"Whatever you need, firefly."

I ignored the way my stomach flipped at that—honestly, it was getting to be a real problem now.

Making sure the app was recording, I asked, "What do you love most about the resort?"

He swiped his forearm across his brow, the move lifting his shirt just enough to showcase a sliver of his abs. "Well, there's this girl..."

I rolled my eyes. "Be serious."

"I am being serious."

"Fine, then stop being an idiot." I blew out an exasperated breath. "What's your favorite thing to do around the Cove?"

He began stacking some of the wood he'd chopped in his arms and glanced my way, sweeping a heated gaze over me that I felt even through all my layers of clothing. "Currently? Watching you get yourself off."

Those handful of words sparked a memory I'd spent days repressing—him standing in the doorway to my bedroom, his eyes fixed on me, his hand wrapped around that thick, magnificent cock as he'd gotten himself off while watching me do the same.

I'd thought it'd been a genius idea to make him suffer like that—being able to look but not touch—but the joke had been on me because what I'd intended as payback had backfired. It had only made me hungrier for him.

And something like that couldn't happen again.

"Okay, I'm done." I stopped recording and pocketed my phone. "It's cold out here, and you're acting like an ass."

Without waiting for a reply, I stomped back toward the house, grateful Brady always made me carry emergency supplies in my trunk so I wasn't trudging through nearly a foot of snow in my four-inch heels.

"Addison, wait."

"Not interested." I flipped him off over my shoulder, which did absolutely nothing since I was wearing mittens.

"Just give me a second," he said. Except he didn't need it because he was far closer than he should've been, considering my head start and the fact that he was lugging who knew how much wood.

Once inside, I kicked off my boots and shed the rest of my gear, glaring at him as he unloaded the logs next to the fireplace. "Did you agree to do this to actually help the resort, or are you just interested in wasting my time?"

"Of course I did it to help the resort."

"Then stop fucking around. This promo isn't about us. *We* don't matter. It's just about you."

"I don't know how much clearer I can make this, Addie, but there isn't *me* without *you*."

"Don't," I snapped, holding up a hand as if I could stop those words from ever reaching my ears. "Don't you dare do that."

"What? Tell you the truth? Talk to you, uninterrupted? For more time than we've had in a decade? I've got you here for days, firefly, and I'm damn well going to use every second of them to figure out what went wrong."

I breathed out an incredulous laugh. "To figure out what went wrong? I'll tell you what went wrong—you somehow went from asking me to marry you to ignoring me for a fucking year. *That's* what went wrong."

"What?" He looked as if I'd slapped him. "I never—"

"I can't help but wonder what would've happened if you'd ignored me right from the start."

"We grew up together, Addie. There was no ignoring you."

"Maybe not. But what if you'd just ignored me that night? When you overheard me talking to your sister about cashing in my V-card with anyone who was willing to do it."

His jaw ticked, as if the idea of me being with someone else was too much for him to handle. Yeah, well, the feeling was mutual, but at least he didn't have it shoved in his face every time he went on social media. "I don't regret that. I could never regret it."

"Of course you don't! You weren't the one who got dumped the morning after."

"You know why I had to do that. Morgan had just been diagnosed. And I had to bust my ass to prove myself in the pros. I wasn't in the right headspace to give you what you deserved."

"And what do you think would've happened if, instead of swooping in and claiming me for yourself before tossing me aside, you'd just let me be? Dropped me off at college without a broken heart and let me live my life without the shadow of you in it."

He shook his head, his eyes blazing with an intensity that was hard to ignore. "It wouldn't have mattered. You and I are inevitable, Addison."

"Inevitable?" I said on a laugh. "We aren't *anything*, Chase. You made sure of that. But I'll tell you what is inevitable—you fucking any and every puck bunny who throws herself at you."

"I haven't touched another woman," he said without hesitation. And if I hadn't seen the pictures for myself, the conviction in his voice might have swayed me.

I scoffed, working hard to keep the tears at bay because I didn't want to give him the satisfaction of seeing how much this affected me. "Well, congratulations. You want accolades for not having sex in the past year, when you were injured most of that time anyway? What a fucking feat. Someone get this man a medal!"

"Jesus Christ, will you shut up and let me talk a minute?"

"No!" I snapped, needing to get the hell out of here because the tears were building—whether from anger, frustration, or hurt, I didn't know. And it didn't matter because they were coming, regardless. I spun around before he could see the first tear fall and stormed off down the hallway. "Leave it alone, Chase, and give me some goddamn space."

CHAPTER EIGHTEEN

CHASE

I HAD SEEN Addison mad more times than I could count—you couldn't be passionate like she was without some anger in the mix. And when she got well and truly pissed, the tears came. It was something she hated about herself—when her anger was interrupted by tears she couldn't control.

While I had no doubt she was pissed off at me for whatever bullshit alternate reality of our relationship she'd concocted, I knew what she'd really been after when she'd run away had been to hide.

So I'd let her.

For now anyway. But that shit wasn't going to last. While she was stuck here with nowhere to go, my gloves were coming off and we were hashing this out. By the end of our snow-in, she was going to know exactly how fucking gone I was for her. No more hiding. No more underplaying it. No more flippant marriage proposals so I could brush them off as a joke in case she said no.

I was all fucking in, and she was damn well going to hear it.

Unfortunately, she'd locked herself away in one of my guest rooms, barking a sharp, "Go away!" when I'd knocked on her door to see if she was hungry.

Earning me absolutely zero points, I'd ignored her harsh command, opened the door, and dropped off some sushi for her inside. She'd been here for hours, and Addison was a fucking beast when she didn't get fed. I was already facing an uphill battle when it came to her—I wasn't about to add hangriness to the list of shit stacked against me.

But I also wasn't going to push.

So, after dropping that off, I'd let her be. For hours and fucking *hours*.

It was just getting absurd now. It was late, my knee ached like a motherfucker, and I wanted to go to bed. With her, preferably.

I knocked softly on the door and waited for a response. When I didn't get one, I tried again before turning the knob and poking my head inside.

While the room was set up with furniture—a bed frame with a headboard, a dresser, and two nightstands, the guest room mattresses hadn't yet arrived. Which meant she was curled into a ball on the floor, like the dramatic little diva she was.

"Go away," she said, not bothering to face me. She was no longer wearing the clothes she'd come here in. Instead, she had on one of my old sweatshirts that was so big it looked like a dress on her. The movers must've accidentally put away some of my stuff in here, but I sure as hell wasn't mad about it —seeing her in my clothes made my dick hard.

I *was* mad about her lying on the fucking floor, though.

"You're not sleeping there."

"Looks like that's exactly what I'm doing," she said. "Now leave me alone, and let me get to it."

I leaned against the doorframe, crossing my arms as I stared at her back. "Don't you think you're being a little ridiculous?"

"No. I don't."

I scrubbed a hand down my face and groaned. "Addie. Just come to bed. It's a king—you can put up a pillow wall between us if it'll make you feel better."

"I'm fine right here. In case you didn't know, the carpet in the brand-new home of a professional hockey player is very plush."

Despite my irritation, I snorted a laugh and walked over to her, squatting down at her back. "You're acting like a brat about this."

"So why don't you leave me alone and let me act like a brat all by myself, then?"

She had the tenacity of a bulldog, and I knew there would be no changing her mind. So, with a sigh, I stood and headed back to my room. I grabbed the down comforter off my bed before bringing it into the guest room and laying it on top of her.

"My room's at the end of the hall when you get tired of this," I said.

"Don't count on it."

I wasn't going to. Which was exactly why I planned to come back in thirty minutes when I knew she'd be dead to the world and carry her there myself.

While waiting for her to fall asleep, I headed downstairs, calling my parents to make sure they were settled at home and didn't need anything.

"Hello?" my mom answered, sounding wide awake despite the late hour.

"Hey, Mom. You and Dad doing okay over there?"

"My sweet boy, always looking out for us. Yes, Dad and I are doing just fine. We're settled in with no plans to go anywhere. And Aiden's new book just arrived yesterday, so your father is quite engrossed right now. I don't think we'll have any problem amusing ourselves while we're snowed in."

I snorted. "Thanks for that."

She laughed, completely unrepentant of her overshare. But I was used to it. Morgan and I had seen more than our fair share because our parents couldn't keep their hands off each other through our adolescence. And after, actually. When my parents were in their midforties, and Morgan and I were nearing our teen years, the twins had been the find-out portion of the fuck-around equation.

"How about you, sweetheart?" she asked. "You okay in that great big house all by yourself?"

I cleared my throat. "Actually, I'm not by myself."

"Oh? Is Levi with you?"

"No. Addie is."

There was a pause on the other line, then all background noise ceased, as if she'd shut off the TV so she could give me her full attention. "*Addison*, huh? You don't say." Amusement saturated her tone, and I could practically see the sparkle in her eye. "Well, isn't she lucky to have you there looking out for her? I wonder what you two will fill your time with while you're stuck together..."

She didn't even bother to hide the hopeful note in her voice. For years, she'd made not-so-subtle hints about the fact that she thought Addison and I would be a perfect couple—how she'd gotten that when all she'd seen was Addie biting my head off, I'd never know, but moms were scary intuitive like that. And though I didn't disagree with her, I'd also never been able to tell her what was going on between the two of us. I loved my mom more than just about anything, but she couldn't keep a secret to save her life. And Addison had made it perfectly clear no one in Starlight Cove was supposed to know about us.

"Not sure we'll be doing much of anything. Right now, she's curled up on the floor in an extra bedroom because she's mad at me and too stubborn to sleep in an actual bed."

My mom blew out a *pfft*. "That girl is always mad at you. But you know what I say, a little fire in a relationship keeps things spicy. Not that you two are in a relationship, of course..." She trailed off, the pause weighted. "Unless you have something to tell me?"

I snorted and shook my head. "No, Mom. Nothing to tell you."

She heaved a deep sigh, as if I'd crushed all her dreams with that statement. "That's too bad. But I want you to know that even though the plant nursery is all set up, it's easily moved. If, for some reason, we would need the space for something else... Like, perhaps a different kind of nursery."

"Smooth, Mom."

"What?" she asked, all faux-innocence.

"Addison's currently not speaking to me," I said dryly. "I think talking about babies is a little premature."

Mom huffed. "Well, I'm not getting any younger. I want some grandkids to spoil! And God knows with the jackass Morgan married, I'm not gonna get them from her. And the twins just started college, so they better not be giving me grandbabies just yet. You're our only hope."

I sank back into the couch and rolled my eyes toward the ceiling. "I'm a professional hockey player, still under contract, who spends three-quarters of a year out of town. And you're forgetting the most important fact—I don't even have a girlfriend."

Now was not the time to let my mom in on the fact that while I hadn't necessarily had a girlfriend, I'd been Addison's for years.

Mom blew out another long-suffering sigh. "So you say. But I hear snowstorms are a great time to change that..."

"All right, Mom. Settle down."

"Fine. I'll let you get back to whatever you're doing over there. Don't you dare let her sleep on the floor, Chase Matthew."

"You know I wouldn't."

"And for God's sake, stop irritating the poor girl! Hate sex is fine once in a while, but it won't sustain a relationship."

I huffed out a laugh and scrubbed a hand over my face. "You're relentless, you know that?"

"You'll find that any mom anxious for grandbabies is rarely anything but."

After finishing up our conversation and ending the call, I shot off a message to my rehab coordinator, letting him know I was shut in for a few days, so I'd miss my PT appointment tomorrow and we'd have to reschedule our call.

Once that was taken care of, I made my way back into the guest room and found Addison curled in a ball, shivering, the fluffy down comforter shoved in the corner.

"You stubborn little shit," I murmured, shaking my head.

Grabbing the comforter, I threw it over my shoulder before squatting down to scoop her up from the floor. She weighed next to nothing, but my knee still let me know exactly what it thought of my doing this, a sharp pain reverberating down my leg as I carried her to my room.

Addison slept like the dead, so it didn't surprise me that she didn't stir even after I laid her down and tucked her in beneath the covers. I stripped out of my clothes, leaving on my boxer briefs, and climbed in with plenty of room between us, intent on staying on my side of the bed.

My intentions didn't matter, though, because as soon as I settled on the mattress, she rolled over and scooted closer to me. Her hands were like ice on my bare chest as she sought out my heat, and a satisfied sigh left her as she cuddled close.

"You couldn't just use the damn comforter?" I murmured into her hair. I inhaled deeply, sucking her Addison scent into my lungs as I wrapped my arms around her and tucked her shivering form into my side.

"It was the principle of the thing. And I'm still mad at you," she mumbled into my chest. But the way she curled into my side, hooking her leg over my hips to get as close as possible contradicted her words.

I ran my hand up and down her back, loving the feel of her draped over me, her head tucked in the crook beneath my chin, her body naturally fitting against mine, like two puzzle pieces slotting into place. "You can still be mad at me while I'm holding you. It's never stopped you before."

She didn't respond, but soon enough, her breaths were even, her body heavy against mine as she once again fell into sleep, and I couldn't help but lie there and bask in it. This wasn't something we'd ever had. Our time together had always been comprised of stolen moments. Hours here or there when we could sneak away from prying eyes and ears. But holding her while she slept was something I'd imagined thousands of times. Wondering if she was a bed hog—absolutely. Or if she snored—yes, if you counted the tiny little snuffles coming out of her nose as snoring. Or if she talked in her sleep—sadly, no.

Even though she was mad at me, and even though these weren't the best circumstances, I was going to savor every single moment of this night, sleeping with her curled in my arms.

CHAPTER NINETEEN

ADDISON

HIS HANDS WERE EVERYWHERE and nowhere all at once. Gentle, barely there caresses over my skin—the dip of my waist, the curve of my hip, the back of my knee—but never where I needed. Never where I ached.

It was so dark, I couldn't even make out his silhouette. I only knew his satisfied sounds and the sensations he was dragging out of me as he swept his hands over my body. A flick of his tongue over my nipple, the ghost of his fingers down my spine, his shoulders pushing my thighs apart, and then hot breath on my pussy before his tongue was finally, *finally* licking me and dragging a moan straight from my—

I startled awake, slowly blinking into the dark room. My body was thrumming with need, my nipples hard and my panties an absolute mess. It took me only a moment to realize *I'd* made the sound that had woken me. My hand was tucked between my legs, rubbing my clit through the lace of my panties, but it wasn't enough.

It never was.

Waking up like this—on the brink of orgasm, thanks to nothing more than the memory of a man who'd haunted me for years—wasn't anything new for me.

So, I did what I always did. I slipped my hand beneath the material of my panties and stroked a finger through my wet slit, my low moan barely a breath in the otherwise still and silent room.

"Those noises better be for me, firefly."

I startled at the low, raspy voice, layers of awareness slowly seeping into my sleep-drunk brain. The appointment with the agent. Getting snowed in at Chase's new home. Me curling up on the floor in one of his guest rooms, and him carrying me to his bed sometime later. Then falling asleep once again, this time in his arms...

Arms that tightened around me now.

Chase's chest was warm against my back, and he pressed his nose to my neck, inhaling deeply. Just the feel of him behind me shot fireworks through my body, every nerve ending responding to him as if they'd been waiting for it. Waiting for *him*.

My clit throbbed beneath my stilled fingers as I remembered exactly what had woken me. Those moans *had* been for him. The dream had been a memory of the last time we'd been together, when he'd been home over Christmas more than a year ago. When everything had changed. He'd snuck into my bedroom in the middle of the night, just like he'd told me he would, and had woken me up with an orgasm, courtesy of his mouth.

I bit my lip to stifle a whimper as my pussy clenched around nothing. As subtly as I could, I pressed my fingers harder against my clit, so desperate to come, I didn't even care that he was lying at my back.

He hummed into my neck, his breath sending goose bumps skating across my skin. "My baby's all worked up, isn't she?"

I made a sound of protest—as if I were in a position to deny anything, with my panties a mess and my fingers wet from the evidence—but he cut me off before I could respond.

"Don't even try to deny it. You've got your hand between those perfect thighs, playing with my little pussy as if I'm not lying right behind you, ready to give you exactly what you need."

I shuddered out a moan, the pulse of my clit a constant reminder of just exactly what I hadn't accomplished in my dream.

"Are you making it nice and wet for me?" He brushed his lips up and down the column of my neck, his tongue tracing soft circles behind my ear. "I want to know what got you so turned on you had to be a naughty fucking girl and finger yourself while you're lying next to me..."

And fuck me, but I always forgot how much his mouth affected me. His words, all growly and rough, said with a mixture of desperation and command, were usually my undoing, and tonight was no exception.

My fingers were *right there*, and it wouldn't take much. A shift of my wrist, some tight, targeted circles over my clit, and I'd go off.

But where was the satisfaction in that?

Especially when he was right here, the too-large-to-ignore proof of just how much he was affected by me tucked tight against my ass, his hips subtly rocking against me as if he wasn't even aware he was doing it.

"Did you have a dirty dream, baby girl?"

"Yes," I breathed.

"Tell me." From the way the words seemed to be torn from his throat, it sounded more like his last dying request than any kind of demand.

After long moments, I admitted, "It was about you."

He muttered a curse under his breath, like he hadn't even allowed himself to hope for that. He pressed his cock harder against me, and I was ashamed to realize I was arching back into him and meeting his thrusts, my body aching for relief.

I stilled, embarrassed, and he wrapped a hand around my hip, digging his fingers into my flesh. To hold himself back or urge me on, I wasn't sure.

Into my neck, he said, "Don't stop now. Tell me exactly what got my pussy so worked up."

I didn't know if it was because we were both soft and sleepy in a cocoon of darkness, a safe space for secrets whispered into the night. Or because the anger had already drained out of me. Or because it had been more than a year since I'd had a non-self-induced orgasm. But I found myself wanting to tell him exactly what had gotten me here. Exactly what had made my panties wet and my nipples hard and my body primed and ready.

For him.

"Last Christmas," I whispered. "When you woke me up licking my pussy."

He hummed into my skin, brushing his lips down the column of my neck before sinking his teeth into the juncture where it met my shoulder. "You mean when you gave me orders to do just that?"

Fine, I *may* have told him if he wanted to sneak into my room that night and wake me up to get some, he'd better do so with an orgasm courtesy of his mouth. Especially if he expected me to take the monster between his legs...

"Do you want to hear the story or not?" I asked.

"I really fucking do."

I closed my eyes, remembering it like it was yesterday. It was easy enough, considering it'd been my most reached for fap material in the time since. "I was already coming by the time I was awake enough to know what was happening."

"You tasted so fucking good... I licked you up like you were my last fucking meal, didn't I? I never waste a drop."

My body tingled all over at the memory, at his words, goose bumps erupting across my skin. "You had to press a hand over my mouth to muffle my scream because you made me come so hard, so fast."

He made a self-satisfied sound, his cock twitching against my ass. "Every time, isn't that right, baby?"

He wasn't wrong. He always got me off. Without fail. And I was sure the biggest reason for that was because Chase had always, since that very first time, treated my orgasms as if they were more important than his own—as if they were the key to his very fucking survival.

I nodded into the dark, my fingers twitching between my legs, desperate to sink inside. Desperate to make myself come.

"Then what happened?" he asked.

I bit my lip, unsure if I could voice the rest of this. Certain I might spontaneously combust if I did.

"Don't get shy on me now, firefly." He slipped a hand under his sweatshirt I wore and pressed it flat against my stomach. His hand was so large, his pinkie slipped just under the hem of my panties right next to my hand already tucked inside, his thumb grazing the underside of my breast. "You want to show me instead?"

His voice was so low, so gravelly, so thick with desire—for *me*—I didn't even take a full breath to think about what I was doing or what it would mean in the light of day before I rolled over and pushed him onto his back.

He went willingly, settling his hands on my hips when I straddled him. His eyes glittered in the mostly dark room as he stared up at me with hunger and desire and something else I couldn't name. I rocked my pussy over the bulge in his boxer briefs, moaning at how fucking good it felt, that phantom ache inside that always craved him flaring to life.

I ran my hands over his bare chest, tracing the tattoos that covered it and trailing my fingers over every dip and contour I knew by heart. From his collarbone to his defined pecs, to the abs that had been splashed across every social media site a hundred times over. His body was a finely tuned machine, a fucking work of art, and I wanted to spend hours studying every inch of it...get lost in it for days. Wanted to drown in him and never come up for air.

Without taking a moment to second-guess myself or to think about how this was an epically bad idea...how I swore I wouldn't do this with him again...I whipped his sweatshirt over my head and tossed it to the side, along with my panties, before settling astride him once again.

"Oh fuck." Chase dug his fingers into my bare hips, his gaze darting over every inch of me the moonlight showcased. "Tell me I can touch you, Addie. Please, *please*, baby, let me touch you." His words were strained, the tension coming off him in waves. And in that moment, I wanted nothing more than for him to do exactly that. Wanted to feel his hands on me. Everywhere. Fall into him again like I always did.

Get lost for just a little while in this thing between us.

I gripped his wrists and brought his hands up, placing them on my breasts and arching into him. "Touch me."

With a groan that sounded like it was torn straight from his soul, he cupped my small breasts exactly the way he knew I liked, brushing his thumbs over my nipples until they were stiff peaks under his touch. "Missed these perfect little tits so fucking much."

He leaned up, circling my nipple with his tongue before lightly scraping his teeth against it. Then he sucked as much of me into his mouth as he could, his tongue laving over my hardened peak, and I arched into him. Desperate for more. Desperate to come.

"*God.*" Holding the back of his head tight to me, I ground

down harder against his cock, my pussy throbbing and needy, aching for something only he could give me.

"That's my girl. Rub that greedy little cunt all over me. You're soaking through my boxers, aren't you? Making a mess all over me." He groaned, guiding my hips against him, rocking me back and forth over where he was thick and hard for me. "Tell me what you need."

I knew being with him like this wasn't the best idea. That I'd probably regret it in the morning. But even knowing that didn't stop me from diving headfirst into this.

It never did.

"You," I breathed. "I need you."

"You have me. *Always*." He licked a line between my breasts, nipped at my jaw, and then brushed his lips over the shell of my ear. "Tell me what you need right now. You want my fingers? My tongue? That cock you keep marking as yours? Or are you going to be my greedy fucking girl tonight and beg for all three?"

CHAPTER TWENTY

ADDISON

HIS WORDS HUNG in the air between us, and I sucked in a breath. I had no doubt in my mind I'd be doing exactly that before this night was through.

When I didn't respond, he tightened his fingers against my hips. "You've gotta tell me, Addie. This is your show tonight. I want everything you do, so take it. Whatever you want. Use me however you need, baby girl."

His words sent a shudder rolling through me. Sometimes I liked when he took all the options away from me and did what he wanted. Told me what to do or didn't give me a choice in the matter. I spent the majority of my life doing exactly that, being that person for everyone else, so it was a nice respite not to have to think about anything but my own pleasure.

But right now, I needed it. Needed his big body at my mercy. Needed to know I was in control of everything that happened tonight.

Especially when I hadn't felt in control of anything between us in more than a year.

The trouble now, though, was I wanted it all. I wanted to ride him—wanted to sink down on his perfect cock, gasping at the unrelenting stretch as he filled me like no one else ever had. Wanted his fingers in me while he kissed me within an inch of my life, making me go off with seemingly little effort, as if my body was an instrument he'd been playing his whole life. But more than anything, I wanted what I'd been thinking about in the first place... What had gotten us right here to this moment.

"I want your mouth."

Chase groaned, and before I could so much as blink, he hauled me up until I was hovering over his face, my knees sinking into the pillow on either side of his head. "Thank Christ. Been dreaming about tasting your come for *months*. Now, put your hands on the headboard and give me what we both want. Suffocate me if you have to, but you better not lift that sweet pussy off my face until you've come all over it."

Jesus. I was already breathless, and we hadn't even started yet. A shudder worked its way through me, and I barely managed to get out, "Thought I was in charge..."

He grinned up at me, shooting me that devilish fucking smirk that melted me without fail. "You're about to smother me with your cunt while my cock is leaking all over itself because of you. Believe me, baby girl, you're definitely the only one in charge tonight."

I didn't know what it was about seeing this man at the mercy of someone half his size. Giving up all control so I could have it when he knew I needed it. But more than that, it was that he'd known it, period. He'd always had a way of doing that. Of studying me so intently, he could give me what I craved before I even realized I was craving it.

I gripped the headboard and spread my legs wider above him, slowly sinking down until I was close enough for him to lick a path straight through my seam. At the first contact of his tongue against me, I tossed back my head on a moan, rocking my hips against his face, every nerve ending in my body primed and waiting for release. *God*, it'd been too long since I'd felt this, and I wasn't sure once would be enough.

As if agreeing with my thoughts, Chase groaned, cupping my ass in his large hands and holding me tight to his face while he devoured me. Before long, I was lost to the pleasure, my body having a mind of its own. I rocked over him, rolling my hips in a frenzy and rubbing my pussy all over his face.

The thought made me pause, my movements stuttering as the reality of what I was doing caught up with me and embarrassment seeped in. But he only dug his fingers tighter into my ass, guiding me to keep doing what I was, his eyes determined as he stared up at me from between my thighs.

He pulled back just enough to say, "Don't you dare stop. Grab my head and take what you need. Rub this sweet cunt all over my face. Ride my tongue and show me how much you love to come all over it, baby girl. I want you dripping down my chin by the time you're done."

I barely managed to choke out his name, need clawing its way up my throat. My pussy throbbed, the ache deep inside unrelenting, and I couldn't stop myself—didn't *want* to stop myself—from doing exactly what he said.

Gripping the headboard with one hand, I brought my other down on his head to hold him right where I wanted him. And then I lowered myself, rocking against his face, and he ate my pussy like it was his favorite meal. He rubbed his lips back and forth, his scruff scraping over every inch of me. Over my lips, down my seam, teasing my clit...the sharp pricks of it paired with the smooth, gentle glide of his tongue shooting me faster and faster toward my release.

He groaned into me, his tongue working harder, hands cupping my ass and holding me tight to him. Making sure I took everything I needed, just like he'd told me. His gaze stayed locked on mine the whole time, his eyes hot and hungry...*ravenous*, and I couldn't look away. I couldn't do anything but stare down at him between my thighs, mouth agape, as he took me straight to the edge of reason and shoved me over the cliff without mercy.

Moaning, I held his head in place and ground my pussy against him, our eyes locked as I shuddered through my release. But even as the waves of bliss crashed over and through me, my body still somehow ached for more. Ached for *him*.

Rather than lick me soft and sweet, slowly bringing me down off my high, Chase never let up. Even as I arched my back, desperate to either get closer or farther away, he held me to his mouth, not allowing me a second of reprieve. He guided my hips against him, urging me faster and working me through one orgasm and straight into another, groaning when I found my pleasure once again.

When he was finally satisfied and I was a boneless mess barely clinging to the headboard—and the threads of reality, if I was being honest—he lifted me off him, lowering me until I once again straddled his hips.

He slipped his hand around my neck, threading his fingers into my hair, and brought my face to his. "Fucking delicious." His lips shone with my come, his chin coated with the proof of how much I'd enjoyed his mouth, and I wanted to lick up every drop. Wanted to taste myself on his tongue. Taste the two of us together.

"Do it," he said, his voice rough and low, his cock straining against me. "Taste how fucking much you love to come all over my face."

My clit throbbed at his words, aching for more despite what he'd already given me. I loved that he knew exactly what I wanted without my having to say anything. I couldn't help but rock over him, grinding myself against his thick shaft as I cupped his face in my hands.

With our eyes locked, I dragged my tongue over his chin, collecting everything that was left of the orgasms he'd coaxed out of me. I sucked his top lip, then the bottom, before sliding my tongue inside, moaning at our combined taste.

He groaned into my mouth and fisted the hair at the base of my skull, holding me tight to him. He tasted me as if he never wanted this kiss to end. As if he'd never get enough.

I wasn't sure either of us would.

I wanted forever with him like this. Just our bodies speaking to each other in the quiet of the night. Nothing and no one to break through our bubble of bliss.

Not even ourselves.

CHAPTER TWENTY-ONE

CHASE

IN ALL THE times I'd been with Addison, I'd never taken a single one for granted. I was a lucky motherfucker, and I knew it. Considering everything we'd gone through over the past ten years—the separation and the fights and the heated not-so-makeups—it was a fucking miracle I found myself here. With her. Again.

"Chase..." she said against my lips, her voice barely more than a whisper. "I want you inside me."

"*Fuck.*" My dick twitched at her words, at the soft, breathy plea of them, and I groaned into her mouth, desperate to give her exactly what she needed. Without breaking from her kiss, I reached to my nightstand for a condom, blindly riffling through the drawers for the box I'd stashed there, grateful I'd been feeling hopeful after the toy incident and stocked up.

Unwilling to wait like the impatient little thing she was, Addison shoved my boxer briefs off and was now grinding away on my bare cock, rocking her clit over the head, her pussy growing wetter with every pass. She whimpered and moaned into my mouth as she used my body to crank herself higher, and knowing just how close she was only urged me on faster.

I nearly shouted in relief when my fingertips finally connected with the box, cursing myself silently that I hadn't had the foresight to open it earlier. If I'd known this was where my night would lead, I would've set out a whole fucking row of condoms on the nightstand to have at the ready.

"What's taking so long?" Addison asked, impatience ringing in her words.

"New box," I grumbled, finally tearing into it and pulling out a condom.

Before I could rip it open, she grabbed it from me and did it herself. And because she took great pleasure in driving me out of my mind, she rolled it down my shaft in slow strokes designed to tease. To torment. To make me fucking desperate for her. And I was.

Her hands felt so good on me after a year with nothing but my own to keep me company. I hissed out a breath, clenching my eyes closed as my dick twitched, eager as fuck to go off, especially with the memory of her coming on my tongue.

"Wait." I reached down, wrapping my hand around hers where she gripped my shaft, squeezing hard to stave off the orgasm that was already breathing down my neck. "*Shit*."

It'd been too fucking long, and considering I also hadn't had the forethought to jack it tonight before climbing into bed, I was going to have to work my way through every hockey drill I could just to stop myself from blowing too soon.

"You better get yourself under control, big boy." Addison settled over me again, bracing her hands on my chest as she slid my cock through her pussy lips. "Because I want at least another two."

"You'll get them, you horny little demon." I didn't care what I had to do to make it happen. I was damn sure going to give my girl exactly what she needed.

I rested my hands on her hips, allowing her to set the pace. The trouble was, she fucking loved to torment us both. Could spend hours doing just that. She stared down at me, satisfaction and desire written across her face, as she rubbed her clit against my cock, never taking me inside.

"Is this really how you want to come?" I asked through a tight throat, every ounce of my self-control focused on not spilling all over her. "With your cunt empty and aching for me?"

She parted her lips, her eyes going unfocused as her movements stuttered over me.

"I didn't think so." I palmed her ass and squeezed tight, my fingers just grazing between her cheeks. "Now stop fucking around and take me deep."

"You said it was my show."

"It is," I agreed with a nod. "But you and I both know what you want, so take it. Take your cock and put it right where it belongs, inside my perfect little pussy."

My words sent a shudder rolling through her. But instead

of putting us both out of our misery and sinking down immediately, she used the head of my dick to circle her clit, before sliding it back to her entrance and slipping just the head inside. Then she pulled off me and started the circuit all over again.

By the fifth pass, both of us were panting, our bodies slick with sweat, and I was damn near out of my mind with need.

"*Baby*," I groaned, digging my fingers into her ass in an effort to keep myself grounded. "Put me out of my fucking misery and give me what I've been jacking it to for a year."

I didn't know if it was my words or if her patience snapped, but finally, *finally*, she shifted and lowered herself onto me. I kept my gaze locked on hers to watch the emotions play across her face as she took me inside. With her mouth open on a silent moan, she curled her fingers against my chest, eyes wide as she stared down at me like we hadn't already done this a thousand times. Though with how long it'd been, it *felt* like the first time all over again.

Inch by agonizingly slow inch, she took me deeper, lifting up before sliding back down to ease the way. It didn't matter how wet she was—didn't matter if I used an entire fucking bottle of lube on her—stuffing my cock into Addison was always a feat, but now more than ever. It'd been too damn long, and I was too damn big.

She whimpered, determination and undiluted need written across her face.

I brought my thumb to her clit, rubbing in fast circles as she worked her cunt down on me. "You can do it, baby. Let me inside."

"Fuck, Chase," she breathed, rocking her hips as she struggled to take all of me.

I reached up, wrapping my hand around her neck and tugging her face down to mine. I captured her lips with my own, my other hand still working her clit. Every second of this in-between felt like heaven and hell wrapped up in one mindfuck of a package. With every glide of my tongue against hers, she melted into me, her body softening and taking more of me.

I groaned into her mouth the deeper I sank. Against her lips, I murmured, "That's my fucking girl. You love when I fill you up, don't you? Love being stuffed so full of my cock it's all you can feel."

"*God*," she choked out, eyes wide as her hips finally settled against mine.

"There you go. *Shit*," I said under my breath, the tight fist of her cunt nearly strangling my dick. "Goddamn, my little pussy's so fucking perfect. You were made to take me, weren't you, baby girl?"

She didn't answer—didn't nod or acknowledge what I'd said—but I could see the desire in her eyes. The undisguised want. The tiny flicker of hope that I meant it.

I slid my hands up to cup her tits, sweeping my thumbs over her nipples. "Take what you need. Use your cock to get yourself off. Let me feel it."

She whimpered and pushed against my chest to sit up, giving me an unobstructed view of her beautiful body. And then she began to move. Rather than riding me up and down, she slid her hips back and forth, keeping me as deep as possible. The slow, steady grind of her clit against the base of my dick rather than frenzied bouncing was the only reason I didn't shoot off immediately. And after years of watching her ride me, I'd learned this was a surefire way to make her come.

Addison was never shy about taking her pleasure. Had never been. But I'd never let her be. I'd made sure every time we were together that she knew nothing she wanted was wrong. Nothing to be ashamed of. She could have any fucking thing she wanted with me, without question, because I was game for it if it intrigued my girl. All she had to do was take it.

Her movements quickened, and she collapsed forward on my chest, breathing hard as she ground her clit against me at a fast, frenzied pace.

"That's it, baby," I murmured against her ear, already feeling the fluttering pulse of her pussy, her short little gasps puffing against my neck. I gripped her ass in my hands and squeezed hard, encouraging her movements. "Grind that sweet little clit on my cock while you take every inch. Make yourself come all over me."

She whimpered, her movements turning sloppy, sporadic. And then, all at once, she broke. Her entire body tightened, and she pressed her open mouth against my neck, sobbing out a moan as her pussy squeezed my dick through her release.

"*Fuck*," I breathed, screwing my eyes shut and clenching my ass so I didn't blow. "Goddamn, baby girl. Your pussy feels so good. So fucking good."

After the last shudder quaked through her body, she went

boneless on top of me, her breaths hot against my skin, her pussy still strangling my cock.

I ran my hands up and down the damp skin of her back, my lips against her temple. "Don't tell me you're done. You made me promise you two more."

Without moving an inch, she murmured, "And I'm still waiting for you to make good on that."

I huffed out a laugh, sliding my hands over every inch of her body I could reach. "Don't say it unless you mean it."

She lifted her head and stared down at me, one brow raised. Her makeup was smeared under her eyes, her lips red and swollen, her hair an absolute mess—my beautiful disaster. "I do mean it. Make me come again."

My dick twitched inside her, and one corner of her mouth lifted in a smirk as if she'd won. We'd apparently slipped into one of our silent games now—whoever came first was the loser.

But I'd never lost, and I didn't intend to start tonight.

I nipped at her bottom lip, capturing it between my teeth and tugging before soothing the sting with my tongue. "You didn't ask nicely."

"I never do."

I shrugged as if I wasn't dying to come. As if my cock wasn't currently buried in the hottest, tightest heaven it had ever had the privilege of feeling. As if my balls weren't drawn up tight, ready to explode with the barest movement. "I can wait."

"You sure about that?" She very purposefully rotated her hips in a slow circle, and I groaned. "One of us has already come a couple times. And the other one of us is you."

"That may be true, but we both know I'm the one who can hold out the longest. And that greedy little clit of yours gets you in trouble." I could last all fucking night if she wanted me to—and she had. Many times. Whereas she got needy—which I fucking loved—until she was completely satisfied. And the soft, subtle shifts of her hips against me proved she wasn't anywhere near satisfied.

I ran my hands down her back, over the curve of her ass, squeezing her cheeks and giving one a sharp smack before banding my arms tight around her, not allowing her to move.

Then the real fun began.

I tortured her. Exploited every spot on her body that made her nipples harden, made her pussy wet. I nipped across her collarbone. Sank my teeth into her shoulder. Scraped my teeth along her earlobe. I brushed my lips down her neck and swirled my tongue in the hollow of her throat. Showered attention on her perfect little tits, sucking each tip into my mouth.

Soon enough, she was whimpering and trying to shift her hips against me, desperate for friction, but I clamped a hand down on her ass and stilled her.

I dragged my tongue up the column of her neck, my lips brushing against the shell of her ear. "Beg for it."

Her pussy clenched at my words, squeezing the life out of my dick, but she shook her head. Didn't stop her from shifting and trying to grind her clit on me again, though.

I smacked her ass one more time and stilled her movements. "Beg, Addison. Beg me to fuck you, and I will. Beg me to make you come, and I will."

"Chase," she said. Whined, really. Outside of the bedroom, it would've been a barked command. But in here, she was soft for me. Pliant. In here, she surrendered control, even during the times she thought she needed to be in charge.

"That's not begging."

She bit her lip, her eyes pure fire as she stared down at me like she didn't know if she wanted to fuck or murder me. "Would you just do it already?"

I shrugged as if I wasn't aching just as desperately for her. "Or I can leave you hanging, slide out of your perfect cunt, and jack myself until I come all over your tits. Either one works for me."

While the interest gleaming in her eyes told me she loved that idea, the insistent rocking of her hips proved she wouldn't be satisfied with anything less than coming on my dick again.

"You know what you have to do, baby girl, and I'll give you exactly what you need."

"Give it to me," she whispered. "Make me come."

"Those sound like orders to me." I gripped her ass and lifted her off me before sinking deep again, moans torn from both of us. "Beg for it, and I'll give it to you, just like I promised. My little pussy wants it so bad, doesn't she?"

"Please," she choked out, but that wasn't near enough.

Just to torture us both, I lifted her off me again and thrust deep, giving her a preview of exactly what I'd do to her if she'd stop being so fucking stubborn.

"*Yes.*" She moaned loud and low, her eyes heavy lidded as she stared down at me, hunger and awe shining bright in her gaze. "More. Please, Chase. *Please*. Give me what I need."

My dick twitched inside her at the pleading note in her voice, and I couldn't hold back any longer. On a groan, I gripped her tightly, suspending her above me, and snapped my hips up as I thrust into her from below. It was fast and frenzied, nothing like the slow grind she'd used to make herself come on me the first time. But she loved this just as much, because she wasn't in control of it. She was a rag doll, being used for my pleasure, but she also trusted me to get her exactly where she needed to go.

"Oh my fucking God." She curled her fingers into my chest, her wide eyes locked on mine while I fucked her like I'd never get enough.

Because I could live three thousand lifetimes, and I still never would.

"You hear how wet you are, baby girl?" I ran my hand over her ass until I could reach her pussy from behind. She was a soaked mess, and I gathered it on my fingers before trailing them up to her ass. "You hear how much you want to come all over my cock?"

"*Chase.*"

"Do it, baby. Come on me and give us both what we want." I circled my middle finger around her puckered hole, clenching my teeth as her pussy tightened around me at the light touch.

But I didn't come this far to lose tonight.

I sped up my thrusts, slipped the tip of my finger inside her ass, and that was all it took. She broke apart on a sobbed moan, her entire body tightening as her pussy pulsed around me, her body shuddering over mine.

"Fuck. *Fuck*. Missed this. Missed you. So fucking much." I could barely get the words out as the orgasm ripped through me. I held her close as I came, spilling myself inside her, her name on my lips.

Wondering, just like I always did, how I'd gone this long without her. And hoping I'd never have to again.

CHAPTER TWENTY-TWO

CHASE

UNSURPRISINGLY, I woke to an empty bed. I'd been expecting this. First and foremost because when shit got real, Addison's first response was to avoid, avoid, avoid. For another thing, we'd never had to do the whole morning-after awkwardness. We hadn't slept a full night in the same bed since I'd taken her virginity before dropping her off at college the very next morning. When I'd told her we couldn't be anything.

Back then, I'd thought I'd had to choose between pursuing something with Addison or giving my all to hockey to make sure my sister had the best medical care available to her. I'd been a dumb kid who'd thought in black-and-white, and I'd paid for that over these past ten years. It was a misconception I was no longer burdened with.

Being our first sleepover in ten years on its own would've been enough to send Addison running. But combining it with the uncertainty I knew she'd be feeling, and this morning was shaping up to be a perfect storm for second-guessing.

I scrubbed a hand down my face and tossed back the covers. While my dick was up and ready for action, I figured Addison probably wouldn't be very receptive to me walking out there naked, so I tugged on a pair of gray sweatpants before heading downstairs.

It didn't take long to find her. Though, the boxes strewn across my floor like casualties gave a big clue to her whereabouts. While the movers had already unpacked the vast majority of my things, there was some shit they just didn't need to have their hands in, and I hadn't yet had a chance to take care of it. Addison, apparently, didn't have that same problem.

The great room looked like a hurricane had torn through it. Empty boxes were stacked in haphazard towers, packing paper was strewn everywhere, and bubble wrap littered the floor.

And in the middle of it all, there she sat, my tiny tornado.

Her rustling and sorting had masked my entrance, making her none the wiser to my presence. So, I leaned against the wall, arms crossed, and just observed. I rarely got to watch her like this, without her being aware, so I was going to take full advantage of it. She sat cross-legged on the floor and muttered to herself—something I couldn't make out—as she dug in a half-empty box, unapologetically going through my shit.

I didn't care. There wasn't anything anywhere she

couldn't see. No part of my life she couldn't shine a spotlight on or dissect.

She wore the same sweatshirt she'd had on last night, and I could finally appreciate it now when she wasn't a shivering bundle of stubbornness curled on my floor. My dick twitched at the sight, already hungry for a repeat of last night. I fucking loved her in my clothes. The only way it could've been better was if she were wearing my jersey. But then, it would've been game fucking over as soon as I saw it. I'd have fallen to my knees in front of her, bunched the material up at her hips, and begged to lick her pussy while she wore my name across her back.

Great. And now I was hard as a fucking rock, imagining just that.

After watching her in silence for a while, I started to feel like a creep, so I cleared my throat. "Whatcha doin' in here, firefly?"

She screamed loud enough to be heard all the way in town, flailing and sending the stack of boxes next to her toppling over. I couldn't help the laugh that burst out, and she shot a glare my way. "You asshole."

With a grin, I pushed off the wall and strode her way, stepping over the debris as I went. I squatted down next to her, leaning this way and that to try to catch her eye, but she avoided my gaze like a fucking professional. "Addie?"

No response.

"Addison."

Nothing.

Such a beautiful, stubborn, pain in my ass...

"Firefly, will you—"

My phone rang from the pocket of my sweats, cutting me off. I swore under my breath and pulled it from my pocket, wishing I would've just left it upstairs. I blew out a sigh when I saw my agent's name on the screen. Considering the two missed calls from him and the fact that we obviously hadn't connected yesterday thanks to his grounded flight, I couldn't ignore it.

I held out my phone and said, "I gotta take this."

Addison didn't acknowledge me, but I didn't miss the way her eyebrows twitched when I sat next to her and accepted the call.

"Marty," I said in lieu of greeting.

"Finally!" my agent boomed. I'd known the man for ten years, and in all that time, I'd never heard him speak at a decibel below earsplitting. "After that mess of a storm and you not answering your damn phone, I was beginning to wonder if my star player was okay. You doing all right up there, kid?"

"Things are a little chilly in here right now," I said, my eyes locked on Addison as she pretended to ignore me. "But I'm all right."

"Good, good. Sorry our plans got screwed up with the weather, but I hope you were able to wow her for us."

Somehow, I didn't think he was referring to the number of orgasms I'd given her last night. "Trying to..."

"*Trying*? As in, still doing so? The meeting go a little bit longer than you planned?" he said, amusement and the underlying *attaboy* clear in his tone.

Regardless of whether his assumptions were true, I didn't like him thinking about her like that at all. "The storm shut down everything, including her way out," I said, sharper than was probably called for if Addison's widening eyes were anything to go by.

"Right, right. Well, since it sounds like you're stuck there for the foreseeable future, how about we talk a little bit about these other opportunities I've got in the pipeline for you?"

I didn't want to do this. Now, especially, with Addison sitting right next to me. It wasn't that I didn't want her to know about this part of my life. It was just that I'd tried so hard for so long to keep her out of it. To make sure she still saw me as just a guy from Starlight Cove. Not a professional hockey player worth millions who was turning up his nose at endorsements that would gain him millions more.

I also just didn't want to think about endorsements right now. All my focus needed to go to healing my body so I could play again—and Addison. That was it.

But I'd promised Marty if he'd set up the endorsement for the resort, I'd consider the other opportunities he had available, so I was stuck.

"Fine. What've you got for me?"

For the next ten minutes, I listened to him rattle off various businesses that wanted a partnership and the obscene paycheck that came with them, while also keeping an eye on Addison's reactions. Based on them, it was clear she could hear some of what Marty was saying. Namely, when any specific dollar amounts came up.

I already felt like I was fighting a losing battle being back here, attempting to win her over in a way I'd never had to before. In a way I'd never allowed myself to even try for. And I worried this was only going to be another strike against me —the reminder of my life away from Starlight Cove. Away from her.

"Is this something we can discuss later?" I finally asked.

"Not too much later," Marty said. "I want to get these locked in while they're biting. They're interested right now, even while you're on LTIR, so let's not give them a chance to second-guess this."

Read: it was a fucking miracle someone wanted me when I was on long-term injured reserve, my body was fucked, I couldn't play, and my future in the sport was unknown.

"But this absolutely cannot wait until you're back in Vancouver," he continued. "I want to get these contracts signed before you're on the ice again."

Addison's shoulders stiffened more with every word that came out of his mouth, and I couldn't get him off the phone fast enough. Because I had done such a stellar fucking job of keeping her separate from my life in Vancouver, she didn't know what any of it meant. And she probably thought I was a first-class asshole for so casually discussing multimillion-dollar paychecks without jumping at every single opportunity.

"Got it," I said, my eyes still locked on Addison. "I'll call you next week, so we can discuss it more."

After I ended the call, there was a beat of silence. Two. Three.

Then, she said, "Don't let me stand in the way of millions.

If you want me to give you some privacy, just say so. I'm sure you've got a gigantic tub in one of these bathrooms that I can soak in for a few hours."

Was that why her shoulders were so stiff? She thought I didn't want her hearing me make these deals? What would she think if I told her I wasn't sure I wanted to make them at all? How would she look at me then? If she knew I was willingly turning down the opportunity to earn the kind of money that would be life-changing for anyone. The kind that would alter the future of the resort. The future of their entire family. That would give them the kind of legacy money I'd worked my ass off and sacrificed my body for.

But before I could tell her any of that, she froze in her aggressive sorting through one of the boxes. And then she snatched a small card from inside, her eyes scanning across it as she read. Then she plucked another. And another. And another. They just kept coming, and her anger ratcheted up with each one.

I furrowed my brow, staring at them as if that would clue me in to what they were. Probably cards from the dozens of pity deliveries I'd received after the team's confirmation I was going on LTIR. But I didn't know why they'd make her so mad. Truthfully, I hadn't read any of them. My teammates didn't have shit like that delivered, and neither did my family or friends. That meant I didn't give a single fuck about whoever they were from, so they were easy to ignore.

There must've been a miscommunication somewhere, because I'd told the movers to get rid of all that shit, but instead, it all ended up across the country in my new living room.

Finally, after several long moments of Addison getting increasingly more pissed off, she slammed the cards down on the floor before standing and hefting the entire box into her arms. "Well, you can save some of that wood for later. I've got all the kindling we need right here."

CHAPTER TWENTY-THREE

CHASE

WHEN ADDISON GOT a murderous gleam in her eye, everyone needed to hold on to their fucking hats because shit was about to go down. I was surprised actual lasers didn't shoot out of her eyes and incinerate the box she was currently fixating all her anger on.

"What the hell's in there, and why do you want to burn it?" I reached for the cards she'd tossed on the floor, scanning them for a hint at her sudden mood shift.

The first card had a message written in bubbly pink letters.

I'll give you a rubdown anytime you need to get that knee...and other things...feeling better.

I flipped to the next one.

I bet a blow job would take your mind off the pain...

And the next...

Call me anytime you need a release. You can just lie back and let me do all the work.

I snorted and rolled my eyes at the desperation pouring off these cards. The sad thing was, the messages weren't even from the same woman. Trixie, Melody, and Sabrina all just wanted to make sure I was taken care of. I'd never met these women a day in my life, and they still thought it was fine to send me shit like this. But that was par for the course as a professional hockey player. At least none of them had broken in to my home in order to greet me naked in my bed. Again.

Without answering my question, Addison spun on her heel and stormed off in the direction of the fireplace, box in hand.

I laughed, rising to my feet to follow her. "What are you doing, firefly?"

"I'm cold," she said flatly, dropping the box on the floor.

I braced my arm on the mantel and watched her with amusement. "We haven't lost power, so I can just turn up the heat if you want."

Shaking her head, she gestured to the already burning fire she must've started when she woke up. "No need. This will work just fine." She reached into the box and grabbed something from inside.

Before she could toss the stuffed animal to its fiery death, I wrapped my fingers around her wrist and stilled her movements. "What did this poor teddy bear wearing a mini Lockhart jersey ever do to you?"

She pressed her lips into a flat line and narrowed her eyes at me. "I didn't realize you were so attached."

Though I'd tried to keep my smile under wraps, there was no use tamping it down anymore. Not when it became perfectly clear what was going on here.

"What the hell are you smiling about?" she demanded, all fire and venom.

I grinned widely down at her. "You're jealous," I said, not bothering to keep the satisfaction out of my voice.

Did I like the fact that my girl thought she had something to be jealous about? Fuck no. Did I like the fact that my girl felt she had enough of a claim over me to get jealous in the first place? Fuck yes.

"I am not," she snapped, her words sharp and her scowl sharper.

"Oh, you definitely are."

Through clenched teeth, she said, "No, I'm not."

"You are," I insisted. "But you don't need to be."

She scoffed and rolled her eyes. "No? How often do you get messages like this?"

I shrugged. "No idea."

"So you get them so often, you can't even keep track?"

"I don't pay attention to how often I get them because I don't give a single flying fuck about them." I stepped closer to her and reached out, tucking a stray lock of hair behind her ear. "Apparently I've done a shitty job of letting you know this, but you're the only one I care about."

Her eyes darted between mine, and she was trying so hard to hide the hopefulness there. I understood her trepidation. For years, Addison had set the pace in our relationship. Since she hadn't wanted anything serious, I'd followed her lead. But in doing so, I'd pretended for years I wouldn't cut off my own fucking legs just to be with her.

And now, here I was, challenging every preconceived notion she had. Combating any doubt she had about us. But Addison was like a cornered animal when it came to dealing with emotions—her first instinct was to lash out. Her second was to retreat. Which was why I wasn't surprised when she turned on her heel without another word and stalked out of the room, heading straight for the stairs.

"We're not done, Addison," I called after her.

She didn't respond, just quickened her pace. Unfortunately for her, even with a fucked knee, I caught up with her and was on her heels before she was halfway up the staircase.

"I mean it," I said. "I'm tired of you running away every time I try to talk about this."

Once she got to the top of the steps, she turned to face me. "I'm not run—" Her words cut off as I lifted her over my shoulder without breaking my stride and headed down the hallway to my bedroom, her fists pounding on my back the entire way.

"Put me down, you giant oaf! Just because I'm fun-sized doesn't mean you can toss me around like a sack of potatoes anytime you want."

"You fucking love when I toss you around." I flipped her onto the bed and braced my hands on either side of her shoulders, pinning her in place. "And just because you don't want to listen doesn't mean you get to run away every time I try to tell you something. I've let you do this on your timetable, you beautiful little brat. And now it's time to do it on mine. We're talking about this whether you're ready or not."

She huffed out a disbelieving breath. "Oh, *now* you want to talk? I've been trying to talk to you for *months*, and it's been nothing but crickets. And now you finally decide it's time to hash shit out when I literally can't leave? Real nice."

"What the fuck do you mean, it's been crickets? I've been trying to get you to talk to me for a year, and you've been ignoring me."

Addison's mouth dropped open. "Excuse the fuck out of me? *I've* been ignoring *you*? You are a big, fat liar." She pulled her phone out of her pocket and navigated to something before flipping it around and shoving it in my face. "*See*?"

I reared back until I could clearly decipher what she was showing me. It was our text thread, but it looked drastically different from mine. Where mine was a sea of blue without any gray to break it up, hers was a whole lot of...nothing. Just a couple texts from her... One in early January, one in April, and one in June after I'd been injured.

But nothing from me.

That didn't make any fucking sense. I remembered each of those texts, and I knew for a fact I'd responded. Not only that, but I'd sent her hundreds of messages over the year. Any time I thought about her, missed her, wanted to talk to her...

Basically, every fucking day, multiple times a day. But then why didn't they show on her—

Realization slammed into me, and I breathed out a disbelieving laugh as I stared down at this woman I loved more than the fucking world but who drove me insane. "Jesus. I thought you were just being a stubborn little shit like usual, but you actually blocked me."

She shoved my shoulder, her mouth hanging open. "I did not!"

"No?" I asked, brow raised. "Then how do you explain not getting any texts from me?"

"Uh, maybe because you didn't send any?"

"Try again, firefly. I sent you at least one a day, every day. Except when I was too hopped up on pain meds to be aware of anything other than my next dose."

But Addison was nothing if not a skeptic, and that was written across every line of her face.

"Don't believe me? I know how much you're going to hate this, but I'm happy to prove you wrong." I pulled my phone out of my pocket and handed it to her. "Here. Password is your birthday."

Her gaze snapped to mine, shock and disbelief mingling there, whether from my password choice or the fact that I was giving her full access to my phone, I didn't know. I didn't have anything to hide, and I was tired of the bullshit. It was clear we'd both been on different pages this past year. Hell, we'd been in entirely different books.

And it was well past time to set that shit straight.

CHAPTER TWENTY-FOUR

ADDISON

CHASE'S and my relationship had never been anything but casual. In all our years of doing this, we'd never talked about what it was and what it wasn't. And based on the number of pictures I'd seen of him with other women fawning all over him, I'd assumed it landed heavily on the latter.

It *wasn't*. Period.

I'd accepted that. Hell, it was my doing in the first place. When I'd come back to Starlight Cove after graduation, I hadn't wanted any distractions as I dove headfirst into trying to save the sinking ship that was the resort. And Chase was the biggest distraction of all. So we saw each other a handful of times a year, hooked up—in secret—when we did, and went on living our separate lives the rest of the time.

I assumed his phone was full of all the secrets he kept in our time apart. Call logs and text threads and DMs with all the women I'd seen him photographed with over the years.

And yet he'd just handed me his phone, passcode

included. A passcode that, apparently, was my fucking birthday.

Feeling the weight of his stare on me, I shoved down the shock, put in my birthdate to unlock his phone, and navigated to his messages. Over the months of silence, our text thread had slowly slipped farther down the line in my app to the point where I now had to scroll to find his name.

But not in his.

Our thread was right on top, as if he'd recently texted. And it looked so different from what I'd seen for months that I couldn't make sense of it at first. But then I started scrolling. And scrolling. And scrolling some more.

He hadn't been lying.

There were hundreds of messages here, all of them unanswered, but that hadn't stopped him from continuing to text. Daily, for the most part. There were even responses to the couple of texts I'd sent him last year before pride hadn't allowed me to send any more.

January 4

ADDISON:

We need to talk

CHASE:

Yeah, we do. I've got back to back games in Detroit and Chicago. Friday?

January 5

CHASE:

Had to throw down at tonight's game, but the fucker had it coming. Gonna crash and dream about my girl.

January 7

CHASE:

Back in Vancouver and ready to talk whenever you are, firefly.

January 12

CHASE:

Are you avoiding having the conversation you said we needed to have?

January 17

CHASE:

Can I assume the Rage Machine playlist choice today was for me? Can't work through this shit if you don't talk to me, Addie...

I couldn't read fast enough, desperate to inhale every word he'd typed, every thought he'd sent, every glimpse into his mind over the course of the year we'd been separated.

Some messages were sweet...

March 22

CHASE:

I need to hear your voice

August 11

An image of three specks of light in a field at dusk.

CHASE:

Miss catching fireflies with you, firefly.

And some were decidedly not...

May 27

CHASE:

Wish I were celebrating with you. Remember that time you let me lick champagne off your tits before I bent you over the counter and fucked you from behind? Think I'll replay that in my mind tonight for my goodnight jerk.

September 16

CHASE:

Woke up from a dream of you sucking my dick. Now I'm hard as a rock and pretending the poor substitute of my hand is your perfect mouth.

But the ones that were the hardest to read were when he'd, apparently, responded to the minimal texts I'd sent him, and then he received a whole lot of nothing from me in return.

May 29

ADDISON:

It finally happened

The resort is booked

For months

CHASE:

I knew it was only a matter of time. I'm so fucking proud of you.

June 13

CHASE:

Tried calling but I just got your voice mail. Again. Didn't want to tell you over text, but I want you to hear it from me first. Don't freak out, okay?

I've got a medial meniscus tear in my right knee, and I need surgery. They said it's pretty straightforward, and I should be good as new by training camp.

I barely held in a sob at that. I'd spent months being upset at him, thinking he'd thought what we had wasn't even worth a mention of his injury to me, when he'd actually tried to contact me about it several times.

June 16

ADDISON:

Hope your surgery goes well

Heard your mom's heading there to help

But lmk if you need anything

CHASE:

I need you to come play nurse. I miss you so much, baby.

I couldn't stop the tears from welling up as I continued to read his messages, trying to reconcile what I'd thought had happened with what had *actually* happened. I'd spent the past year thinking he'd decided to ignore me and throw away what we had because he hadn't gotten his way in having me drop everything and move to be by him. When the reality was so fucking far from the mixed-up version I'd been clinging to all year.

"Well, firefly?" he prompted. "I know how much you hate being wrong, but don't keep me waiting."

"Why did you keep texting?" I asked through a tight throat, voicing the one question that rose above the rest. "Even when I wasn't responding..."

"Why wouldn't I? I wasn't going to give up on us."

"There was never an us." As much as I'd wanted otherwise, our lives were on two separate tracks.

"We have *always* been an us, Addison."

I blew out a humorless laugh, chuckling through the tears that clogged my throat. "Always, huh? And where were *we* when you were out fucking anything with a pair of tits shoved into a too-small jersey?"

A grin kicked up one side of his mouth as he stared down at me, still bracing himself above me. "I love when you get all possessive over me because it tells me you think of me as yours. But let me make this perfectly clear..." He lowered himself until his face hovered above mine, his gaze locking me in place. "Yours is the only pussy I've had, firefly."

I rolled my eyes, trying to break this tension. Trying to ground myself when his words were sending me flying. "And I've already told you what an amazing feat it was that you managed to go a year without sex when you were injured half the time."

He made an amused sound in the back of his throat. "You assumed it was just this year, but I never said that."

"What's that supposed to mean?"

He lifted his left hand from where it had been braced next to me on the bed and held it in front of me, palm out. Whereas Chase's torso was covered in tattoos—so much so, I secretly played the *let's see what new ink he's gotten since the last time I saw him* game whenever we were together—his hands were untouched.

Or I thought they were...

Except the underside of his left ring finger was inked with roman numerals, and I didn't know if they were new or if I'd just never seen them before.

"What is it?" I asked.

He brushed his thumb over the black symbols. "The day I became yours."

My gaze flew to his, and I had to tamp down the flurry of butterflies swirling in my stomach at his words. "What?"

"You heard me. And I have never—not once in the time since—been inside anyone else. I haven't kissed anyone else. Fuck, Addison, I haven't even *looked* at another woman. How could I when you're all I see?"

His words cracked my chest straight down the middle, and my breaths came in short bursts. Logically, I understood what he was saying—my brain didn't have any trouble deciphering his words. But my heart? My heart was cautioning me to wait just a damn minute.

I'd been here before...when I'd thought things would be different between us. When he'd found me at that college send-off party. When we'd swiped a key from the main inn and snuck into one of the many unoccupied cottages. When he'd undressed me slowly. Gently. Reverently. When he'd kissed every inch of my body, made it so good for me, I thought for sure I was dreaming because it hadn't been anything like what my friends had experienced. When he'd been inside me for the first time, his gaze so full of what I'd thought was love...

And then he'd dropped me off the next morning with little more than a wave and a *see you around*, talking about how he'd needed to focus on his career and he wanted me to enjoy my college experience without the shackle of a long-distance boyfriend.

So yeah. I'd learned to be cautious, not allowing myself to be vulnerable with anyone. Least of all him.

But this... If what he said was true, this changed

everything.

I grabbed his hand and held it close to my face, thoroughly inspecting the tattoo. It arched around the base of his finger, resembling half a ring. I was a little rusty on my roman numerals, but I was pretty sure those spelled out the day before Chase dropped me at college.

The night he'd kissed me for the first time. Touched me for the first time.

The night I'd first felt him inside me, before he'd left me brokenhearted on the front lawn of my dorm the following day.

While I'd been crying over losing him, he'd already considered himself mine.

"You're lying," I whispered, unable to hide the tremor in my voice.

"I'm not."

"You expect me to believe that you—a professional hockey player who looks like you do—have been perfectly content getting twice-a-year pussy?"

"I've been perfectly content getting *you*," he said without an ounce of hesitation. "However you'd have me."

"You're lying," I said again, my voice barely a whisper as I held his hand clutched between mine. A part of me hoped he actually was lying because if he was telling the truth...if his words were sincere...it meant we'd wasted so much time. *Years*.

"You know I'm not." His voice was low and calm, as if he hadn't tipped my entire fucking world upside down. "It's always been you, Addie."

CHAPTER TWENTY-FIVE

ADDISON

THERE WAS no stopping the tears from falling now. Chase caught the first one with his thumb, the second with his lips. I could've discounted his words alone, but that was harder to do with permanent ink staring back at me that underlined everything he said.

Shock rolled through me first, and then so many emotions, I could barely name them all. Disbelief that what he said was true. Anger that he'd waited this long to tell me. Regret over all the years we'd lost. But above all, I felt possession. Over him. Over us. And for once, I didn't try to tamp it down. Didn't try to beat it back into submission, thinking I had no right to it. To claim him. But that tattoo on his finger proved otherwise.

He was mine. He'd *been* mine.

With that knowledge thrumming through my veins, matching the frantic beat of my heart, I couldn't hold myself back anymore. I threw my arms around his neck and tugged him down on top of me, crashing my mouth against his.

His lips were salty from my tears, his tongue soft and sweet against mine. I'd just had him last night, and I wanted him again already. Though that was nothing new with us. For years, we'd taken what we could get, as many times as we could get it, no matter how quick we had to be.

But right now, we didn't have to be fast. There was no clock ticking away at our time together. No firm stop we had to abide to.

There was only him and me and this new reality between us.

"Addie." He pulled back enough to cup my face, not allowing me to look away. "Tell me you understand what I mean. Tell me you know it's only you."

Chase didn't take life too seriously. Even after his sister's diagnosis, he'd been the one who'd kept everyone's spirits up. When Morgan had lost her hair and he'd shaved his in support, he told her he'd done it to even things out between him and the rest of the male population. When he was taken down with the injury that led to his surgery in July, he was joking with reporters hours after being helped off the ice. And by some miraculous feat, he'd always been able to pull a smile from my brooding asshole of a brother.

Now, though, his gaze pinned me in place, his eyes intense and serious as he stared down at me. And if I'd had any doubts before, he brushed them away as easily as flicking his wrist with those handful of words.

"I know," I said.

With a groan, he captured my lips again with his own, and then we were in a frenzy, desperate to strip each other's clothes off as if we were racing against the clock. Needing to feel each other, skin on skin, with an urgency I'd never felt before.

But as soon as we were both lying there naked, me spread out on the bed before him while he stared down at me with hunger and awe and something else swimming in his eyes, everything shifted. Settled. Slowed.

He took his time kissing down my body, making pit stops at all his favorite places along the way. He sucked on each of my nipples, lavishing them with attention until I was squirming beneath him, my pussy throbbing and so wet I could feel it on the insides of my thighs. Only then did he shift lower and settle between my legs, spreading them wide with his shoulders.

He groaned low in his throat as he brushed a thumb over my slit. "Jesus Christ, look at you. My perfect pussy's soaking wet, isn't she?" He spread my lips wide with his thumb and forefinger, blowing a gust of air against my already throbbing clit.

"Chase..." I reached down, bracing my hand on his head and not-so-subtly encouraging him to lick me.

"Yeah, baby?"

"Quit teasing." I attempted to guide his face forward, but I might as well have been trying to shove a brick wall for all the good it did me. "Lick my pussy already."

He turned his head and sank his teeth into my inner thigh before soothing the sting with his tongue. "I don't think so.

You got to call the shots last night, but now it's my turn, and I want to play with my food for a while." He licked along the crease where my leg met my body before shifting to do the same on the other side. So close, but not nearly close enough. "Now, be a good girl and let me enjoy my breakfast in peace. I'm fucking starving."

If his goal was to drive me out of my mind, he succeeded. He tormented me with his tongue, licking me absolutely everywhere but the one spot I desperately needed him. I couldn't come without direct clit stimulation, and he knew it. Knew it and was exploiting it. Working me up into a rambling, incoherent mess as I begged him to make me come.

"Is that what you want, baby girl? You want to come all over my tongue?"

"You know I do," I said through panting breaths. My body was strung so tight with need, it wouldn't take more than the barest glance against my clit, and I'd go off like a rocket.

"I'm not sure I want to be done yet. You taste so fucking good."

I stared down at him, this big, rough-looking man whose face was covered in my pleasure because he was feasting on me like I was a five-course meal. "What do I taste like?"

His eyes sparkled as he kept his gaze locked on mine and gave a slow, deliberate lick through my seam, stopping just short of my clit. With a low groan, he said, "*Mine.* You taste like mine."

My heart thudded painfully in my chest, hope blooming inside. I'd wanted that for so long, even when I'd been lying to myself and pretending otherwise.

"Yours," I agreed, and that was all it took to make him snap.

With a growl that vibrated against my oversensitive skin, he finally gave me what I'd been begging for and lapped at my clit before sucking it between his lips. I exploded into a thousand tiny pieces, colors bursting behind my closed eyelids as I arched off the bed. He licked me through every wave of my orgasm, and then he slipped his fingers inside my pussy and shoved me straight into another.

When I was a breathless, boneless mess on the bed, he finally crawled up my body, a grin splitting his face. His lips were shiny with the proof of what he'd done to me, and I couldn't wait another second to feel him inside me.

Despite how utterly wrecked he'd made me, I pushed against him, guiding him onto his back. He might not be concerned about his knee right now, but I sure as hell was.

He went willingly, settling back against the headboard as he stared at me with half-lidded eyes. "You wanna ride me again so you can take what's yours?" He wrapped his hand around his cock and gave a slow, deliberate stroke. "Then climb on up, baby girl, and claim it."

Fuck *yes*, I wanted to claim it. Wanted to claim *him*. Wanted the whole fucking world to know he was mine, even though that wasn't in the cards right now. Even though the facts hadn't changed—I lived in Starlight Cove, he lived in Vancouver, and neither of us had plans to change that.

But for now, this was enough.

I straddled his lap as he reached toward the nightstand,

no doubt to grab a condom, but I stilled him with a hand on his arm. "I want you just like this."

"Just like what?" he asked, his brow furrowed as if he couldn't make sense of the words.

What didn't make sense was using condoms when I had an IUD and neither of us had been with anyone else in years. There'd been so much between us for so long, I couldn't stand the thought of even one more barrier, as inconsequential as it might be.

"Did you mean it?" I asked, desperate for the answer. "Has it really only been me this whole time?"

His gaze softened and he reached up, wrapping his fingers around my nape, his thumb brushing the underside of my jaw. "You know it has."

From the way my stomach flipped, my insides a swarm of chaotic butterflies, I wasn't sure I'd ever tire of hearing that. "Then I want you inside me. *Just* you."

"*Fuck*," he groaned. Closing his eyes, he rested his forehead against mine. His cock twitched between us, telling me exactly what he thought of that idea. "Jesus, baby. You're going to let me inside you bare? Gonna let me slide in this sweet little cunt with nothing between us?"

"If you want to."

He breathed out a pained laugh. "Yeah, I fucking want to." He glided his hands up the outsides of my thighs until he palmed my ass. Then he lifted me so I hovered above him, his cock straining toward my pussy. "Take it, baby girl. Take what's yours. Let me feel how hot my little pussy is without anything between us."

A shiver skated down my spine as I wrapped my fingers around his length and placed him at my entrance. And then slowly, oh-so slowly, I sank down onto him. It didn't matter that he'd just been inside me hours before. Didn't matter that he'd eaten me out and served up two orgasms courtesy of his tongue. Didn't matter that I was soaking wet at the thought of having him like this. The thought of *claiming* him like this. He was huge, and no amount of foreplay changed that.

I whimpered at the fullness and rocked my hips to take more of him inside. He felt so good, so fucking good, that it stole my breath. I sank down and back up again, repeating the move over and over, taking a bit more of his cock each time.

He allowed me to set the pace, staring at me through half-lidded eyes while he whispered words of praise with every inch of him I took. "That's it, baby. You're doing so well. Breathe with me. Just breathe and let me inside."

His words were my undoing—whether they were filthy or sweet, they always managed to crank me higher. By the time he was as deep inside me as he could get, we were both panting, sweaty messes. He'd always felt good, but this...this was something altogether different. To feel him inside me...to *know* there was nothing between us brought out something primal in me. I wanted more. I wanted everything he could give me.

When I shifted my hips, needing to move, he tightened his grip on me, pinning me in place.

"Don't." He breathed out a pained laugh and dropped his head back against the headboard, his eyes squeezed shut.

"Can't even tell you how fucking good you feel. *Jesus Christ*, baby girl. If you don't want this to be over before it's even begun, give me a second."

I hummed and leaned forward, settling against his chest, my pussy pulsing at the subtle shift of him inside me. Against his ear, I murmured, "Are you telling me the guy who's had enough willpower to spend the past ten years only fucking me or his right hand can't help me come before he goes off? Maybe I should've brought that toy you bought me."

"Should've known you'd goad me, you gorgeous little brat."

I bit my lip, not bothering to hide my smile because my taunt worked. Palming my ass, he shifted beneath me, his cock hitting even deeper inside me, and our groans split the air.

"Fuck, you're so perfect." Bringing a hand between us, he circled my clit with his thumb, his gaze locked on where I was spread tight around him. "Look at you taking my cock. So fucking gorgeous. My pretty little cunt is swallowing me whole, isn't she? Taking it like a good fucking girl."

With a whimper, I shifted my hips, and this time, he didn't stop me. One of his hands gripped my ass, guiding me over him while the other was wholly focused on my clit. Chase and I'd had a lot of sex. Rough sex, frantic sex, hungry sex. We'd laughed and we'd yelled and we'd cried. But none of it had ever been like this. None of the other times had ever felt like our souls were locking together.

None of them had felt like my ruin and my salvation all at once.

"*Shit*," he cursed under his breath. "I'm so fucking close. You feel so good. Too fucking good. Tell me you're ready to squeeze my cock. Tell me you're ready to come, baby girl."

Thankfully, he didn't wait for my answer before he pressed harder against my clit, rubbing in the fast, tight circles he knew would get me off. He cupped his other hand around my neck and tugged my face to his for a kiss. It was sloppy, all teeth and tongue, while I rocked over him, riding him to our bliss.

"Addie..." he said, urgency threaded through the single word.

"So close—"

"Fuck, baby. I'm—" He cut off on a low, rough groan that seemed to be torn straight from his chest. He stared at me with heavy-lidded eyes, mouth parted as he came, his cock twitching and warmth spreading deep inside me.

Frantic now, I reached down and joined my fingers with his, rubbing myself faster, harder. That, combined with the thought of him spilling himself inside me, pushed me straight over the edge.

"Oh, fuck yes," he growled. "That's my girl. Come all over this cock and claim it as yours."

I was breathless, lost in ecstasy as I did exactly what he said, managing only a single word as I came around him. "*Mine*."

He wrapped a hand around my neck, tugging my face to his and capturing my lips in a passionate kiss. I rocked against him, dragging out every ounce of our orgasms while he held me as close as two people could get.

We stayed like that for long moments, our hands everywhere they could reach, our mouths never separating. For the first time in our history, he didn't have to immediately pull out of me and deal with the condom. For once, we could take our time.

When I was spent and exhausted, I collapsed next to him on the bed, immediately feeling the loss of him inside me. And immediately feeling the remnants of what he'd left behind. It was different than I was used to, but I definitely didn't hate it.

"You made a mess of me."

"Did I?" he asked, interest heavy in his tone. He pushed me onto my back and spread my thighs wide, taking in just how thoroughly he'd used my pussy. "Jesus Christ," he groaned, his voice nothing but gravel.

Before I could glance down and see the mess we'd made, Chase shuffled closer on his knees, and I gasped. "Wait! Your knee!"

He breathed out a laugh. "What knee?"

"Your *injured* knee."

"Believe me, it's the last thing I'm thinking about."

"What are you thinking about, then?"

He shook his head, shooting his gaze to mine before returning his attention to my pussy. Finally, on a whisper, he admitted, "Shoving my come back inside you."

My stomach flipped at his words, and I couldn't deny the answering throb in my clit. My *God*. I hadn't allowed myself to even entertain the thought of having kids, now or in the future, because I hadn't wanted anyone but him and I hadn't thought we were anything. But the idea of him filling me up did something visceral to me I couldn't explain.

I *wanted* him to mark me like that, whether the goal was to knock me up or not. I wanted it so bad that my nipples tightened, my pussy aching with a throb that was hard to ignore.

"Holy shit," he said, awe threaded through the words. "You like that, don't you, baby girl?" He wrapped his fingers around his already hard cock and shuffled closer. After draping my knees over his, he ran the head of his cock through the mess we'd made. "Love the thought of me filling this sweet pussy with my come."

I stared down between us and watched as he gathered his release with the head of his cock. And then, with our eyes locked, he slid deep, shoving it all back inside me.

"Oh shit," I whispered, my pussy squeezing around him already, desperate for another release.

"Gonna come so deep inside you again." He caught my bottom lip between his teeth and tugged before licking away the sting. "Gonna fill you up, baby girl. All fucking day."

He fucked me, slow and sweet, growling words of praise and filth as he worked us both toward our releases. Where before, we'd only ever had stolen moments...hours here or there when we could get lost in each other, now we had what felt like an endless amount of time stretched out before us.

And we took full fucking advantage of it.

CHAPTER TWENTY-SIX

ADDISON

I COULDN'T REMEMBER a time in my life when I hadn't been in love with Chase Lockhart. Of course, I'd spent the majority of that time denying it. Even to myself. Because anything else hurt too much. But I couldn't deny that I'd spent hours—days, probably. Maybe even a grand total of weeks—dreaming about what a life with him would look like.

But as we lay in front of the wall of windows on a cloud of pillows, the fireplace crackling and the box of puck bunny deliveries long gone, I wasn't sure I'd ever imagined something as good as this.

We'd spent most of the day in bed. After our second round, when I'd tried to get up and, you know, *do* something, Chase had hooked his arm around my waist and tugged me back into his chest. He'd murmured into my hair that we had too much time to make up for, so he had no intention of letting me leave the bed. It was only after I'd promised to wear his jersey, sans panties—and after he'd sat me on the kitchen island and ate me out to a screaming orgasm—that he'd agreed to move the party out here.

Now, I was curled into his side, his arm around me, my head resting on his chest as we stared out at the still-falling snow.

At this point, I had more questions than answers about what we were, but part of me didn't want to burst this bubble we found ourselves in. Worried it could all come crashing down around us.

But the other part—the bigger part—was desperate to know him without any secrets between us.

"How come you don't talk about this?" I asked, gesturing to the ice pack he'd just wrapped around his knee.

He pressed his nose to the top of my head and inhaled deeply, lifting his shoulders in a shrug. "Not much to say. Besides, someone told me they didn't hand out pity, so what's the point?"

I poked my finger into his side, causing him to jerk away from me with a yelp. "First of all, you run into fights with grown-ass men, but jerk away from a little finger?"

"That's not a *little finger*. That's your demon finger, and you know my ticklish spots."

"Second, you wouldn't want me to feel sorry for you anyway. And just because I'm not going to pity you doesn't mean I don't want to know about it."

"There's not much to tell. First time was a medial meniscus tear that surgery fixed pretty quickly. It was grueling to recover and get back in playing shape by training camp, but I made it happen."

And his undelivered messages showed he'd told me back in July that he wasn't going to be able to come home because of that.

"And this"—he gestured to his knee—"was a lateral meniscus tear and just plain fucking unlucky."

"What it was was a cheap shot and a shitty call by the refs," I grumbled. "Everyone saw it."

Chase's body stilled under mine, and he shifted so he could catch my eye. "Addison Grace. How do you know what kind of play it was?"

I froze, my fingers stuttering on his chest. Fuck. "Uh...Levi?"

"Was that supposed to be a question?"

"I mean, Levi," I said with more confidence this time.

Chase rolled us so I was flat on my back, and he hovered over me. "Nice try, but that commentary was all you."

"So?"

"So... Someone has been watching my games while pretending for ten fucking years that they hated hockey."

"I have no idea what you're talking about."

A smile slowly spread across his face until he was openly grinning at me like a big idiot. "You beautiful little liar. Your brothers know about this?"

"Know about what?"

"How obsessed you are with me."

"I'm not—" The words were barely out of my mouth before Chase attacked me, his fingers digging into my sides until I was a squirming, squealing, gasping mess. "Okay, okay! Stop!"

He stared down at me, fingers poised and ready. "Okay, you admit to being a dirty liar?"

"Okay, I'll answer your question."

He must've realized that was as good as he was getting from me, so he relented and stared at me with one brow raised.

I blew out a long sigh. I'd managed to keep this locked down for ten fucking years, and then I got some good dick and I was suddenly spilling state secrets. "No, they don't know. It's my dirty little secret. I sneak into my room to watch your games."

"How many?"

"How many what?"

"How many games of mine have you watched?"

I rolled my lips in, not wanting to admit this. But when he wiggled his fingers, ready to strike again, I relented. "Fine!" I snapped with a huff. Then, quieter, I mumbled, "All of them."

"All seven hundred plus, huh?"

"Yes, all right? All seven hundred plus. Are you happy now?"

"Immensely," he said, a broad smile spread across his mouth. "And no one's ever caught you?"

"Almost, but no." I shrugged, a smirk tugging at the corner of my lips. "That could have something to do with the fact that I told Levi I was watching porn the last time he almost caught me a couple years ago."

Chase barked out a laugh. "Oh shit. How'd that go over?"

I dropped my voice an octave, mimicking my brother. "Jesus, Addison. You don't have to tell me absolutely every-fucking-thing." I giggled, recalling the look of horror on his face. Priceless. "He hated it, obviously. But guess what? He hasn't bothered me about it again."

"You really are a devious little genius, you know that?" He stared down at me, his eyes shining with something that looked an awful lot like love, and my stomach flipped.

His phone buzzed where it sat on the table, breaking the spell between us. He reached for it, holding it out between us —he really didn't have anything to hide—and I glanced down at it. A text thread filled the screen, the name at the top reading Lindy—Aleksander Lindell, the captain of his team.

Instead of responding to the new text asking how Chase was doing—which was below a string of also unanswered texts from his captain—he tossed the phone onto the table. Then, he relaxed back into our pillow fort and tugged me into his side once again. I came willingly, hooking my leg over his as I absent-mindedly traced the tattoos on his abdomen.

I bit my lip, unsure if I should ask this, but the masochistic part of me desperately needed to know where he stood. After several long moments of silence, I finally asked, "You miss it?"

"What?" he asked. "Hockey?" At my nod, he pressed his lips to my temple and murmured, "Yeah. I do."

I could've guessed that was what he was going to say, but I couldn't deny the splinter that lodged in my heart at the confirmation. I hated that he couldn't play right now. Hated that he wasn't busting his ass on the ice with the rest of his team as they fought for a spot in the play-offs.

And a tiny, selfish part of me hated that his love for the game would take him away from me again.

"When do they think you'll be able to go back?" I asked, barely more than a whisper.

I didn't want to even voice the question that had been a niggle in the back of my mind since he'd shown up at One Night Stan's. Part of me was desperate to stick my head in the sand for as long as possible, live in this bubble of bliss where it was just the two of us and nothing could interfere.

The other part of me was preparing for the inevitable crash when he left, worrying that everything would go back to how it had always been—the two of us living separate lives on opposite sides of the country.

"I don't know. They want me rehabbing it through the season before they'll even consider another surgery. After that..." He didn't finish the sentence, leaving everything unsaid hanging in the air between us.

After that...he'd be gone. Back to Vancouver, leading the life of a professional hockey player and all that entailed.

And I'd be here in Starlight Cove, spending my days once again trying not to think about a man I was so head over heels in love with I couldn't think straight. And spending my nights praying I'd get to see him in my dreams.

CHAPTER TWENTY-SEVEN

ADDISON

BRADY'S ESTIMATE had been scarily accurate. By the time the secluded road leading to Chase's cabin was cleared, we'd been snowed in for fifty-six hours. Where, initially, I'd been counting down the minutes until I could leave, in the end, I'd been wishing those minutes would tick by a little slower, just so I could stay a bit longer.

Despite wanting to remain wrapped up in the bubble Chase and I had been in where it felt like nothing could touch us, real life waited. That meant that I had resort shit to do, and he had a knee to rehab, plus hockey commitments to get back to.

Not to mention, I had to have a major debrief session with my bestie.

While Aiden was supervising the front desk, Avery and I grabbed some lunch—and by that, I meant we each had a pint of ice cream...gossip wasn't the same without our favorite guys, Ben and Jerry—and I spilled everything. From the call with the agent's office to showing up at Chase's home not realizing it was his to Brady's call and my entrapment. The dream that led to me attacking Chase in the middle of the night, finding the puck bunny gifts, our fight...and our reconciliation.

"And then, in the middle of it all, we figured out he's somehow been blocked this whole damn time." Digging out a spoonful of ice cream, I shook my head, still not understanding how the hell that had happened.

"Wait, what?" Avery said. "How could he be blocked when you didn't—oh shit. Um...we did do that, didn't we?"

I snapped my gaze to hers and narrowed my eyes. "We did do *what*? And what do you mean, *we*?"

With a grimace, she shifted in her seat. "You remember when you came to visit me at my mom's after Christmas? When you and Chase got into that fight?"

How could I forget? It was the last time he and I had been in the same room up until he'd strolled into One Night Stan's. The night that had changed everything... When he'd casually suggested we should just get married in order to spend more time together, and I'd lost my shit because I couldn't just leave my whole life behind because he *missed* me. What he hadn't said aloud was that I should follow him around and be happy being a WAG.

"When we got super drunk and woke up the next morning in a sea of burrito wrappers?" I asked.

"That's the one," she confirmed.

I shook my head. "Honestly, no, I don't remember a whole lot about that night. At least not after I got to your place."

"Well, at about three a.m., after we'd drunk our weight in margaritas, you said you needed to just cut him out of your life once and for all so you could stop thinking about him. So"—she shrugged as if she hadn't changed the entire trajectory of Chase's and my relationship—"I cut him out of your life. And then I...sort of forgot I did that. We really did have a fuckton of tequila that night."

I huffed out a shocked breath, mouth agape as I stared at her. "Avery!"

"What?" she asked, all wide-eyed and not so innocent. "I thought I was being a good friend and doing what you needed! You can't blame me for that."

"I can, and I do."

"Well, how the hell was I supposed to know he was secretly pining for you the entirety of your relationship and that he'd get a tattoo to prove it? I was just being all Bestie Revenge Warrior for you." She jabbed her spoon in my direction. "And I'd do it again in a heartbeat—you would, too. We already established that during the Great Blocking Pact of sophomore year when that guy broke my heart and you weren't having it."

"Oh my God." A mixture of a laugh and a groan slipped out as I dropped my forehead to the counter. "I can't believe that's what happened. I forced myself to hate him for a year, and for what?"

"Maybe you needed that separation," she said, her tone

gentle. "If you'd been distracted by him, maybe the resort wouldn't be doing as well as it is. Your attention would've been divided, so you wouldn't have been able to put all you have into it."

I couldn't deny her logic. I'd been distracted enough when Chase had been injured, and I'd forced myself to lock that away when I hadn't heard back from him. But if I had? If I'd been in contact with him all year...if we'd been able to actually talk about where we'd left things?

Well, I didn't know where any of us would be now.

"So, what does this all mean?" she asked around a mouthful of Chocolate Therapy.

I inhaled deeply before letting it out on a slow sigh. "It means we wasted a lot of time."

"No." She shook her head. "What does it *mean*? Is he staying in Starlight Cove now? Is he going back to Vancouver? If he is, does he want you to go with him?"

I didn't have an answer to any of those questions. Mostly because I hadn't asked. While Chase and I had ten years of history, those years had been tumultuous at best. And two days of understanding, connection, and real conversation couldn't possibly make up for that.

"I don't know," I said. "I didn't ask."

"Are you going to?"

I couldn't meet her questioning gaze as I admitted what I feared most. "What if he's not staying? What if he doesn't want me to go with him?"

"But what if he is? What if he does?" She placed her hand

on top of mine and squeezed. "Look, you know I'm not Chase's biggest fan. But that was because I had to witness the fallout. I was your sounding board any time he pissed you off, and I was there every time shit got bad, picking up the ravaged pieces of you."

I rolled my eyes. "Don't be dramatic. I wasn't *ravaged*."

Avery stared at me blankly. "At one point, I had to physically shove you in the shower because it had been eight days, and you stunk up the entire dorm room."

"I was eighteen. Give me a break."

"I'm just saying. Shit happened. But I see how you are around him. You can pretend all you want—and God knows you do—but you orbit each other. I don't think you even realize it, but you are intimately aware of him every time he walks into the room. And that man's eyes never leave you, not to mention he permanently marked his body with something that's only meaningful to the two of you." She shook her head. "How your brothers haven't figured you two out is beyond me. I can only assume it's because they've blocked out the possibility of their baby sister having sex, so they ignore anything and everything associated with it. But I digress." She shrugged and glanced at me as she scooped a bite of ice cream. "I don't know. I feel like it's worth asking."

She was right. Of course she was right. But logic didn't have a place here. Not yet, when it felt like Chase and I were still on rocky ground. Maybe after we had more time under our belt in this new normal. It was only February. A lot could happen in two months.

"What's worth asking?" Levi asked, strolling into the kitchen and startling a yelp out of me.

I shot Avery a wide-eyed stare, one that clearly conveyed, *Oh shit, did he hear us?* She pressed her lips together and gave the subtlest shake of her head.

"Um..." I hedged, trying to come up with something plausible and latching on the first thing that came to mind. "How many times the puck bunnies have broken in to Chase's house or hotel rooms."

Levi snorted and grabbed an apple from the fruit bowl on the counter. "You wouldn't believe me if I told you. Though maybe I should. That'd definitely be the final nail in the coffin of your high school infatuation."

I snapped my gaze to his. "What do you mean, my high school infatuation?"

He rolled his eyes and lifted a brow. "You didn't think it was a secret, did you?" Without waiting for me to answer, he shook his head. "I'm just glad it passed. Because I wouldn't be the only one who lost my shit if you came home with a guy like Chase."

Because, apparently, according to Levi, my other brothers would be boneheaded idiots about it, too.

"A guy like Chase, huh?" I asked, my voice deceptively calm. "You mean someone who's determined and committed enough to make it as a professional athlete? Someone who's kind enough to work his ass off and send home money so his parents wouldn't go bankrupt because of Morgan's treatment? Someone who's funny enough to make even your grumpy ass crack a smile? Someone who's loved by our whole family? Someone like that?"

Levi's eyebrows inched up his forehead more with every word that came out of my mouth until he was staring at me with wide eyes by the end of my diatribe. "Shit," he said, shooting a *what the fuck* glance at Avery. "Apparently you guys really bonded during the storm."

Avery choked on her ice cream and then proceeded to cough hard enough to bring tears to her eyes. She muttered a quick, "Sorry," before grabbing a water and sneaking out of the room, leaving just me and my dumb brother.

"I didn't mean anything by it," he said with a shrug.

"You did. You meant that even the guy who's been your best friend since you were in diapers—the one who's like another brother to you—somehow isn't good enough for me. I sure hope Chase doesn't know how little you think of him."

"That's not what I meant, and you know it. Stop trying to use your voodoo girl word tricks on me just to get me in trouble."

"I don't have to use anything on you. You're getting yourself in trouble all on your own. Fortunately, no one else is here to listen to your shitty commentary."

"What's your deal?" he asked, his brow furrowed as he stared at me. "Are you seeing someone like Chase or what?"

I put the lid on my ice cream and shoved it back into the freezer, suddenly having lost my appetite. "Well, if I were, I sure as hell wouldn't tell you now."

I strode out of the kitchen without a backward glance,

because I wasn't sure I'd be able to keep my mouth shut if I stayed a second longer.

That was another thing Chase and I hadn't discussed... what—or even *if*—to tell Levi. But right now, with everything between Chase and me so precarious, I didn't want to go there. Not yet anyway. My brother finding out about the two of us was the last thing I wanted or needed to worry about.

CHAPTER TWENTY-EIGHT

CHASE

WALKING BACK into my old high school rink was a complete mindfuck. So much had changed since I'd set foot inside these walls. The last time I'd been here, I hadn't been a professional hockey player, Morgan hadn't had a deadly diagnosis hanging over her head, and I'd still been pretending Addison wasn't my whole fucking world.

I felt like I'd lived a hundred lifetimes these past twelve years.

Between my sister's treatments and eventual remission, the trials and tribulations of ten years in the NHL, and the constant push and pull with Addison, so much had changed.

I'd changed.

What I'd once wanted for my life was no longer cutting it. I hadn't realized how much I'd missed normal life—something I hadn't had since I was a kid. But being here—with Addison, hanging out with Levi, popping over to my parents' spontaneously, being close enough to see the twins over a short break—had shown me exactly what I'd been missing in Vancouver.

And exactly what I'd be missing when I left.

The rink, recently expanded and refurbished, was now the size of an NHL rink and featured all the upgraded amenities usually only found in professional arenas. I would've killed to practice in a place like this when I was a kid. The only problem was that the rink was designated almost exclusively for team use.

I loved that the hockey team now had a state-of-the-art facility to practice in, but what about the rest of the town—or even the surrounding towns? Since the resort's rink had closed down, local residents no longer had an easily accessed place for recreation, and that killed me. Especially since the resort was where I'd cut my hockey teeth, first with my dad and then with my friends, honing my skills and learning the game from the ground up.

With my bag slung over my shoulder, I walked toward the lone figure standing near the boards, feeling like I was stepping back in time.

Coach Brower turned and greeted me with a warm smile and a backslapping hug. "Chase. It's good to have you back, kid."

"Hey, Coach," I said, returning the embrace. "It's good to be back."

"Thanks for coming. I really appreciate you taking the time."

"I should be thanking you. I've been going stir-crazy, dying to get back on the ice."

"This your first time out since the injury?" he asked, his brows drawn down as he dipped his gaze to my knee.

"Yep. Been a couple months, so hopefully I don't make an ass out of myself in front of the team." I'd prepped as best as I could, preemptively icing and popping some painkillers to get ahead of any possible repercussions from being out there. My physical therapist had given me the green light but paired it with strict orders to listen to my body and adjust accordingly.

"I have no doubt you'll be fine." Coach chuckled and shook his head. "You sure have come a long way from a small town in Maine, haven't you, kid? Ten years in the NHL and everything that comes along with it. Must be one hell of a ride."

Yeah, and sometimes that ride felt like a hundred-foot-drop roller coaster without any guardrails or safety harnesses. "That's putting it lightly."

He clapped a hand on my shoulder and squeezed. "It's gotta be difficult where you're at right now. I know more than most how much injuries can really fuck with your head. But they can also make you appreciate things differently, as long as you're willing to look."

Coach was speaking from experience, not just blowing smoke up my ass. He'd had a career-ending injury in college before he'd even had a chance to be drafted. And as much as that must've sucked for him, altering his plans in the blink of an eye, I couldn't lie and say I wasn't grateful for that roadblock. Because without his guidance and support over my years playing for him, who knew where I'd be now.

The same could be said for me and this injury that just kept on giving. Without it, I wouldn't have been back in Starlight Cove, winning my girl over and making up for a hell of a lot of lost time.

"I'm getting better at that," I said.

"I believe it. You never were one to let the obstacles keep you down. Most determined player I've ever had the privilege of coaching. Though I do have one this year who's nipping at your heels."

"Oh yeah?" I glanced out to the ice and watched the boys practicing breakaway scenarios, my gaze immediately finding the player Coach was talking about. While the whole team looked good this year, there was definitely one who stood out from the rest. "Damn," I murmured.

"Nolan's really something, isn't he? And he's a freshman. You believe that? Fifteen years old and on the varsity team."

My eyebrows rose. While a freshman playing varsity wasn't unheard of, it was definitely unusual for such a young player to be at the level he showcased, especially in our small town where the pool was already tiny. "No shit?"

"Yep. I haven't seen that much promise in a player in a long time." He glanced over at me, a brow raised. "Since you, actually."

"What're his plans? He thinking about joining a travel team or participating in a development camp where scouts will see him?"

Crossing his arms, Coach blew out a long sigh and shook his head. "Doubt it. It's him, his little brother, and their mom, and she's already working two jobs just to make sure Nolan can play for us. Between registration, equipment, and travel fees, the parents have to cough up a pretty penny."

I was all too familiar with that. While I hadn't been raised in a single-parent household, money had still been tight. Though I'd known we weren't rolling in dough, I definitely hadn't realized how dire it was until after the fact. My parents had drained their savings...mortgaged the fucking house, just so I could take advantage of the best hockey development programs available.

My parents had bled themselves dry in the hope of giving me a better future, and I'd never, as long as I lived, forget the sacrifices they'd made to allow me this life. I was just grateful I'd been able to pay them back for all they'd given me, get them out of the hole they'd found themselves in as a direct result of me.

I hated that hockey cost so damn much. Sometimes I wished success were based solely on the roots of it—playing outside on a rudimentary rink, just a bunch of kids and their sticks having the time of their lives. Unfortunately, though, without face time at those development programs, the chances of this kid being seen by someone with enough pull to get the NHL interested were slim to none. Starlight Cove High was at the bottom of hockey hierarchy, a Division III school, and scouts usually didn't bother with it. But the thought of this kid's talents never extending beyond this tiny rink in our tiny town stung.

I pulled out my phone and navigated to the camera app. "Is it all right if I take a video?"

Coach dipped his chin in a nod. "Go for it. They all signed media releases at the beginning of the year."

After filming Nolan nailing a flawless breakaway goal, I shot off a quick message to the team text thread—my first since arriving in Starlight Cove.

CHASE:

Check out the talent on this kid.

Within minutes, my phone was buzzing with responses.

HAWK:

What's in the fucking water up there? If you hadn't locked down your spitfire, I'd take a crack at bringing the next generation of hockey royalty into the world with her.

CHASE:

Unless you want a beatdown the next time I see you, stop thinking about my girl popping out hockey babies with anyone but me.

My dick twitched in my pants at just the thought, and this was definitely not the appropriate location for any such fantasy, so I shoved that shit down and put a pin in it for later.

HAWK:

A couple months without you and I forgot how feral you are when it comes to her.

CHASE:

Happy to remind you anytime.

TOSHY:

Shit, the kid's good. When's he getting signed?

CHASE:

He's 15, so not for a while...

HENSLEY:

Goddamn, 15?! Did you see that smooth AF deke? Davies could learn a thing or two.

DAVIES:

Fuck off, Hensley. But is the kid interested in some one on one time?

LINDY:

The scouting department needs to see that.

And hey, asshole. Respond to my texts once in a while, would you?

I cringed. I'd been avoiding my captain, but I couldn't bring myself to do anything else. Not when shit was still up in the air. Not when I didn't know what my future held. And sure as hell not when I'd started to second-guess the surgery that would no doubt allow me to get back on the ice. But the chances of it buying me any more than a single year playing professionally were slim, and it could cost me in the long run. God knew I had enough scar tissue in that knee already, and any more could make daily life difficult. Was being able to play for what amounted to a blink of time worth having chronic issues the rest of my life?

I shook those thoughts from my head and pocketed my

phone, focusing once again on the kids I was here to see. My shit could wait.

"So, what's the plan for today?" I asked Coach.

"Honestly? Just have fun. They think we're having a standard practice today, so they're going to absolutely lose their minds when they realize you're here."

"Looking forward to it," I said with a grin.

"They've lost their last three games, so spirits are a little low. But every single one of them is a fan. I have no doubt they've been following your career for years—probably since they could lace up a pair of skates. Nolan came to practice one day a couple months back, damn near pissing himself because he said he'd seated you at Ambrosia."

"No shit, that was him? Nice kid." Especially considering how he'd hooked me up that night.

"They all are. And I think just seeing you out on the ice again, even after all the obstacles you've faced—are currently facing—will be great for them."

"Let's hope I can still skate, then."

He laughed and patted me on the back. "I have no doubt. You can head back to the locker rooms and get changed. Come on out whenever you're ready."

When Coach had called me on Monday, a couple weeks after Snowmaggedon, and asked if I'd have any time while I was home to speak to the team and run a few drills or scrimmage with them, I couldn't agree fast enough. I'd been feeling like a caged animal for weeks, desperate to get back on the ice. So I jumped at the opportunity.

It'd been barely two months since the injury had benched

me, relegating me to LTIR and the relentless grind of rehab, but it felt like a fucking lifetime. This was the longest I'd ever gone in my career without being on the ice, and I couldn't wait to get back out there. I just needed to take it easy and listen to my body. And considering what was on the line—not just a future in hockey, but also my ability to live a pain-free life when my career was long gone—I had no intention of ignoring what my knee was telling me.

Once I was suited up, I headed back out to the rink, tipping my chin at Coach when he noticed me waiting in the wings, hanging back until his signal. He gave two quick bursts of the whistle, and the boys immediately skated his direction, gathering around him.

"I have a little surprise for you today, boys."

"Tell me there's a taco truck waiting for us after practice, Coach," a kid who stood half a foot above the rest said.

"Sorry to disappoint, Reynolds, but there aren't any tacos. But I do have someone joining you on the ice today."

Murmurs went up as the team exchanged questioning glances.

"You guys probably know him best as the elite two-way player for Vancouver, celebrated for his exceptional stats—someone with a knack for clutch goals, a guy who can always get the puck on his teammates' tape, and a force to be reckoned with in every aspect of the game. But what I see when I look at Chase is what I see in so many of you—just a kid with a passion for this game we all love."

"You better not be playing with me, Coach," one of the guys called.

"Wouldn't dream of it."

"You're serious?" another one asked, shock in his tone. "Chase freaking Lockhart is here?"

"The one and only," Coach said, dipping his chin in a nod. "Since he's back in Starlight Cove for a while, I thought we should give him a chance to come out here and play...see the upgrades to this facility his generous donations provided."

I took that as my cue to head out on the ice. The cold air hit my face as the familiar scent of the rink enveloped me, and the crisp sound of my blades cutting through the ice reverberated in my ears. Each stride I took was familiar and foreign all at once. Lingering pain echoed in my knee, reminding me of how precarious everything still was.

It was a bittersweet moment, a clash of emotions warring inside me—gratitude for being back on the ice, immediately followed by frustration at the limitations I still faced. The pain served as a stark reminder of exactly what I'd lost with this injury—not just playing time with my team but also the intimate connection to the game I loved.

As soon as Coach's attention fixed on me, the boys followed his gaze. Several whooped, a few called out hellos and holy shits, and one kid in the back shouted, "You were robbed of the Selke last year, man!"

I shot him a grin and a chin nod. "Thanks, kid. I appreciate that."

Coach clapped his hands. "All right, boys, let's make today count. Chase is just one of the team while he's here, so don't go easy on him."

"Throwing me to the wolves, Coach?"

"I think you can handle it." He grinned around his whistle before giving it two short blows, and just like in high school, I moved my ass right along with the rest of the team.

As the drills began, it became perfectly clear each and every one of the players was trying their damnedest to show off. But even without that extra burst of effort, the team was dedicated, full of heart and determination, and that was easy to see. But above all, they had that undiluted hunger and love for the game, stripped of endorsements and contracts and all the BS that came with being a professional.

While I'd never *stopped* loving hockey, things had shifted when I'd gone pro. Priorities changed. It was no longer about just playing because I loved it—it was playing to win. Striving for the next contract. Aiming for awards. Killing myself out there to secure legacy money for myself and my family.

And I'd succeeded in all four, but at what cost?

My body had taken a beating over the past decade, my knee possibly fucked beyond repair, and I'd spent ten years away from the only woman I'd ever loved.

But here, alongside this group of teenage boys, all that extra baggage was swept away, relegated to the sidelines as the pure enjoyment of the game rose above everything else.

After a while, Coach blew the whistle again and called for a scrimmage. And if I thought the team was focused before, it had nothing on what they showcased out on the ice now. The intensity heightened, and each player demonstrated their talents as they battled for the puck. It was a fast-paced game, and I was loving every second of it.

In that moment, the burden of everything resting on my shoulders and the fear of the unknown melted away. The what-ifs my future held no longer weighed me down, the urgency I'd felt for months to get my knee back in full playing condition no longer breathing down my neck.

But still, even while I was out there, having the most fun I'd had in longer than I could remember, a whisper in the back of my mind took root. I might've been able to hold my own against some damn good varsity hockey players, but my knee still throbbed like a motherfucker the entire time, and I'd only been playing at half capacity.

Which meant, as it currently stood, there was no fucking way I could hack it in the NHL. Not without another surgery.

CHAPTER TWENTY-NINE

ADDISON

FEBRUARY WAS USUALLY a slow month at the resort. In past years, we'd scraped by on a couple reservations if we were lucky. My brothers had always kept the resort afloat during that time, sinking their own money into this place so our mom's legacy wouldn't die, the bones of our family right along with it.

Fortunately, things on that front couldn't have been more different this year. We were booked solid. Even Cottage Thirteen, which I'd reluctantly agreed to start taking reservations for because my brothers had been right—it didn't make sense to hold it for fantasy scenarios that were never going to come true. But despite our calendar being booked up for months, I couldn't silence the whisper in the back of my mind that kept telling me it wasn't enough.

I wasn't doing enough.

I needed to set things in place *now*—events, articles,

promotions, different marketing strategies—so we'd never face that uncertainty again.

While I'd never had the funds to be able to contribute like my brothers had, I'd done whatever else I could. Had given the resort my everything for years, in part as repayment for all my brothers gave me. But also because this place had always felt like it was a part of my very soul. I loved this resort...the history and the memories and the dreams for it my mom had once shared with me.

When I'd been maybe sixteen, Mom and I had been walking along the beach at sunset, just the two of us. She'd told me that while she had no intention of pushing this life on me or my brothers, she would love nothing more than to see it passed down, just like her parents had done for her, and continue on with the next generation. That one of us would take the reins and run the resort, all while raising a family in the home we'd grown up in.

For years, that had sat in the back of my mind, and I'd wondered which of us—if any—would fall into those shoes. And then last night, I'd dreamed of being so pregnant I looked like I had a basketball stuffed under my shirt. I was walking along the beach with a man in front of me holding the hand of a toddling kid, another perched on his arm. I hadn't even been surprised when the man had turned around and it was Chase's mischievous smile beaming back at me.

I'd woken up this morning with a dull ache in my chest, my heart instinctively knowing what I'd lost before my brain had even caught up. Because that dream wasn't a possibility, considering the man who'd starred in it hadn't called Starlight Cove home in more than a decade.

That fucking dream had derailed me all day, and I needed to focus. I was currently spread out in the parlor, my laptop, iPad, and phone all within reach as I shot off an email to Harper—we'd been going back and forth on ideas for possible articles on the resort and hadn't yet settled on anything. My only saving grace in getting stuff done had been the fact that my brothers hadn't interrupted me all day—a fucking miracle.

Requests from guests had been slow, so Avery sat in here with me, curled in a chair in front of the fireplace with a book in her lap. As I shuffled some papers, she looked over at me, one brow raised before pointedly glancing to the clock on the wall that read well past five. "You about done over there? Finally ready to—"

"Oh!" Mabel came to a sudden stop as she strolled into the parlor, decked out in head-to-toe winter gear. "I wasn't expecting anyone to be here."

"I live and work here, Mabel," I said. "I think it's probably safe to expect me here at all times."

"Well, yes, but I figured you'd be where everyone else is," she said. "I was just going to grab some snacks before heading over..."

Avery laughed and shook her head. "You better grab them quick so Aiden doesn't see you. You know he said he was going to start sending you a bill."

Mabel blew a raspberry and swatted her hand through the air. "He loves me too much to do that."

"Where are you heading?" I asked.

Mabel glanced at us over her shoulder as she rummaged through the snack bowl, her brows raised. "You haven't heard? I figured you'd have given the okay."

"The okay for what?"

"Chase grabbed the hockey team and got them to clear out the brush covering the old rink. Since we're in a cold snap, they whipped up a backyard rink. There's a pickup game between the old studs and the young bucks starting in ten. And I, for one, am not going to miss it."

Uhh...*what*? Mabel was right—I should've been the one giving the okay for something like that, yet I hadn't heard a damn word about it. I shot a glance at Avery, who only shrugged in response, clearly as in the dark as I was. Since fucking when didn't I know about shit going on at the resort?

Had I voiced aloud my want to get the rink back in working order, or was this just a coincidence? Chase might have dickmatized me these past several weeks as we'd been sneaking around, hooking up whenever the possibility presented itself, but I was almost positive I hadn't shared my plans. After running into obstacle after obstacle, I'd given up on having a usable rink this year. But apparently, Chase wasn't so easily deterred. Though there was something altogether different about their clearing out the space and flooding it for a quick pickup game than making the rink fit for continued, consistent public use.

"Well, are you two just going to sit here by yourselves or join in the fun?" Mabel asked, already on her way out. "I don't know about you, but I'm in the mood to watch those men beat the boys and serve up some eye candy while they're at it."

Avery closed her book and stood with a laugh. "What does George think about your roaming eyes?"

"He loves them." Mabel shot us a wink. "As long as I bring the sugar home to him, if you know what I mean."

After bundling up to face the bitter cold, the three of us piled into Mabel's already-running car and drove to the side of the property that had been my escape for years but hadn't seen the light of day in more than a decade. It was so bizarre to find the path lined with cars, snowmobiles, and ATVs when it'd been barren for so long. Warmth bloomed in my chest at the sight, an inkling of what this area could be once again settling deep.

I'd spent more hours than I could count out here with my brothers and Chase, running circles around the outside of the rink and begging them to teach me how to skate. It was Chase who'd finally succeeded after my brothers had gotten frustrated with me and given up. But I'd been only eight...maybe ten, and I'd been scared of falling.

If only I'd known then that falling for the boy who'd skated backward and held my hands, showering me with words of encouragement and praise, would hurt that much worse.

What had been nothing but a barren wasteland the last time I'd been out here had been transformed into something straight out of a movie. String lights hung from posts someone had haphazardly erected around the space, a hot chocolate station was set up on the other side of the rink, and a scattering of overturned buckets and logs served as makeshift seating for the onlookers. It was a poor facsimile of what it had once looked like—what it *could* look like—but the blueprint of it was there, and it was beautiful.

"You girls have fun," Mabel said. She pulled out a sparkly pink flask from her pocket and held it up between us with a grin. "I'm going to add a splash of hot chocolate to my Bailey's."

With a laugh, Avery and I waved her off before making our way through the crowd toward the rink until we had a clear view of the group on the ice. About twenty guys were out there, half high schoolers and half adults—including each one of my damn brothers.

My first instinct was anger that they'd known about this and hadn't said a word to me, but that evaporated just as quickly while I watched them having fun and joking around.

Beck and Ford were on the ice in front of where Quinn and Everly sat on a couple logs outside the perimeter. Ford said something that caused the four of them to crack up, and my lips twitched in response.

Brady broke away from the group he was talking to and skated over to Luna. Instead of leaning down for a kiss, he tugged her straight off her upturned bucket and into his arms, holding her suspended above the ice. She tossed her head back on a laugh and wrapped her arms around his neck. And then she kissed him as if the two of them were alone in their own little world.

Even grumpy asses Aiden and Levi were grinning as the two of them joked around with Chase and a couple of his teammates from high school.

"Oh my fucking God, would you *look* at him," Avery hissed, her eyes glued to Aiden. "Christ on a cracker, if there weren't witnesses, I'd climb that man right here, I swear to God."

"*Avery*," I said, my tone heavy with exasperation. "What did we say about that?"

"What? It's the truth. Fuck me running, I can't wait for him to do *extremely* naughty things to me tonight."

I groaned. "You are the literal worst."

As if he'd heard her plans, Aiden lifted his head, his gaze finding Avery immediately. He said something to the group before skating over to us. My best friend and my brother were probably making out next to me for all I knew, but I couldn't drag my eyes away from Chase, whose focus was directed at me.

He wore his old high school jersey—it was smaller on him now than it'd been back then, but I couldn't deny the flicker of heat that bloomed low in my belly at the sight. I'd had an embarrassing number of teenage fantasies featuring him in that jersey...me in that jersey...the two of us together with the jersey crumpled on the floor.

And absolutely none of those were scenarios I should be thinking about out here, surrounded by what felt like half of Starlight Cove.

Levi elbowed Chase to get his attention, and he finally

tore his gaze away from me, but not before shooting me that smirk I loved so damn much.

I blew out a long sigh, part of me wanting him to skate over to me like Aiden had for Avery. To pick me up, hold and kiss me like Brady had done with Luna. But we weren't there yet.

I didn't know if we'd ever be.

I dragged my gaze away from Chase and glanced over at Avery and Aiden in time to hear my bestie proposition my brother for some role-play.

"Can you bring this home?" Avery bit her lip as she ran her hands all over my brother's chest. "Maybe wear it tonight?"

"Okay, first of all," I cut in, "knock that shit off. We've talked about this! I don't need to know anything at all about my brothers' sex lives."

"I thought you weren't paying attention." Avery shrugged, completely unrepentant.

"And second..." I narrowed my eyes and jabbed a finger in Aiden's direction. "You're on my shit list. You didn't even think to mention this to me? We're going to be having words tomorrow."

"Can't wait." Then he tugged Avery as close as she could get and held his mouth just above hers. "And I'll wear whatever you want tonight, bunny. But first, I have a game to win."

Before I could tell him to get the hell out of here, he gave Avery a kiss, smacked her ass, and skated off to join the fray as they readied for the face-off.

"You two are so disgustingly in love," I grumbled.

Avery shot me a wide grin. "I know. Isn't it great?"

I blew out a long sigh. Yeah, it was. Not only did I love that my bestie had found her forever with one of my brothers —which meant we'd be sisters-in-law at some point—I also couldn't deny that something inside me was soothed at seeing my family so happy. So content. Especially when they'd been anything but for so long.

I also couldn't deny just how much I wanted that to be me.

As the game started, I shoved all that aside, my attention focusing on the action on the ice. I'd watched enough of Chase's games to know exactly what he usually looked like out there. And while he skated with what anyone else would probably see as ease, making his skates look like an extension of his body, I could see the cracks in his facade. He wasn't as fast as he usually was. Wasn't as nimble or agile, either.

It was obvious to me his knee was bothering him, but you'd never know it from the giant smile on his face as he teamed up with my brothers and a handful of his old teammates. He was having the time of his life playing against those kids. And as much as I loved seeing him like this, my heart ached because I knew it wouldn't last. It was a blip in time, just a small snapshot of an exceedingly long stretch of days...*years*...when he wouldn't be here anymore.

Pretty soon, he'd go back to Vancouver. Fierce determination would replace that smile, and emptiness would once again replace the spot he'd taken up in my bed.

While we'd been careful since the nor'easter, he'd stayed at the inn a couple of times, sneaking in late and leaving early just like he'd done for years when we'd gotten by on nothing more than stolen moments.

Except now, unlike our previous encounters, I had a glimpse of what it could be like if he stayed. And I wanted it.

More than I was willing to admit to myself.

CHAPTER THIRTY

ADDISON

LATER, after most of the onlookers had left and Avery was long gone, having dragged Aiden off to no doubt have her way with him, I hung back. I strolled around, pretending I was there to clean up and make sure everything was set back to rights and that I wasn't sticking around for Chase and only Chase.

He was talking to a kid from the hockey team, maybe fifteen or sixteen years old. The kid's mom, who I knew from around town, and his younger brother stood close, soaking in everything Chase was saying to them.

I slowly made my way over, gathering scattered items left behind as I went and giving them time alone. The kid was looking at Chase with stars in his eyes, and I didn't want to interrupt that hero worship.

"Maybe we can do this again next year," Chase said loud enough to carry over to me.

"Really?" The kid's eyes were bright and full of excitement, his tone stripped of all teenage angst and replaced by pure, undiluted hope.

That killed me because I was intimately familiar with that hope. I'd felt it more times than I could count. I'd also been crushed by it when Chase inevitably left to go back to his real life, no longer able to stay in this make-believe dreamland vacation. And this visit back home was shaping up to be one hell of a long vacation… One I was getting way too comfortable in.

Even though I'd been silent on my approach, Chase lifted his head when I was close, as if he'd sensed me. With a smile tipping up one side of his mouth, he held out his hand toward me. "Addie, come here for a second."

On autopilot, I reached out and allowed him to tug me in next to him, the kid's mom's lips twitching as Chase tucked me right into his side.

"Marissa, have you met Addison? She's the one in charge of this whole place."

"Of course." Marissa offered me a warm smile, even as her youngest child tugged incessantly on her arm. "But it's been a while. I'm usually working, so I don't get to the town festivities as much as I'd like. I knew your mom, though. I worked here one summer in high school." She shook her head, her eyes bright with wonder and a hint of sadness. "You look just like her."

"Thank you." I'd heard that enough in my life that I was used to it by now. It no longer stung as much as it had in the early years following her death. I didn't see the similarities, even when I looked at photos of my mom when she was my age. But I didn't mind the comparison. My mom had been gorgeous—vivacious and funny with a smile that could light up the whole room.

"I used to come out here all the time when I was little. I definitely miss it." Marissa patted her youngest son on the head. "And Zach would love something like this again. He wants to be a carbon copy of Nolan, but it's hard to find a place for Zach to practice since the school rink is in use so often. Not to mention not having reasonable rentals—so many kids in town miss out because there aren't any other alternatives besides buying your own, and that isn't an option for many. Thanks again for doing this with them, Chase."

"Happy to. And I'm going to look into those development program scholarships I was telling you about."

"Thank you." Marissa's eyes shone with gratitude. "I really appreciate you doing that for us."

"Yeah, thanks, man," Nolan said. "And sorry I pulled that deke on you."

Chase boomed out a laugh and shook his head, clapping Nolan on the shoulder. "Never apologize for that. You keep playing like a boss, no matter what. I'll be in touch, all right?"

With a wave, they headed to their car, leaving just Chase and me out here alone in the falling snow.

I squeezed his hand where it was still wrapped around mine. "What kind of scholarship are you looking into for him?"

Chase shifted his gaze to the family who'd just climbed into their weathered car before returning it to me. "The brand-new Chase Lockhart scholarship I just made up?"

I breathed out a laugh and shook my head. "You're keeping all kinds of secrets. The '*scholarship*,'" I said with air quotes, "and all this."

He grinned, completely unrepentant. "The kid's good, Addie. Really fucking good. Better than I was at that age. But his mom's already working two jobs, just scraping by, so there's no way they can afford some of the development programs he needs to be at for a better chance of getting noticed by the pros."

"And that's where you come in?"

He shrugged. "What good is having all this money and these connections if I don't do something worthwhile with them? I busted my ass for it, broke my body for it... I want to see some good come from it."

At the mention of breaking his body, I glanced down at his knee before scanning his features, reading every line on his face. "And how's that body doing, after the school visit earlier in the week and now all this?"

"Gonna pay for it, for sure, but it was worth it just to see them out here. The facility at the school is amazing. Seriously. I couldn't have dreamed up a nicer place for those kids to practice." He blew out a long breath and glanced at the rink they'd set up in a couple hours. "But there's no heart. All of those kids are too young to remember this rink before it closed, so I wanted to bring them out here. Show them the true soul of hockey—being outside in the fresh air, just a bunch of kids with sticks goofing around, playing their hearts out."

"Well, I think you succeeded." I elbowed him in the stomach. "Still would've liked to be let in on the secret."

"Sorry, firefly. I wanted it to be a surprise. And I have a confession."

"What's that?"

"That's not my only secret."

"No?" I asked, brows raised.

"Nope." He grabbed a bag he'd set on the perimeter and pulled out a pair of skates from inside, holding them up between us. "I had ulterior motives to getting this rink ready. I wanna skate with you again."

"Here?" I glanced around at the deserted space. I was freezing, my toes nearly numb and my nose like an icicle. "Now?"

"Here," he confirmed. "Now. I've wanted to for years, but we've never gotten the chance."

He tugged me closer until our bodies were flush. Then he leaned down and kissed me. His lips were warm, his tongue soft and smooth as he slid it against mine, heating me up from the inside out.

When I was breathless and aching for him, he pulled away just enough to murmur, "C'mon, firefly. Skate with me."

How could I say no to that?

I rested my hands on his chest, feeling the strong thrum of his heartbeat, and stared up into his ice-blue eyes. With a nod, I said, "Okay."

He flashed me a grin before guiding me to sit on an upturned five-gallon bucket. "Sit your cute ass down, and let's get you geared up."

After I complied, he squatted in front of me and tugged off my boots before replacing them with the skates he'd brought for me, a perfect fit. Once he'd finished lacing me up, he tugged me to my feet.

"How do they feel?"

"Perfect. But weird." I wobbled, not used to finding the balance needed to stay upright on the blades. "I haven't worn a pair of skates since the last time we were out on this rink."

"When was that?" he asked. "Twelve...thirteen years ago?"

A lifetime ago.

"Something like that."

"There's no time like the present to get back out there, then."

I blew out a sigh. "I'm for sure going to land on my ass before this night is through. You gonna kiss it and make it better?"

"I'd love to." He guided me out on the ice, his hand wrapped tightly around mine. Grinning down at me, he skated backward and pulled me right along with him, just like when he'd taught me to skate all those years ago. "But don't worry, baby. I won't let you fall."

As we glided around, just the two of us out there in the falling snow, the stars and the twinkling string lights glittering above, I knew it was already too late.

I'd fallen a long time ago.

CHAPTER THIRTY-ONE

CHASE

MY BODY WAS WRECKED, but my soul was fulfilled. Playing hockey had always given me a thrill, ever since I'd laced up my first set of skates. It'd been my life for so long, and I loved every second of it. But there was something so different between hustling on the ice as a professional and just playing for fun. Fucking around with my friends... watching those kids have the time of their lives.

And being reminded once again just how *good* Nolan was, even in a casual pickup game.

I'd sent off that video of him to the scouting department earlier in the week, just like Lindy had suggested, and I'd received a call not even an hour later, asking for details about the kid. It seemed I wasn't the only one who saw promise in him. Pride swelled in my chest, knowing *I'd* been the catalyst for that. That I'd identified a possible future NHLer—someone whose modest life could forever be changed, much like my own had been—all thanks to a video I'd taken and a single email I'd sent. Thanks to the contacts I'd made over my years in the league.

After Addison and I had skated for what felt like hours and she was almost a popsicle, we headed back to the inn, no sneaking necessary. Aiden and Avery were already locked away on their side of the house, so I followed Addison upstairs as she dragged me through her bedroom and straight into the connected bathroom.

"Much as I love this on you," she said, running her hands down the front of my old jersey, "it's gotta go."

She slipped her hands under the garment and pushed it up my chest. I helped, gripping the back of the neck and pulling off the jersey before tossing it into a puddle on the floor. She bit her bottom lip as her gaze skated across my bared chest, and I couldn't deny how much I loved seeing that desire in her eyes.

The rest of our clothes followed suit, and soon, the floor was littered with our discarded garments. Addison tugged me behind her into the steaming shower, pulling my body flush against hers. My dick was already hard—had been from the second she'd slipped her hands under my jersey—and there was no hiding that fact as it bobbed between us, pointing directly at her.

With the hot water beating down on us, she trailed her hand along my chest, not stopping until she wrapped her fingers around my shaft and gave a soft, slow stroke, designed to do nothing more than tease.

"Fuck." The curse was barely more than a breath as I crowded her up against the shower wall. I dipped my head to capture her lips in a kiss, and she met my tongue stroke for stroke, her hands around my neck, her body flush against mine.

Today had been a perfect day—playing hockey, seeing the excitement on those kids' faces, talking with Nolan and his mom about opportunities, skating with my girl under the stars, and now this. What if *this* was my life? Not the rigorous, fast-paced, daily grind I was so used to in Vancouver. But something softer. Slower. Sweeter.

I lifted Addison up, ignoring the pain in my knee, and pinned her against the wall with my hips. I swept my lips along her jaw, scraping my teeth against her earlobe. "Tell me you want it, baby."

"I want it," she whispered, rocking her hips against me, her ankles locked at the base of my spine.

I pressed a kiss below her chin. "Tell me you need it."

"More than anything."

I traced the shell of her ear with my tongue and gripped her ass, lifting her to slide her pussy up and down against my shaft. "Tell me you can't fucking live without it."

"Chase," she breathed, her head resting back against the tiles, eyes heavy lidded. Her tits brushed my chest, her nipples hard little peaks I wanted to devour, and her pussy was so hot and wet against me, I couldn't hope to hold in my groan.

"Tell me, firefly." I shifted her until my cock lined up with her entrance and sank just the tip inside her warm, wet heat. "Tell me you're just as lost to this as I am. That you crave me in the middle of the night, wake up with your cunt aching and empty. That you want it more than anything."

Want me *more than anything...*

She stared up at me, desire blanketing her gaze. But that wasn't all. Apprehension was also written in those depths, and I hated it. Hated that she still didn't know how fucking much I wanted her. How much I loved her.

But I couldn't tell her now. Not in here, while we were both naked and I was about to fuck her. When I told her, she wouldn't be able to blame my declaration on horniness instead of the bone-deep devotion I felt for her.

Finally, she swallowed and gave a short nod. "I am. I do."

A relieved breath whooshed out of me, and I bent to capture her lips in a kiss as I pulled her down on me, sinking deeper inside her. She moaned into my mouth, rocking her hips in a slow roll against mine.

It wasn't fast and it wasn't frenzied, despite our not being able to wait until we were in a bed. It was slow. Intimate. Like we had all the time in the world. Like the unknown wasn't still waiting for us outside this steamed-up shower stall.

She had one hand wrapped around my neck, holding my face to hers. Our foreheads pressed together as I rocked inside her, her fingers dancing across her clit. And when she came around my cock, the pulsing waves of her pussy pulling my orgasm from me without any hope of holding back, I tried to convey every ounce of love I had for her in my whispered words of praise against her lips. As I told her without words that she meant the world to me.

She meant *everything* to me.

CHAPTER THIRTY-TWO

ADDISON

LAST NIGHT HAD BEEN DANGEROUS.

Not in the real, literal sense, but in the *oh shit, I'm going to be decimated when this inevitably ends* kind of way.

Chase and I had skated for what felt like hours, just the two of us under the stars with the snow falling softly around us. When my feet had been blocks of ice and my nose as red as my hat, we'd headed back to the inn.

After what Avery had said about mauling Aiden, I'd known we wouldn't have to worry about being caught. So I'd dragged Chase upstairs and straight into a hot shower, leaving the jersey that had starred in so many of my fantasies on the floor along with every stitch of clothing we wore. He'd whispered the sweetest things in my ear, and I'd seen something different in his gaze. Something that spoke of permanence. Something that spoke of forever.

Then I'd woken up this morning to an empty bed. Again. And the pang in my chest had only grown in the time since.

It was stupid—*I'd* been the one to tell Chase he needed to be gone before Brady did his patrol of the resort grounds at ass-o'clock every morning—but I couldn't help but feel slighted that Chase and I had to survive on these stolen moments. Especially when we got so few of them in the first place. Especially when he was going to be gone before I knew it.

On top of that, I was still irritated that none of my brothers had thought to clue me in on the impromptu ice-skating rink in our backyard. Or worse, that they'd thought about it and actively discounted it. It was hard not to feel like an afterthought in this family of nearly all boys, the five of them leaving me out, whether on purpose or not.

I'd had all night to stew, as well as the entire walk over to the diner for this morning's meeting, and I hadn't calmed at all.

Avery was getting something set up for one of the guests, so it was just me and my brothers today. Beck stood behind the counter pouring a cup of coffee for Ford, who sat on one of the barstools. Levi was at his usual place in the corner, his nose buried in a book. And I was spread out at my table in the middle of the space, ready and waiting to give everyone a piece of my mind.

Brady and Aiden strolled in at last, cutting it awfully close to the start of the meeting. They both pulled out chairs at the table next to mine and let out identical groans as they sat.

Levi lowered his book and glanced at them with a raised brow. "Feeling your age today, boys?"

"Watch it, you little shit," Brady muttered without any heat.

Levi chuckled. "Not sure why you two old men thought you could keep up with the rest of us yesterday, but you're paying for it, huh?"

Without sparing Levi a glance, Brady flipped him off.

Aiden scoffed. "You're only four years younger than me. You telling me you didn't have any aches and pains this morning?"

Levi didn't say anything, but that was answer enough, and everyone knew it.

"Well, I, for one, feel like I'd been run over by a Mack truck," Ford said, lifting his coffee mug as if to cheers.

"Same," Beck grumbled as he dropped off coffees for Brady and Aiden. "I don't know how the fuck Chase does that every damn day."

I blew out a long-suffering sigh. "If you guys are done with your old-man gossip, I'd like to transition to something different, if that's all right with you all."

The five of them exchanged questioning glances—asking for permission about anything wasn't in my wheelhouse, and they were understandably confused.

Finally, Aiden dipped his chin in a nod. "Go for it."

"Great," I said with false cheer, my hands folded on top of the table as I glanced at each of them. "I'd just like to know why the fuck no one bothered to tell me something like this was going on at the resort."

"Goddammit," Ford muttered. "Rookie mistake. We should've known that was a trap."

Brady lifted his hands. "I didn't even know it was happening. Aiden dragged me over there."

"And I got roped into it on my way back to the inn," Aiden said. "I tried calling Avery to let her know, but she didn't answer."

Ford shrugged. "I didn't find out anything about it until they needed me to help set up the stakes for string lights."

Beck leaned back against the counter, his arms crossed, and lifted his chin toward his twin. "I only went because Ford made me."

I narrowed my gaze on each of them before turning toward the only person who'd yet to speak up. The rest of them followed suit, all of us glancing at Levi, who Chase had told me last night had given him the green light to use the rink in the first place.

Levi took a sip from his coffee mug, totally unconcerned that five pairs of eyes were on him. Finally, he glanced up and shrugged. "So I didn't tell you. So what? You want me to check in the next time I need to wipe my ass, too?"

I chucked a pen at his head, missing by a mile. "Are you intentionally this much of an ass, or am I just lucky?"

"What's the big deal? You hate hockey—said it takes more skill to play table tennis, if I remember correctly. Why the hell would you want to watch a bunch of guys playing a pickup game?"

"It's not that I wanted to go watch," I snapped. "And it's not about the fucking hockey game. It's that I should've known it was happening in the first place. But this was just one more thing the five of you tried to keep from me.

Either we run this resort as a family, or we don't. Which is it?"

"Wait." Brady leaned forward, his brow pinched. "What do you mean 'just one more thing'? What else did we keep from you?"

Well, shit. I hadn't meant to say that. I'd let my emotions get the best of me—not to mention Levi bringing up my fabricated hate for hockey and making me all flustered.

I shook my head. "Forget it."

"No," Aiden said. "What did you mean?"

I glanced at each of them and knew there was no getting out of this. "Fine. What about Dad? You didn't want to tell me about him, either."

It was quiet until, finally, Aiden blew out a long sigh. "We didn't go out of our way to tell you about the rink because we figured you had other shit to deal with. You're always putting out one fire or another, managing a new promotion or event or whatever the fuck keeps you working your way through those dick-shaped stress balls like they're candy. You didn't need to worry about this, too. We had it handled. And we all know you would've worried about it right before you took it all over and added yet another thing to your plate."

I huffed out an indignant breath. "I would not!"

Brady and Aiden both stared at me with identical expressions as if to say, *are you kidding me right now*, but it was Ford who piped up with, "Face it, little D. You've got control problems."

"Oh yeah?" I snapped, sharper than was absolutely necessary. But if they wanted to get into this shit, we were going to get into it. "Well, did you ever stop to think that maybe that's because none of you let me control *anything* when I was younger? You took everything out of my hands and didn't give me a choice in the matter. So when I came back after college, I decided enough was enough and took control of everything I could. Except, even with doing that, the same shit is still happening. I'm one of Dad's kids, too, and I deserved to hear about it directly from your mouths, rather than having to eavesdrop to be in the know."

"We didn't want to tell you about Dad because you shouldn't have to worry about it," Brady said, his voice gruff.

"But you guys should?"

Beck shrugged. "We're used to it."

"And we made damn sure you weren't," Aiden said.

I threw my hands up in the air, frustrated all over again. "Because you guys don't think I can handle shit. I've been back here for six years, busting my ass every damn day, and it still feels like I'm trying to prove myself."

Silence descended on the diner as everyone stared at me. After several long moments, I started shifting in my seat, the awkwardness nearly unbearable. "Stop looking at me like that, you big, hairy trolls."

Levi exhaled a heavy sigh and shook his head, as if *I* were the one causing the issues here. "You're an idiot."

"He's not wrong," Beck agreed.

My mouth went slack as my gaze pinged between each of them. "Ex*cuse* me?"

"Addison," Aiden said on a sigh. "I have no fucking idea why you feel like you're still proving yourself to us. You did that on your first day home when you walked in and took over. You worked eighteen hours straight, getting this mess in order, and managed to secure our first three bookings of the summer by the end of the day."

"*You* are the one who single-handedly brought this resort back to life," Brady said. "You're the heart of it, just like Mom was. The five of us are just along for the ride."

A knot the size of Australia formed in my throat, and I couldn't swallow fast enough, attempting to shove it down deep. Desperate to keep my emotions in check, especially in front of them. With the exception of Ford, my brothers weren't talkers. They didn't discuss their feelings, they weren't super comfortable when I discussed mine, and they definitely didn't heap praise on me.

Which was probably why this hit so hard.

I hadn't realized how badly I'd needed to hear those words until they'd spoken them aloud. Until they'd put to rest the fears I'd been unnecessarily carrying for years.

That I wasn't enough. Hadn't contributed enough. Hadn't repaid them for all they'd given me...all they'd done for me.

I also hadn't realized how fast the waterworks would come because of those big, dumb, lovable jerks, or how futile it would be trying to keep them at bay. My eyes filled, and I had about ten seconds to get out of here before they'd spill over.

Knowing I was fighting a losing battle, I gathered up my things as fast as I could. "Well," I said, my voice wobbling as I spoke through the tears I refused to let fall. "Since I do so damn much around here, I'm due for a break. And you five idiots can work through the budget meeting on your own."

I hustled to the front door and pushed through it just as the first tear fell, grateful for the cold bite of winter against my face.

"We love you, too, little D!" Ford called just before the door shut, and I breathed out a watery laugh even through my tears. Grateful beyond belief that they were mine and I was theirs and we were making this dysfunctional little family of six work, despite our history. Despite everything that had been stacked against us.

CHAPTER THIRTY-THREE

CHASE

A COUPLE OF DAYS LATER, I stopped by my parents' house for a home-cooked meal. Mom bribed me to come over by making my favorite—roast beef with mashed potatoes and gravy—and now she was tending to her plant babies while Dad and I took care of the dishes.

"When do you think Mom's going to give me a break and stop dropping not-so-subtle hints about me giving her grandkids?"

"With how often you've talked about Addison since you've been back home, basically confirming her suspicions of something between you two?" Dad shook his head and chuckled under his breath. "I'd say probably just as soon as you make a pregnancy announcement."

"So, I've still got a while, then..."

While the thought of knocking Addison up had become a near-constant fantasy since the first time I'd gone bare inside her and every subsequent time we were together—not to mention every time I was alone—that wasn't our reality. Not yet anyway. Ever since being snowed in together, we'd been making strides, and things seemed to be settling between us.

But every once in a while, I still got glimpses of her pulling back. Pulling away. Doing her Addison thing and retreating when shit got too real. Which was why I hadn't broached the subject of us continuing this when I went back to Vancouver. Of finally coming clean to her brothers. To Levi. To the whole fucking world.

"You played quite a game the other day," Dad said, elbowing me in the side. "How was it being out there again?"

I grabbed the pan he handed me and began drying it off. "Honestly? Fun as hell."

"Yeah?" He shot me a grin. "I could tell. Looked like you were having the time of your life."

"I was. I haven't been able to just fuck around on the ice in years. I missed it."

"I'm glad you got out there, then. Get back to your roots a bit. It was good to see. Your mom and I love watching you on TV, but nothing beats watching you at the rink I taught you to skate at."

Before I could respond to that, my phone buzzed in my pocket. I tossed the dish towel over my shoulder and pulled it out to check the screen.

LINDY:

Rumor has it you're coming back to see the medical team in a few weeks. We're gonna catch up if I have to pin you to the fucking wall, and you're going to tell me why you've been ignoring every damn one of my texts.

I blew out a sigh and slipped my phone back into my pocket, leaving his text unanswered. I knew it was shitty to keep ignoring him, but I couldn't bring myself to respond. What the hell was I supposed to say? That my knee was still fucked? That, while I'd had a hell of a good time out on the ice, I'd barely held my own against a bunch of high schoolers? That I wasn't sure I wanted to gamble having mobility in my knee for the rest of my life for the chance to play professionally for maybe another year? That I couldn't see a way through this? That I had no idea how I could possibly be a contributing member of our team if my body didn't start cooperating?

"What was that all about?" my dad asked, tipping his chin toward my phone.

I shook my head, reaching for another dish from the sink. "Nothing. Just Lindy checking in."

"Not gonna respond?"

I lifted a single shoulder in a shrug. "Not sure what to tell him."

Dad hummed, keeping his attention on the bowl he was washing. "You could give him an update about your progress. Let him in on what your physical therapist is telling you or where your mind is in all this."

I blew out a humorless laugh. "I'm sure he'd love to hear that. My physical therapist reminded me this morning that it took years to fuck up my body this bad, so it makes sense that my recovery is also going to take some time."

And time felt like the one thing I didn't have. Whether it was time left in the NHL, time here in Starlight Cove, or time with Addison... It was all slipping through my fingers, faster than I wanted, and I had no idea how to stop it.

"As for where my mind is, I'm not even sure I can articulate it. It's a clusterfuck in there. Part of me wants to do everything I can to get back on the ice with them, no matter the cost."

"And the other part of you?"

"Is constantly thinking about life *after* that and what kind of permanent damage I'll do to my body if I pursue surgery just so I can keep playing."

"Nothing wrong with telling him exactly that."

"Right. Just what the captain wants to hear a couple months after I signed a multimillion-dollar contract. That I don't know when—or even if—I'm going to be back to play. Don't know if I want to have the surgery that'll allow me more time with them."

"You're not the first player this has happened to, Chase. There are a dozen other guys going through this right now. But I bet they're not beating themselves up about it, so why are you?"

I braced my hands on the counter, curling my fingers over the edge, and hung my head. With my gaze focused on the sink and not on my dad, I quietly admitted, "I feel like I failed the team. I failed Addison, too."

"How the hell have you failed them?"

I breathed out a disbelieving laugh and gestured to my knee. "How haven't I? Unless I have a surgery I'm not sure I want anymore because of the ramifications, I'm not getting back out on that ice. Not as a professional player anyway."

Dad shrugged, like I wasn't talking about the end of my career. "So what."

"So what?" I asked incredulously.

"Yeah, so what. So what if you've played your last NHL game. So what if you've just signed a contract you can't complete. You paid your dues for that team, Chase. You worked your ass off for years. Put your body through the damn wringer, day after day, year after year, for them. And I don't care how big that contract you signed was, it wasn't nearly enough for how you're suffering now. How you may be suffering for the rest of your life. So maybe it's time you stopped trying to make this happen."

"What the hell does that mean?"

"Maybe playing professional hockey is no longer the path you're supposed to be on anymore."

If he'd said that to me months ago, I'd have shut it down immediately. Not even entertained the thought, because doing anything but playing professionally wasn't an option. Had never been an option. It was what I'd sacrificed for, this game that I loved so damn much. And I was just supposed to leave it behind?

A glimpse of the future flashed in my mind. I was out there at the resort's rink again, except I wasn't playing a pickup game with the varsity hockey team. Instead, I was teaching my son how to skate while Addison stood on the perimeter, hand resting on her pregnant belly as she watched the two of us with a smile.

I shook the thought from my head and admitted what I'd

really been struggling with for months. "I don't know who I am without hockey."

"Well, I do." He clapped a hand on my shoulder and squeezed. "You're exactly who you've been your whole life. Overprotective brother to your sisters, rock to your mom, the best golfing partner I could ask for, and the biggest supporter of this whole family. And that's just who you are to *us*. Never mind who you are to your friends. To this community. To Addison."

"If I can't play hockey, what am I supposed to do with the rest of my life? This is all I've known."

"It might be all you've known, but it's not all you're good at. Look at what you did with those kids, not to mention the one you were telling me about who has a shot at the NHL, thanks to your eye. What you did for the resort—hell, the whole town enjoyed that. And no one said you had to give up hockey. There are a hundred different things you could do in the sport even after you hang up your skates professionally."

"I'm pretty sure Addison wouldn't be interested in a washed-up has-been for a husband."

"Chase." My dad's voice rang with incredulity. "First of all, you're not a washed-up, has-been anything. And to tell you the truth, I don't think Addison gives a single shit about having a hockey player for a husband. If I had to guess, I'd say she just wants someone who's going to show up for her. Consistently. Relentlessly. Someone who'll be there for her, without fail." Dad raised his brows and clapped a hand on my back. "And there's nothing that says that someone can't be you."

CHAPTER THIRTY-FOUR

ADDISON

I HADN'T SEEN Chase in a couple of days, and I was beginning to wonder if something was wrong. He'd been uncharacteristically quiet following the night we'd had at the resort's rink. I knew he'd gone to see his parents, and he'd been in touch with the scouting department about Nolan, so he'd been busy. But that had never kept him away before.

Was this what I had to look forward to the closer we got to April and his impending move back to Vancouver?

Levi and I had just run some errands, grabbing supplies for the resort's booth at the winter festival this weekend, and I was on my way back to the inn after dropping him at his place. I'd sent Chase a text asking what his plans were tonight and if he wanted to hang out, but I hadn't received a response yet.

Even though I'd driven the road past the rink a number of times since Chase and the team had cleared it out, it was still jarring to see it back to at least part of its original glory. Dead trees and bushes no longer took over the path, and the rink was clear. The buildings still needed a tremendous amount of work, and the Zamboni shack needed to be torn down completely—

I did a double take, my train of thought skidding to a halt at the sight of Chase's truck parked in front of the shack. With a quick glance in my rearview mirror, I altered my course and pulled in next to him. I had no idea why the hell his truck was parked here when he wasn't out on the ice, but I was definitely going to investigate.

After trudging my way through the snow toward the shack, I opened the door and stopped short at the sight that greeted me. A toolbox sat open on the floor, tools scattered around it. The hood of the Zamboni was propped open. And in the middle of it all stood Chase. Despite the cold temperature, sweat dampened his skin even though he wore only a white T-shirt, streaked with dirt and clinging to his broad chest, and a pair of jeans that had seen better days.

At the sound of the door shutting behind me, he snapped his head in my direction, his gaze sweeping over me from head to toe. "Addie. What are you doing here?"

I lifted my brows and pointedly looked at the tools spread out around him. "What are *you* doing here?"

The tips of his ears turned pink, and he cupped a hand on the back of his neck, darting his gaze to the side. "I wanted to see if I could get this thing running again. You'll need one in working order if you want to make the pickup game an annual thing." He cleared his throat. "Or want to make the rink more permanent."

My heart tripped over itself, my feelings a maelstrom of contradictions swirling inside me. Gratitude that he'd taken it upon himself to do this for us, especially when I wasn't even aware this was something he knew how to do. And then there was the regret over the fact that if we did make this an annual thing, he wouldn't be here to witness it.

I'd grown so used to him being in Starlight Cove over these past couple months that I could no longer see my life without him in it. Didn't *want* to. I knew it was a fruitless hope, but I'd been dreaming up scenarios where we could make this work. Wishing that Vancouver wasn't on the other side of the continent. That he wasn't playing professional hockey, or that I wasn't in charge of the resort. Wishing that we, somehow, had different lives entirely. Lives that would allow us to finally be together.

But we didn't. That wasn't our reality. We only had the short time he was here before everything would change again. And as disheartened as that made me, I promised myself I wasn't going to dwell on it. I was going to soak up the time he had here. Revel in our connection while I could. And not waste a single second of it.

So, without thought, I strode up to him, wrapped my arms around his neck, and tugged his face down to mine. I crashed my mouth against his, slipping my tongue between his lips, his moan mixing with my own. If Chase had been caught off guard, he didn't show it. The tool he'd had in his hand clattered to the floor as he wrapped his arms around me, hauling me up against his body, my feet dangling off the floor.

"Missed me that much, huh?" he asked against my mouth,

one of his hands gripping a palmful of my ass and grinding me against his hard cock.

I made a noise of agreement as I slipped my hand beneath the hem of his T-shirt, running my fingers along the sweat-dampened skin of his abdomen, before fumbling with the fly of his jeans.

Chase hissed out of breath when I reached in and wrapped my fingers around his cock, squeezing the thick length before swiping my thumb over the tip. “Jesus. You need me right now, baby girl?”

More than anything, but that said too much. Opened up my chest in a way I wasn’t quite ready for. So instead, I whispered a simple, “Yes,” against his lips.

With a groan, he spun us around and climbed onto the Zamboni before settling me on the bench seat. He braced himself above me, his eyes heavy with desire as he swept his gaze over me. It didn’t matter that I was covered head to toe, winter gear adding so many more layers than we were used to in this scenario, because he looked at me like I was naked. He looked at me like I was the most gorgeous woman he’d ever seen.

He eyed my outfit, my winter coat zipped up to my chin and leggings covering my legs, snow boots on my feet, and frowned. “You’re going to be cold.”

I breathed out a laugh and shook my head. “I promise I’m anything but cold. I don’t care what you have to do or how you have to make it happen, but I want you to fuck me. Right here. Right now.”

He froze for a beat. Two. Three. Before suddenly, he was

in motion, flipping me over onto my hands and knees and tugging my leggings and panties down before I could blink. Then his mouth was there, licking me from behind, his satisfied groan reverberating against my pussy.

"Oh God," I breathed, hanging my head between my shoulders and closing my eyes on a moan.

"You're fucking soaked, baby girl. What got you this worked up?"

I couldn't exactly tell him that finding him repairing the Zamboni for the resort, combined with the unfulfilled dream I had about him staying here, about a life we could have together, had done that, so I went with a half-truth instead. "I don't know what else you expected when I walked in and found you looking like that."

He chuckled against my pussy, bringing his hand around to rub his fingers over my clit. "That was a perfectly formed sentence, firefly. Which means I have some work to do."

Before I could ask him what he meant, he dove face first into me from behind, relentless in his pursuit of my pleasure. I didn't even realize I was climbing my way toward an orgasm before suddenly it crashed over me, my arms no longer able to hold me up. I collapsed onto the seat, my cheek and chest flat against the bench as I moaned, rocking my hips and coming on his tongue.

He groaned against me. "That's my girl. Can't wait to feel that again. Can't wait to have you squeezing my cock." He shifted behind me, fumbling with his jeans until I felt the warm press of his skin against mine. And then he was leaning over me, his chest covering my back as he swiped his cock through my slit before sinking inside me on a slow, steady thrust. "Oh fuck, there it is. Needed this. Needed you, baby."

Chase slipped a hand between my thighs, rubbing my clit in tight circles as he thrust in and out of me at a pace designed to get us both off. As much as I wanted this to last forever, as much as I wanted to freeze time and stay right here with him, my body was primed, my pussy craving release.

"Fuck, I can feel you. You're close, aren't you, baby? My little pussy was desperate for it, wasn't she?" He brushed his lower lip against the shell of my ear, his teeth scraping my earlobe. "Do it, then. Come on your cock and give me what's mine." He flicked my clit harder, faster, and that was all it took before I was flying again.

I didn't bother to hold in my scream since we were in the middle of nowhere without a soul around. Though, I wasn't sure I'd have been able to hold it in even if there were. I was tired of the secrets. Tired of hiding the fact that we were together. Tired of hiding that I loved this man. More than I'd ever loved another soul.

More than I ever would.

And as Chase sank his teeth into the juncture where my neck met my shoulder, pushing his cock deep and letting out a low groan as he spilled himself inside me, I knew that was never going to change. No matter where he went. No matter where I was.

My heart was inextricably linked to Chase Lockhart. *I* was inextricably linked to him. And no amount of time or distance would ever change that.

CHAPTER THIRTY-FIVE

ADDISON

THE WINTER FESTIVAL was one of my favorite times of the year, the reprieve this awful month needed. It meant we were almost done with this dreadful season that I loved in December but loathed with every fiber of my being by the time March rolled around. The festival was held no matter the weather, which meant whether it was fifty degrees or five, it went on, regardless. It had only been canceled once that I could remember—when a nor'easter had torn through, dumping a foot of snow in its wake.

Since the town had been cooped up inside for months, we went all out for this festival. We had live entertainment, ice-sculpture displays and carving contests, food trucks, and—weather permitting—a snow slide for the kids.

Levi had drawn the short straw, so he was my partner for the day shift at the booth before Avery and Aiden took over in the evening. And Levi looked exactly as happy about it as I would've expected.

"You're going to scare off all our potential customers if you keep glaring at everyone," I said with an eye roll.

He let out a long sigh. "I don't know what to tell you, Addison. This is just my face."

"Well, you have the most severe RBF I've ever seen."

"Thanks."

"It wasn't a compliment."

"If it keeps people away, that's all the compliment I need."

Since we had a lull in people stopping by, I refilled the bowl full of Beck's peppermint brownies—a hit every year—as well as the brochures of the resort. And the display of Aiden's newest release was almost bare. I dug under the table for the box I'd stashed there and pulled out the last two books I had with me. He'd told me to bring only one box because he didn't think they'd sell. Luckily, I didn't listen to a damn word he said and had brought three. The other two were stored away in my car, but I was definitely going to have to grab them before the night was through.

"Gonna need you to run to my car and get those other boxes of books," I said. "We're almost out."

"Happy to. Realistically, how long can I be gone for before you throw a shit-fit?"

"If it's more than ten minutes, I'm going to sneak into your apartment and put hot sauce in your body wash again."

"You're such a brat."

"I think you mean she's such a good prankster," Mabel called from the neighboring tent. "Before you scoot out of here, Levi, would you mind watching my booth while I take a quick potty break?"

He closed his eyes and pinched the bridge of his nose but eventually nodded. No one—not even my grumpiest brother—could say no to the older woman.

"Thank you, honey! I knew you could handle this. If anyone happens by, the items really sell themselves. And I'll be gone only a minute." The items she was referring to were the plethora of sex toys she sold at her pleasure parties—or in broad daylight at any and every Starlight Cove festival. Mabel wrapped her scarf tighter around her neck and headed toward the bathrooms with a flutter of her fingers in our direction.

Levi sighed. "I'm not getting paid enough for this."

"You're not getting paid anything for this."

"Exactly." Then, under his breath, he grumbled, "I swear to God, if I have to touch a fake dick today..."

I snorted. "Don't tell me you're intimidated by sex toys."

"I'm not discussing this with you."

"Fine. But you should know that if you have to give a demonstration, I'll be getting photographic evidence to share at tomorrow's morning meeting."

No sooner were the words out of my mouth than a woman walked up and glanced around at Mabel's booth covered in glittery pink streamers with penis garland hanging from the top of the tent.

I elbowed him in the side. "That's your cue."

"I'll pay you fifty bucks if you do it for me."

"Nah, I'm good." I looked up at him, smile bright. "Better hurry, though. You promised Mabel you'd take care of all her dicks."

"You're the fucking worst." With a sigh that sounded like it was pulled straight from the depths of his soul, he made his way next door.

The woman, probably in her forties, smiled at his approach. "Hi. Is there, like, a special handshake I need to do to see the goods?"

I bit back my laughter, and Levi shot me a glare out of the corner of his eye. Then, with a heavy sigh, he bent to retrieve the bin o' dicks, as Mabel called it, from beneath the table before setting it down in front of the woman. While the town council had agreed that Mabel could still sell her *pleasure accoutrements* at any and all town festivals, she needed to keep the more...explicit merchandise out of sight unless asked.

"Wow, that's a whole lot of dicks." The woman laughed as she scanned the bin overflowing with silicone toys. "Honestly, it's kind of overwhelming. Especially when I'm not really sure what I'm looking for."

In typical Levi fashion, he didn't say a damn word. Just let her ramble on as she picked up every dildo, butt plug, and vibrator Mabel had to offer. But this woman—bless her heart—was not at all deterred by Levi's crossed arms or his scowl or his lack of basic customer service skills.

"Hmm...I don't think I want one with all those gadgets. A little too much, you know? And—*wow*—that is one thick penis. My God. Would definitely need some assistance with that sucker. I saw something about a free bottle of lube with a purchase, is that right?"

"Whatever you say," Levi muttered, looking as though he hoped the ground would open up and swallow him whole.

"Still not sure what to get…" She glanced at him, brows raised. "What's your best seller?"

"Um…" Levi pointed in the general direction of the box, not singling out a damn thing. "That one."

The woman picked up a bejeweled anal plug and held it out between them, her brows drawn down. "This one is your best seller?"

I had to press my lips together to hold in my laughter, though from the glare Levi shot my way, I hadn't been successful.

I was so wrapped up in what was happening next door, I didn't realize anyone had come up to my booth until a deep voice asked, "What the hell's happening over there?"

Like I'd been caught with my hand in the cookie jar, I jumped and spun around to find Chase standing there. He looked like sex on a stick with his black beanie pulled down low, a gray hoodie beneath a black winter coat, those crystal-blue eyes focused on me. And my entire body lit up from the inside out. When he looked at me like that, his gaze never straying from me, he made me feel like I was the only person in the world.

Except I wasn't. And drooling over my brother's best friend while said brother was a couple yards away wasn't my brightest idea if we wanted to keep this on the down-low.

As much as I didn't want to, I needed to. At least for now. At least until Chase and I talked about the future. At least until I knew if there even was a future for us…

Shaking my head, I cleared my throat and shot a glance back toward Mabel's booth. "Levi's doing his best impression of a statue while he watches the booth for Mabel. Meanwhile, that poor woman just wants to buy a friend for some fun tonight."

"Hey, you need some help, man?" Chase called, and Levi's only response was to flip him off.

"If I'm looking for penetration with clit stimulation, what would be my best bet?" she asked without an ounce of shame.

Levi rubbed his thumb and forefinger over his eyes and shook his head. "Look, lady, I'm just watching the booth. If you wait a couple minutes, I'm sure Mabel will be able to tell you all you want to know about these dicks."

Chase chuckled under his breath, his eyes positively gleaming as he watched Levi suffer.

"I'm in a bit of a rush." She turned toward me, her gaze questioning. "What about you? Do you have a favorite?"

Levi pointed a finger in my direction. "Don't you dare."

"What?" I asked, all faux-innocence. I had absolutely no intention of discussing my sex toy preferences while in my brother's presence, but he didn't need to know that. "She just asked what my favorite—"

"Nope!" Levi released the bin like it was on fire, hands held up as if that would keep him from touching any part of this conversation, and walked backward out of the booth. "Absolutely do not want to hear anything about *anything*. You're on your own, Addison."

With that, he spun around and took off like the hounds of hell were nipping at his heels. I tossed my head back in laughter, Chase's deeper chuckle mixing in with mine.

"Brother?" the woman asked with a giggle.

I grinned. "One of them."

"I have two myself, and messing with them is the best." She glanced at Chase and raised a brow. "You one of her brothers, too?"

"God no."

"Good." She smiled at me and gestured to the bin. "Now, about that favorite..."

CHAPTER THIRTY-SIX

ADDISON

BY THE TIME Mabel showed up, her arms laden with snacks, and Aiden and Avery on her heels, I was on the verge of combustion. The customer had pressed until I'd finally suggested a toy very similar to the one Chase had bought for me. From the look in his eye, the way he thumbed the corner of his mouth as I told her all my favorite features, he knew it. And he was remembering every second of the night he'd watched me use it. When he'd made me come for him from clear across the room.

My body was on fire, even out here in the cold, and I wanted to drag Chase to the nearest dark corner and work off some of this tension. If I didn't get out of here soon, I was certain I was going to combust.

"Great, you're all here," I said, my voice pitched higher than normal. "That means I can leave."

"Sorry that took so long, honey," Mabel said, setting her snacks down at her table. "Where'd Levi run off to?"

"Saw him over at the beer garden," Aiden said, lifting his chin in that direction.

I glanced at Chase out of the corner of my eye to find he was already looking at me, hunger burning in his gaze.

I cleared my throat, trying to come up with an excuse for us to leave together, because I needed him, and I needed him now. Finally, my attention landed on the single book left on the table.

"Books!" I yelled, and all four of them turned to me with questioning gazes. "Um, we need more of Aiden's books, I mean. They're selling out just like I told you they would."

"I think the booth will survive without them," Aiden said.

Avery squeezed his biceps and smiled up at him. "Actually, we'll probably sell more now that you're here."

"She's right!" Oh my God, why was I talking so loud? "I've got another couple boxes in my car. Levi was supposed to get them, but he ran off like the fake dicks were about to jump out of the box and assault him."

Chase cleared his throat, though his voice still came out low, rough. "I can grab them for you."

My gaze shot to his, and I read everything in his stare. He was just as desperate for alone time as I was. Even if that alone time was in an alley, around a corner, in a fucking car. Didn't matter.

"Perfect! We'll be right back."

"Maybe not *right* back," Chase said, swiping a thumb over his bottom lip as he stared down at me. "I'm pretty hungry, so I want to eat first."

Oh, fuck me. *Fuck. Me.*

"Right. Eating. Yes, we will do that, and then we will be back with the books." I glanced at Aiden and Avery. My brother looked bored, like he'd rather be anywhere but here, but my bestie was smirking at me, a silent *have fun riding that dick* passing between us.

Without another word, Chase and I strode toward the entrance of the festival and the parking lot beyond. We were careful to keep a good deal of space between us, and I didn't dare look over at him. Didn't dare even hardly breathe, too worried I'd suck in a lungful of his scent and drop my panties right in the middle of Main Street.

By the time we got to his truck, my nipples were so hard they were painful, and my panties were soaked. My clit throbbed, desperate for attention from the man in front of me. Desperate for what only he could give me.

He opened the back door and tipped his head that way. "Get in the truck, Addie." His voice was low, gravel coated in honey, and I couldn't scramble into the back seat fast enough.

Before I could get far, Chase grabbed the waistband of my leggings and yanked them and my panties down to my knees, leaving me bare-assed right there where anyone could see. Then he flipped me onto my back, pushed my legs toward my chest, and fixed his mouth against my pussy.

"Oh *God*," I breathed, arching into his mouth.

Chase gripped the backs of my thighs, pressing them to my chest as he licked and sucked at my clit. "Told you I was starving, didn't I, baby girl? Gonna eat you up until you come all over my face."

I whimpered, rocking my hips in time to the strokes of

his tongue. The truck door was wide open as Chase stood outside it, which meant anyone who happened to be walking by could look right in and know what we were up to. True, Chase was parked in the back corner of the lot, near my car, but that didn't exempt us from onlookers.

"Chase—*fuck*." I reached down, pressing my hand on the back of his head and moaning as he focused all his attention on my clit. "Oh my God, someone's going to see."

He pulled back far enough to look up at me, his eyes glittering in the glow of the lamplight, his mouth shiny with my arousal. "Then you better be a good girl and come all over my tongue."

He didn't allow me to answer before he dove back in, his tongue rolling over my clit before he sucked it between his lips. I was so worked up, so ready for him, that all it took was another swirl of his tongue around me, and I did exactly what he told me to.

Squeezing my eyes shut, I held his head to me with one hand and pressed the other against my mouth, attempting to stifle my moans as I came for him. By the time the last wave had washed over me, I was boneless but not anywhere near sated.

Chase yanked my leggings down the rest of the way until they pooled above my boots and then climbed into the back seat. He shut the door before pulling me astride his lap, and from his frantic, choppy movements, it was clear he was just as desperate for me as I was for him.

"Need you, baby girl. Can't wait. Need to feel this sweet

cunt around me." He fumbled with the fly of his jeans, shifting so he could lower them enough to free his cock.

He was thick and hard and so fucking ready for me. I wrapped my fingers around his shaft and swiped my thumb through precome beading at the tip. Loving that he seemed to need this just as badly as I did. Because this constant pull I felt toward him in my chest was scary as hell. Especially when the future was so unknown. Especially when he was leaving in just a few short weeks.

On a groan, he closed his eyes and dropped his head back against the seat. He dug his fingers into my hips, whether to ground himself or pull me closer, I wasn't sure, but I loved that sign of desperation.

"Ride me, baby," he murmured. "Put your cock right where it belongs."

A shudder worked its way through me, just like it always did when he claimed a part of himself as mine. I lifted up, sliding his cock through my pussy lips before slowly sinking down on him.

Chase's long, low groan filled the space as he gripped my hips and helped me ride. "You feel so fucking good. My little pussy's always so sweet for me, taking me so well. Gonna fill you up. Gonna come so fucking hard inside you."

The thought of him doing just that had my pussy pulsing around him, desperate for it. With one hand braced on the seat behind him and the other on the roof of the truck, I rode him as best I could in such a confined space. I didn't worry about the fact that it was twilight, still light enough for people to see inside. I didn't think about my brothers at the festival. I didn't worry about anything but this moment. Here, with Chase, his breath hot on my neck, his whispered words of praise in my ear sending me higher and higher with every one.

"I love this, Addie. Love this so fucking much. Want you all the time. Need you. Always."

That was all it took, and I was coming around him again, my mind having replaced "this" with "you" and sending me spinning. I nearly slipped and whispered those three little words to him as the orgasm swept through me. But instead, I pressed my lips to his neck, directly over the thundering beat of his pulse, and repeated them in my mind instead.

"Shit, Addie." He groaned low and tightened his grip on my hips. "You're gonna make me come."

Wrapping his hand around my neck, he tugged my face toward his and slipped his tongue between my lips. He moaned into my mouth as his cock twitched and warmth spread inside me. Even though I was on birth control, and even though a baby was the last thing either of us needed right now, I couldn't help the shiver that swept through me at the thought of having that with him. A family. A future. Together.

I rolled my hips as I kissed him slow and deep, wanting to extend this moment as long as possible. Wanting to extend it forever.

After a while of nothing but soft kisses and whispered words, Chase pulled back and rested his head against the seat, looking up at me with a dopey grin and half-lidded eyes.

A matching smile swept over my mouth. "You look drunk."

"I am drunk. On your pussy."

I snorted, then leaned forward and draped myself over his chest. "I can't believe you fucked me in your truck."

His lips twitched, and he palmed my ass, squeezing tightly before giving it a soft smack. "I can't believe we made it to my truck. Thought I was going to have to tug you behind a building and fuck you in an alley."

I bit my bottom lip to stifle a grin. "Maybe next time."

His cock twitched inside me, and my smile grew. "Don't play with me, Addie."

"Wouldn't dream of it."

"That's a lie, and we both know it."

Since Aiden and Avery were waiting on us, and I had no idea how long we'd been gone, we reluctantly broke apart. Chase grabbed a few napkins from his glove box and helped me clean up. As much as I loved not using condoms with him, things definitely got messy this way.

Despite the minimal space in the back seat, he helped me tug my panties and leggings back up, setting me to rights as best he could. Then we tumbled out of the back seat, our laughter echoing between us. He leaned against the truck, the fogged-up windows leaving no doubt as to what we'd been doing, and pulled me to stand between his legs.

"C'mere," he murmured, slipping his hand under my coat and sweater to palm my bare back, as if he needed that physical connection, even though he'd just been inside me. He dipped his nose to my neck and inhaled deeply, pressing his lips against my pulse point. "I hope you know that was just an appetizer. I'm still starving for dinner."

"Oh, I know all about your appetite." I slid my arms around his waist, allowing him to wrap me up in his coat, and cuddled close. "Let's get these books to Aiden and then head home. We've got the place to ourselves for a while, so you can make me scream as loud as you want."

A low rumble sounded in his chest, and he pressed his mouth to my ear. "Love the sound of that."

I didn't know how long we stood there wrapped up in each other, the rest of the world slipping away. But by the time I registered the sound of boots on the snow-packed path and the fact that we were no longer alone, it was too late.

Levi's voice cut through the otherwise quiet night, a harsh edge to it I hadn't heard before. "What the fuck is this?"

CHAPTER THIRTY-SEVEN

CHASE

I'D KNOWN this day was coming. I'd been anticipating Addison's and my secret coming out for years, just waiting for the other shoe to drop. I used to be so paranoid about its inevitability, second-guessing every word Levi said to me, wondering if he knew I'd just fucked his sister in the stairwell or her room or down at the beach but wasn't saying anything. I realized now, as I met my best friend's pissed-off glare, how stupid I'd been. Because there was no way in hell he would've kept his mouth shut if he'd known.

With how frequently Addison and I had been together since I'd been home, I was surprised it had taken this long for him to find out. But based on the murderous look he was shooting my direction, he hadn't had even an inkling about what I'd been doing with his baby sister. Which meant he sure as fuck had no idea it'd been going on for years right under his nose.

"Oh shit." Avery skidded to a stop next to Levi, her gaze

pinging between the three of us, her cheeks flushed as if she'd run the entire way over here. "I'm too late, aren't I?"

Ignoring her completely, Levi scowled at Addison, his mouth set in a hard line. "Did you seriously let him fuck you in a parking lot?" he spat, his voice loud enough to be heard at the other end of the festival. "I thought you were better than that. Jesus, Addison, how dumb can you be?"

"Hey," she snapped, hands balled into fists at her side. My little fighter, ready to come out swinging.

I tugged her behind me, putting myself between her and her brother, and shoved hard against Levi's chest. "Don't fucking talk to her like that. You're my best friend and I love you, but don't think for a second I won't lay you out."

"*You're* gonna lay *me* out?" he asked incredulously. "Are you kidding me? You just banged my sister in your fucking truck like she's nothing more than a desperate puck bunny. If anyone's coming out swinging, it's me."

"You're both wrong. *I'm* the one who's gonna throw a punch." Addison stepped around me and glared at her brother. "My God, Levi, get a grip. I'm twenty-eight! You're acting like I'm sixteen and you caught a boy in my room."

"And you're acting like an idiot. What exactly did you think was going to happen here? That you were somehow different from all the other women who throw themselves at him? Didn't we just talk about this?"

I snapped my gaze to his because what the *fuck*? He and I had already had this conversation at the warehouse, and I thought I'd set him straight. Thought I'd been clear that the tabloids reported nothing but lies. But based on what he was saying, that was the furthest thing from the truth. "What, you tried to scare her away from me? Are you fucking serious?"

"You're damn right I did. And don't even try to pretend you wouldn't have done the same fucking thing if you were in my shoes and this was one of your sisters. I can't believe you did this to her. Is the well so goddamn dry in this town that you had to fuck my sister just because she's the first convenient piece of ass you could find?"

"What the fuck did you just say?" My voice was deceptively calm, though I was anything but. Not when he'd reduced Addison's and my relationship down to nothing more than fucking. And sure as hell not when he'd demeaned her like that, belittling her as nothing but a quick lay.

"You heard me." Levi stepped close until we stood toe-to-toe. Not many men could look me in the eyes, but he could, and his gaze was nothing but fire. The last time I'd seen him this furious had been years ago, that anger directed at his father. But this was all for me.

"First of all," Addison said, shoving her way between Levi and me and shooting a glare at her brother. "Fuck you. I'm not a convenient piece of ass. I'm the least convenient person in this whole family, and everyone knows it! Second, if that was all Chase wanted, he would've stopped years ago."

Levi froze at her words, then shifted his cold stare to me. "Years?"

I blew out a sigh and scrubbed a hand over my mouth, knowing just how fucked I was. This was not how I envisioned him finding out about his sister and me, but there was nothing I could do about it now.

"Well...I definitely did not mean for that particular piece of information to come out," Addison said, glancing back at me with a grimace. "But it doesn't matter. You're acting like children. And your friendship is too important to let whatever is going on between me and Chase ruin it, so get the fuck over yourselves." She pointed to an empty bench several yards away. "Now go over there and discuss this rationally like the grown-ass men you are."

She didn't wait for us to respond, just pressed a hand on each of our backs and shoved us in that direction. I glanced at Levi, who met my gaze with an unflinching stare of his own. Then we both did as she'd told us to and headed toward the bench.

"Actually, you know what?" she called from behind us. "Maybe I should just—"

"Nope," Avery said. "You told them to handle it. They don't need a referee." Then, louder to reach Levi and me, she called, "Isn't that right, boys?"

I glanced over at my best friend, whose anger had melted away in the time it'd taken us to walk over here. With my gaze locked on his, I said, "We'll be fine."

He studied me for a long moment before huffing out a breath and shaking his head. "Will we? I'm not so sure. You've been fucking around with my sister behind my back for *years*? And I'm just supposed to, what? Shrug it off?"

I sat down on the bench, waiting for him to join me. Once he did, I said, "Look, man, I'm sorry you found out this way.

But I'm not sorry about being with her. After this long, there was no easy way to tell you."

He breathed out a humorless laugh. "You could've told me from the beginning."

I was pretty sure he had no idea the beginning was a decade ago, and I sure as hell wasn't going to bring that up now. Especially when it involved my taking her virginity. "No. I couldn't have. For one thing, she didn't want me to. For another, it was none of your business."

"My sister sure as fuck is my business."

I shook my head. "Not about this."

"And since when does what she want override our friendship?"

I could've sugarcoated it. Told him what he wanted to hear—that it didn't. But I'd lied to him enough. And now that everything was out in the open between us, I wasn't going to keep even more from him. So, with a shrug, I said, "Since day fucking one."

He paused for a long beat and stared at me, as if the answer surprised him. "And when was that?"

"Don't ask questions you don't want the answers to."

"Oh, that's fucking great."

"What are you really mad about here? That I didn't tell you? Because I can understand that. And I'm sorry that you found out this way, but I can't go back in time and change it." I rested my elbows on my knees, my hands hanging between my spread legs as I glanced over at him. "Or are you mad it's *me* she's with? Because if that's the case, we've got a hell of a lot more problems than this because that shouldn't be an issue. I'm your best fucking friend. Your brother in everything but blood. You know me. You know who I am. And you know I'd never do anything to hurt her."

"No? Then why've you strung her along for years?"

"Strung *her* along?" I breathed out a laugh. "Man, I've been trying to lock her down for *years*."

He was silent for several moments, shock written clearly across his face. Finally, with disbelief heavy in his tone, he said, "You're serious."

"As a heart attack."

"So, what...you're in love with her?"

I glanced over at him and shook my head. "I know this has been a bit of a mindfuck for you, but I'm sure as hell not going to tell you that before I tell her."

If I thought he'd been shocked before, it had nothing on him now. He stared at me, openmouthed, for what felt like forever, trying to read something in my expression. Probably trying to find a crack in my demeanor to prove I was lying. But he wasn't going to find it here.

Finally, he glanced over my shoulder, toward where we'd left Addison and Avery, before meeting my gaze again. "So, you're into her."

I barked out a laugh. "You could say that."

He shook his head and blew out a long breath. "This is a lot to wrap my head around. Shit, man, you were right there with me in high school, scaring off any fucker who looked at her."

"I was. But you and I had very different motives."

He lifted his brows. "Even back then?"

I dipped my chin in a nod. "Even back then."

"You want to be with her."

It wasn't a question, but I answered it all the same. "More than anything."

"And how is that supposed to work? You live in Vancouver."

"I already told you...that's a conversation I owe her before anyone else."

He met my gaze head on, no longer questioning but accepting. Standing, he tipped his chin in the direction we'd come from, one brow raised as if in challenge. "Then what the fuck are you waiting for?"

That was as much of a green light as I was going to get from him. It was also a good fucking question. I'd been avoiding Addison this week, getting my shit in order so I could tell her my plans. Finally come clean about the discussion I'd had with my coach and the medical team. Let her know exactly what my future was going to look like.

What I hoped *our* future could look like.

I pushed to stand, intent on pulling her into a darkened corner or the back seat of my truck or wherever the hell I could, just so we didn't have to talk out in the open where anyone could eavesdrop.

Instead, I turned around and came face-to-face with the rest of her brothers. Not to mention her concerned best friend and Mabel, who held her phone in front of her as if she was recording, as well as what appeared to be half of Starlight Cove waiting in the wings.

And all of them were standing between me and my girl.

CHAPTER THIRTY-EIGHT

ADDISON

I WOULDN'T PUT it past Mabel to have sent out a homing beacon with our exact location, just to get a crowd gathered. She had to have, considering how quickly the rest of my brothers arrived. Aiden made his way over first in search of Avery. Then Brady strolled up, decked out in his sheriff uniform with Luna by his side, his gaze scanning the scene for trouble. Ford and Beck were next with Quinn and Everly on their arms.

I'd been vaguely aware of the growing crowd, but I hadn't been able to pay them much attention. Not when my focus had been entirely on Chase and Levi and their heated discussion. They were far enough away that I couldn't hear what was said, but I could read body language like a fucking boss. And theirs, thankfully, had shifted from the pissed-off vibes they'd both been sporting when I'd shoved them that way in the first place into something more subdued. Acceptance, maybe? One could hope...

Avery was at my side, talking a mile a minute in an obvious attempt to distract me from what was going on a few yards away. But it hadn't helped. I couldn't even recall what she'd said, too focused on the two men as they talked it out before finally standing and turning in our direction.

I didn't know what it was in that moment. If it was the way Chase's gaze found me as soon as he'd turned around, as if we were connected even that far apart. Or if it was the look in his eyes, something that looked an awful lot like love shining through. Or if it was because I had all my favorite people surrounding me, the ones who'd been with me through it all. But I had the sudden and overwhelming urge to let the entire world know Chase was mine and I was his and we were in this—whatever it was—together. Forever, if I had my way.

For so long, I'd called the shots in our relationship just so I didn't have to be vulnerable. Had held him at arm's length to keep myself safe. To keep my heart from getting broken by him again. And look where that had gotten me. Trapped in a web of misunderstandings and regrets where neither of us was happy. And I didn't want to be stuck there anymore.

With my gaze locked on Chase as he strolled toward me, I cleared my throat and spoke loud enough so all those gathered around could hear me. "I have something to tell everyone."

"Oh, this is gonna be good," Mabel murmured, turning her phone to me. Then, quieter, she said, "To all of you just tuning in to my Live, I'm here at the winter festival, and sparks are flying. We've got—"

I tuned out the rest of what she was saying as I met the gazes of my brothers and their significant others, all of them staring at me with interest.

"What's up, little D?" Ford asked, brows raised.

I swallowed down my nerves, steeling myself to finally, *finally* get this out in the open. Stop bending over backward and doing everything I could just to keep Chase and me a secret. I was done. I wanted everyone to know he was mine.

I took a deep breath and, on an exhale, said, "Chase and I are together."

Chase's footsteps stuttered on his way over to me, his brows flying up as he studied me. And then the most beautiful smile swept across his face, and I couldn't help but return it, my heart so full it felt like it could burst.

"I thought she was gonna tell us something we didn't know, but okay," Ford mumbled.

I snapped my head in his direction and pinned him with a glare. "You knew nothing, you lying liar!"

Aiden cleared his throat. "Actually, we all knew."

My mouth dropped open as I glanced at each of them in turn. "No, you did not!"

"Well, everyone but Levi, apparently," Beck said. "How he missed that when you were sneaking off with his best friend—not at all covertly, by the way—I'll never know..."

"Fuck off," Levi said, but his words lacked heat.

I glanced to Brady, my last hope, but he only shrugged.

"I'm the sheriff, Addison. Don't tell me you thought I didn't know."

"That's exactly what I thought!"

Brady shook his head. "If you wanted it to be a secret so bad, maybe don't make out on the ice where anyone can see you. Hell, even Mabel knew. She's been calling it the Zambone-her shack for days."

"It's got a nice ring to it, doesn't it?" The older woman shot me a grin and winked.

Chase snorted a laugh, and any other time, I might've found this amusing, but these fuckers were always stealing my thunder. Figuring out shit like some kind of professional sleuthers. Well, not today.

"Oh yeah? Well, did you know I love him?" I asked, glancing around at each of them. "That's right. I'm in love with him. What do you have to say about—"

My words cut off as Chase suddenly stood in front of me, his imposing form blocking out everyone else. He cupped my face in his hands, his thumbs brushing softly against my cheeks as he swept his gaze over every inch of my face, hope and disbelief shining in his eyes.

And then, before I could say another word...before I could apologize for blurting that out in front of the whole damn town instead of telling him alone, he lowered his mouth to mine and kissed me. Right there, in a parking lot on a cold early March night, surrounded by my entire family and half of Starlight Cove.

But it wouldn't have mattered if the whole world had been watching. Because just like always, when Chase's lips touched my own, everything else melted away. Nothing else mattered when I was in his arms, safe and protected. Cherished.

I wished I'd realized that sooner. Wished we hadn't wasted so many years trying to find our way to each other. Though, maybe this was exactly how our story needed to unfold. Maybe we'd needed that time living separate lives so we knew just how precious it was to be together.

After several long moments, when I was breathless, he finally pulled back and rested his forehead against mine. Then, just loud enough for my ears only, he whispered, "I love you, too, firefly."

CHAPTER THIRTY-NINE

CHASE

"WHERE ARE WE GOING?" Addison asked from the passenger's seat of my truck.

After an awkward goodbye with Levi—he definitely still wanted to punch me, but he'd come around eventually...just not so soon after witnessing his freshly fucked sister stumble out of my back seat with me at her heels—and verifying Aiden had the resort handled for the night, I'd dragged my girl out of there with one destination in mind.

"Our place."

She snapped her head in my direction, brows up. "*Our* place?"

Shrugging, I navigated the truck up the winding path toward the cabin. There was no use denying it—I'd built the home with her in mind. With our *forever* in mind.

Since day one, she and I had always been the end goal. The logistics of it didn't matter—I didn't care *how* we made it work, just that we did. Same as now. Whether we lived in the cabin or used it as a getaway and made the main inn at the resort our permanent residence, that was up to Addison. I'd follow her, just like always. And barring any unavoidable travel, I didn't plan to spend another night away from her. Not when she was finally mine.

"You didn't think I built this huge house for just me, did you?" I asked.

She huffed out a breath and rolled her eyes. "I have no idea why you do half the things you do."

"Then let me clear it up for you, firefly." I put the truck into park and cut the engine before leaning on the center console toward her. "I built it for us. But mostly for you."

She blinked at me. Opened her mouth. Blinked some more. Then she sputtered, "You *what*?"

I breathed out a laugh and pressed a quick kiss to her stunned mouth before climbing out and heading to her side. When I opened her door, she was still sitting there, shell-shocked. And impatient.

"Explain," she demanded.

"Bossy." I reached around and unbuckled her seat belt before tugging her out of the truck and straight into my arms, her ass cupped in my palms. "Let's get you inside first."

"Don't try to distract me with your giant man-hands copping a feel."

I squeezed her ass for emphasis, smiling when she grumbled but ultimately hooked her arms and legs around me. "You love these giant man-hands. And *me*, rumor has it. Pretty sure that's what the *Gazette* is running for tomorrow's headline. *Addison McKenzie Declares Her Undying Love for Hockey Heartthrob Chase Lockhart.*"

"'Hockey heartthrob'?" She snorted and rolled her eyes. "Someone's been spending too much time Googling themselves. And if you don't tell me what you meant, I'm going to take back my declaration."

"Can't. Cat's already out of the bag. I now know exactly how obsessed you are with me."

She gasped. "*I'm* obsessed? You're the one who built a whole house for me, apparently."

"Apparently," I agreed, opening the front door of said house and carrying her over the threshold, grinning the whole way. "I'd do it again, too."

"What you're going to do is tell me what you meant. Be serious. You did *not* build this house for me, Chase Matthew."

"Middle-naming me isn't going to change the fact that I absolutely did, Addison Grace." After setting her on her feet, I shrugged out of my coat before tugging hers off too. And then I led her into the great room, dropped down on the couch, and pulled her straight into my lap. She settled in like she belonged there, her legs on either side of mine, hands resting on my stomach.

With a raised brow, I asked, "You think that soaking tub with a view of the ocean in the primary bath was for me?"

She opened her mouth to respond before promptly snapping it shut, the divot between her brows deepening.

"It's so you can relax once in a while and maybe kick your stress-ball habit. The heated floors? Because your feet are always so fucking cold. The mini freezer stocked with literally only your favorite ice cream? That's all you, baby. Should I go on? Because I can do this all night."

"But..." She darted her gaze over my face before glancing around at the home I'd had built for her. For us. For our future family that I wanted to be a reality sooner rather than later. "Chase...they started building this place last summer."

"And?"

"*And*...we weren't even speaking then."

I cupped a palmful of her ass and squeezed. "*You* weren't speaking. I was pouring my heart out from a blocked number, remember?"

She dropped her forehead onto my chest and groaned. "Oh my God, you're never going to let me live that down, are you? I told you it was Avery! If I'd known, I'd—"

"Stop." I chuckled into her hair, pressing a kiss on the crown of her head. "It doesn't matter. Whatever happened needed to happen to get us where we are now."

"And where's that?" She sat back to meet my gaze, all humor wiped from her expression. In its place was uncertainty. Fear. And I hated that she felt either when it came to me. To us. "How do we do this? How do we make this work if you're not in Starlight Cove?"

"First of all, it doesn't matter if I'm in Starlight Cove or Santorini. Hell, I could be on fucking Mars. Because in every city, in every state, in every country...in every fucking galaxy, I'm yours, firefly. I've been yours. I'll always be yours. And no amount of distance will change that."

She sagged, melting against my chest, and shook her

head, eyes soft as she stared at me. "Oh, that was good. *Really* good. Did you rehearse that?"

I laughed. "No, you beautiful little brat. It just came to me."

"Well, it's definitely going to get you laid." As if to prove her point, she rocked over where I'd been half hard for her since she'd sat in my lap and grinned. "Before we get to that, what's the second thing?"

I reached up and cupped a hand around the nape of her neck, running my thumb along the underside of her jaw. Now that she'd told me she loved me...now that everything was out in the open, I was so fucking desperate to hold her and kiss her. To fuck her slow and sweet, cuddle her to sleep, and then wake up with her wrapped around me in the morning and do it all over again. Every day for the rest of my life, if I was lucky. I somehow had the privilege of calling this beautiful, strong, passionate, fiery, dramatic, loyal, loving, perfectly imperfect woman *mine*. And I sure as hell wasn't going to leave again now that I'd gotten her.

"I'm not going back."

She stared at me, her mouth slack, eyes pinging between mine. Then she gave a little shake of her head, as if she was trying to make sense of what she'd heard. "You're what?"

I shrugged. For all the time I'd spent angsting over my future since I'd been home, this decision had been easy in the end. I chose Addison. But I chose myself too. I chose the future I wanted...the life I'd spent the past decade dreaming of. Working my ass off for. And now it was finally time to live it. "I'm staying in Starlight Cove. Permanently."

"But... But your career!" Addison nearly shouted. "Hockey heartthrob, remember? Not to mention—"

"My knee." The admission of my career's inevitable downfall came easier, now that I no longer felt the weight of the unknown hanging over my head. Now that I'd made a decision for the future, and knowing the choices I'd made along the way had led me right here. To this moment. With her. "I can't cut it professionally anymore. Not with my knee like this. And I don't want to have another surgery that'll buy me maybe a year to play, tops. All at the possible—maybe probable—expense of mobility for the rest of my life. I don't want that. It's not worth it. Not when I want to be able to roll around on the floor with our kids and teach them how to skate."

"Putting the cart before the horse there, aren't you, buddy?"

"Firefly, I'd knock you up tonight if it was possible and you'd let me."

"Okay, settle down, Mr. Horny." She held up her hand as if to pause the conversation, but I could tell from the flush on her cheeks and the heat in her eyes that she wasn't so opposed to the idea, and my cock twitched in my jeans. "You *love* hockey."

"And I had ten years of loving it professionally. But I can still love hockey from here. All while I explore other things..."

"What kinds of things?"

I shifted to pull my phone out of my pocket and navigated to my photo app. I pulled up the picture I wanted—a rough sketch of the resort grounds, how it existed currently...

and what I hoped to add to it. The plans I hoped to put in place.

"What's this?" she asked, brow furrowed as she studied my phone. And then slowly, her features changed as realization dawned. As she recognized the main inn, the cottages, the rink... Her home, just reimagined. Revitalized. She met my gaze, eyes bright, hope shining through. "Is this what I think it is?"

"I don't know. Do you think it's a multi-pad ice-skating complex with renovated bunkhouses, a brand new Zambone-her shack, which I plan to take full fucking advantage of frequently, and a renovated main building, all of which will hopefully house the future Lockhart Hockey Camp for kids?" I gripped her hips and tugged her closer, relishing in how perfectly she fit against me. "Then yeah, it's what you think it is."

"Seriously?" she asked, not bothering to tamp down the excited note in her voice. "You're expanding that area into something year-round?"

"Some of it. The rink—*our* rink—will stay the same. Just for use during winter, but it could be renovated. Brought back to life how it used to be when your mom was here." I gripped her hip, slipping my thumb under the hem of her sweater and running it along her skin. "But that's only if the missus gives me approval to do so."

She breathed out a watery laugh, her eyes growing glassy as she stared at me with happiness and so much love. "Can't be your missus if we're not married."

"You still don't get it, do you?" I held up my left hand,

showing her the roman numerals inked on the underside of my ring finger. "I've been married to you for ten years in all the ways that count, firefly. A piece of paper sure as hell isn't going to make it any more official to me."

I cupped her face, pulling her close for a kiss, and poured everything I felt for her into it. Into every brush of my lips, every stroke of my tongue, every murmured word against her mouth. "I love you, Addie. I've loved you for years. And I'm going to love you for decades more. Right here in the cabin, or right there at the resort," I said, gesturing to the photo on my phone. "Your choice."

"I thought we already covered this." She laid her hand on my chest, over my heart. "I love you, too. And it doesn't matter where we are. Here, there...anywhere. I'm yours. For as long as you'll have me."

"Forever, then?"

She beamed at me and leaned forward, resting her lips against mine as she whispered, "Forever."

EPILOGUE

CHASE

LIFE WAS PERFECT. Seriously fucking perfect.

It'd been months since the winter festival. Months since everything had come to a head. Since the day I could finally call Addison mine.

And now I could call her a hell of a lot more than that.

I held my wife's hand as we strolled out of the café on Main Street following a celebratory lunch, her brothers and their significant others trailing behind us. Today was a big day. The first day of the trial run for the Lockhart Hockey Camp, this time with just local kids. Kids who otherwise wouldn't have been able to attend or afford a development program like this.

I'd gotten approval to use the high school's rink because our new facility wasn't yet ready. But even though this was a trial run, I sure as hell hoped it went smoothly, because construction had already begun at the resort.

"How much longer till those fucking construction trucks

are gone, Lockhart?" Aiden grumbled as we strode down the sidewalk, and Avery elbowed him in the gut. He glanced down at her, eyebrows raised. "What? It's getting mud and shit all over the resort grounds."

"You and I both know you can handle a mess once in a while." And from the look she shot him and the tone of her voice, there was no questioning exactly what kind of mess she was referring to.

"Goddammit, Avery!" Addison snapped, glaring at her. "It's going to be like this for the rest of our lives, isn't it? You saying completely inappropriate things about my brother's and your sex life, and me just having to deal with it."

Avery lifted a single shoulder in a shrug. "Yeah, probably. On the plus side, you get to do that now with Levi."

"The fuck she does," Levi said, shooting a glare at Addison and me.

"I don't want to hear it, either," Brady said. "As far as I'm concerned, you're still a virgin."

"Ditto," Beck, Ford, and Aiden all said in unison.

"Well, if I have to hear about all the freaky shit you guys are doing, it's only fair that you have to hear about me!" Addison said.

Even through Luna's, Everly's, Quinn's, and Avery's laughter, five sets of nearly identical arguments shot up from all of her brothers, the emphatic *fuck no* coming through loud and clear. And I realized, once again, just how fucking lucky I was that they'd accepted Addison's and my relationship with minimal drama or roadblocks.

Like I'd figured, Levi had gotten over the shock of

Addison and me being together sooner rather than later. His only stipulation was that he didn't want to hear it, he didn't want to see it, and he didn't want to know anything at all about what Addison and I did behind closed doors.

And we'd tried. We'd really, really tried. But when I wanted to fuck my wife, not even my best friend was going to stand in my way.

After another round of congratulations from everyone, they said their goodbyes and headed off, finally able to go about their days without worrying who was watching the resort. Because I was selfish and wanted as much time with my wife as humanly possible, I'd pushed for them to hire a part-time employee so they could take time away—and have time together—without having to be on call and drop everything to run back to the resort should a guest have a problem. Despite both Aiden's and Addison's control tendencies, it'd been going surprisingly well.

"Can I catch a ride with you over there?" Levi asked, lifting a chin in our direction.

The camp was scheduled to start this afternoon, and my best friend and my wife both wanted to be there to cheer me on. In fact, I was pretty sure my mom, dad, the twins, Mabel, and a dozen others would be there as well.

Seriously, how fucking great was my life?

"Yeah, we're parked around the corner," I said.

"Let me just run up and grab my gear, in case we do a pickup game."

With a nod, I tugged Addison behind me as the three of

us headed across the street and toward the *Starlight Cove Gazette*'s corner shop, above which was Levi's apartment. I held the door open for my wife, swatting her ass as she walked through the door before capturing her hand again.

"Seriously," he grumbled at the top of the stairs. "I think I liked it better when you were hiding shit from me. I swear I can't look at you two without seeing your hands on some part of her body."

He unlocked the door as he glanced back at Addison and me and to where I rested my left hand on her stomach, the roman numerals of our impromptu wedding date inked on the outside of my ring finger. As he opened his apartment door, his brows drew down, his attention still locked on my hand possessively, protectively, palming Addison's stomach, before he snapped his focus to her face, then to mine, his eyes wide. "Wait, are you preg—"

"Oh honey, I wasn't expecting you home until tonight!" Mabel's voice called from inside his apartment, interrupting Levi's question. Which was probably for the best since Addison and I hadn't yet figured out how we wanted to drop that bomb on her family.

But as I'd already told her, the lid wasn't staying on long. Not only did I get to call her my wife—and I did, repeatedly and often and to whoever would listen—but now...this was so fucking much better.

"Are you...reorganizing my brother's kitchen cabinets?" Addison asked Mabel, disbelief heavy in her tone. Then, to Levi, she said, "Seriously...is she reorganizing your cabinets?"

"Not the first time," he said.

"When he puts the spices in the same cabinet as his cups, what am I supposed to do?" Mabel asked. "It just doesn't make any sense."

Levi blew out a long sigh and crossed his arms over his chest. To us, he said, "She's taken it upon herself to be my surrogate mother."

"Well, with no one else here to help, who else is going to do it for you? I, for one, am happy to provide my assistance. And actually, that's why I'm here."

"To reorganize his kitchen?" Addison asked.

"No, to let you know you won't be lonely living here all by yourself anymore." She beamed at us. "At least, not for a few weeks."

"Um, what?" Levi asked, all his attention focused on Mabel.

But mine wasn't. I glanced around the apartment, cataloging a few things that were out of place. Like the rose-gold MacBook on the coffee table, a pair of women's flip-flops next to the door, and the purse tossed on a chair in the living room.

"A roommate," Mabel enunciated slowly, as if hearing was Levi's problem.

"I don't have a roommate, Mabel. I live alone. I like to live alone. And you might be my landlord, but you can't just rent out a room in my apartment without my consent."

"Oh, but I can. Because, technically, it's still my apartment."

"The lease I signed says otherwise."

"Did you read the lease, honey?" She pulled a sheaf of papers from her bag, flipped to the page she wanted, and handed it to Levi, pointing in the middle of the page. "Because it says right there that you are renting one *bedroom* in this apartment. Not the whole apartment. So technically, the living room, kitchen, and bathroom are all shared spaces. And the extra bedroom is free for me to rent! I had a friend in need, and who was I to say no to the sweet girl?"

"Jesus Christ, Mabel, are you serious?" Levi asked. "I don't want a stranger living in my apartment."

"That's the best part! She's not a stranger. In fact, you all go way back, so I knew it wouldn't be a problem."

Things became clearer, the puzzle pieces finally clicking into place as I recalled who else was going to be at the rink today, interviewing players and my old coach for her article. And then, before I could warn Levi, before I could prepare him for what I was pretty sure was coming, Harper Davidson walked out of the guest bedroom, stopping short at the sight of us, shock written on her face. Apparently, Mabel hadn't filled her in on who the other tenant was. Or even that there was one.

Levi froze next to me, his shoulders going rigid, his jaw set in a firm line as he stared at the girl who'd once owned his heart.

I split my gaze between them and said the only thing I could that summed up this entire clusterfuck. "Oh shit."

THANK YOU FOR READING POSSESSIVE HEART! Want to see Chase and Addison get married? For their wedding, as well as more glimpses into their future—complete with little hockey babies running around—scan the QR code below to receive their bonus epilogues spanning five years delivered straight to your inbox!

ACKNOWLEDGMENTS

Sometimes books pour out of me like a waterfall. Other times, I have to chip away at a dam before even the slightest trickle starts to flow. My unwavering thanks to the following people who handed me pick axes:

Christina... How lucky am I that my plot whisperer, alpha reader, and bestie are all the same person? Your brain amazes me, and what we create when our brains get together is nothing short of magic. Thank you for holding my hand through my (inevitable) 60% breakdown and for reminding me, yes, I can write. No, it doesn't suck. Yes, people will love it. You're the best.

Zoe York for fueling my Input by sending me random hockey videos, answering any seemingly inconsequential (but *very* consequential to my brain) question, brainstorming, and just generally making this small town book that happens to have hockey in it as authentic as possible.

Emerald Elite for endless hours discussing these characters and this tiny little town, for plotting sessions and world domination plans while we slummed it at our retreat mansion, and for being my trusted *oh honey, no* friends, as well as steadfast cheerleaders. Being part of a group who would mention my name in a roomful of opportunities is something special and rare, and I'm grateful we have it.

Molly O'Keefe for stopping my downward spiral into despair with an hour Zoom call. I don't know how you do it, but I'm not entirely convinced you're not a word magician. Your input was invaluable and made this book so much better.

Lisa Hollett for rolling with the punches...even when I throw a *lot* of punches at you. Postponed deadlines, shifted projects, and heaping more work on you, just to name a few. Your feedback was exactly what I needed when I needed it.

Everyone in Brighton's Brigade for your giddy posts, comments, messages, and memes as you waited (not so patiently) for Addison and Chase. Your excitement for these characters and this series fuels my writing days, especially when I've climbed aboard the struggle bus. I can't thank you enough for your support.

Last but never least, my guys. I love you all beyond measure and am so grateful to call you mine.

OTHER TITLES BY BRIGHTON WALSH

Starlight Cove Series

Defiant Heart

Protective Heart

Fearless Heart

Reckless Heart

Possessive Heart

Holidays in Havenbrook Series

Main Street Dealmaker

Havenbrook Series

Second Chance Charmer

Hometown Troublemaker

Pact with a Heartbreaker

Captain Heartbreaker

Small Town Pretender

Reluctant Hearts Series

Caged in Winter

Tessa Ever After

Paige in Progress

Our Love Unhinged

STAND-ALONE TITLES

Dirty Little Secret

Plus One

ABOUT THE AUTHOR

Award-winning *USA Today* and *Wall Street Journal* bestselling author Brighton Walsh spent a decade as a professional photographer before taking her storytelling in a different direction and reconnecting with her first love—writing. She likes her books how she likes her tea—steamy and satisfying—and adores strong-willed heroines and the protective heroes who fall head over heels for them. Brighton lives in the Midwest with her real life hero of a husband, her two kids—both taller than her—and her dog who thinks she's a queen. Her boy-filled house is the setting for dirty socks galore, frequent dance parties (okay, so it's mostly her, by herself, while her children look on in horror), and more laughter than she thought possible.

www.brightonwalsh.com

tiktok.com/@brightonwalshbooks

instagram.com/brighton_walsh

facebook.com/brightonwalshwrites